SCRIPT OF LOVE

LOST CREEK, TEXAS HILL COUNTRY
BOOK THREE

ALEXA ASTON

OLIVERHEBERBOOKS

PROLOGUE

BROOKLYN—DECEMBER

*H*olden Scott turned the final corner, walking briskly up his quiet Brooklyn street, headed toward the brownstone he'd rented for the past five years. Usually, he had his cell phone in hand, dictating into it as he walked each morning. He had read a few years ago that movement sparked creativity and had taken to talking into his phone on his walks. Holden dictated story ideas. Character sketches. Even entire scenes. He faithfully transcribed everything once he arrived home, no longer struggling to recall a plot point or witty line of dialogue. The habit had made him a much more efficient, productive writer.

No. Author. Anyone could be a writer, but an author was someone who saw his work published. Thankfully, he'd had success out of the gate, one of the fortunate few who did.

He had come out of the renown Iowa Writers' Workshop with a completed novel, immediately pitching it to several New York agents recommended to him by Dr. Ingram, one of his favorite professors in the program. Evan McGill had quickly signed Holden and gotten him a high, six-figure deal for that novel. *Capitol Crimes* had been an instant bestseller, and Evan had then sold the book's rights to a major Hollywood studio, where up-and-coming director Wolf Ramirez turned it into a blockbuster hit.

Holden had wanted to do something completely different his second time. Where his first novel had been a thriller with a ticking time bomb plot, the second was a murder mystery set in a quiet Texas town close to Austin. *Hill Country Homicide* had released to excellent reviews and had sold briskly over the last year. Evan was now fielding offers from studios to also turn it into a movie.

He jogged up the stairs to the brownstone, inserting his key in the lock. "I'm home," he called, secretly hoping no one would answer.

Locking the door behind him, he went to the kitchen, chugging a bottle of water he'd left on the counter so it wouldn't be so cold going down.

Madison wasn't home, for which he was grateful. Things were no longer working between them, at least, romantically. They had met at the Iowa Writers' Workshop, a two-year residency program, and become fast friends from day one, sharing their writing with one another and offering critiques. When the workshop ended and they'd graduated with their Master of Fine Arts degrees, their relationship was just heating up. Since

Madison was from Scarsdale, she told Holden they should move to New York together. She had been the one to find the brownstone for them to rent, and they had moved in with high hopes for both their careers and their relationship.

Unfortunately, Madison had yet to sell anything. Although he used to read every word she wrote, he'd seen nothing from her in over a year now. On the other hand, she gave him excellent notes, some of which he implemented into his manuscripts. He had told her she would make a fine editor and encouraged her to pursue the editorial end of the literary business. Her temper had flared, and she had told him she was a creative, not a hack who edited others' work.

That had been the moment he sensed the shift between them.

From then on, she'd kept her work to herself, disappearing for hours each day with her laptop. She told him she went to different places to write. Coffeehouses. Benches in Central Park. The public library. Holden had no idea if she really spent her time writing, especially because he'd seen train tickets in the trash to places beyond the city and the clothes on her side of the closet continued to increase.

They had started out splitting everything equally, him drawing from the advance he'd received on his novel, while she had freely accepted money from her wealthy family. Eventually, he had taken over paying the rent and all the bills, not wanting to accept any money from her parents since he disagreed violently with their politics and lifestyle. The three days they'd recently spent with her family in Scarsdale over Christmas had cemented the fact that he never wanted to be a part of the Parmalee family.

He knew Madison wanted to get married from the numerous hints she had been dropping recently, but Holden hadn't been ready to put a ring on it, especially since he felt them drifting apart. At this point, he felt nothing romantic toward her. She had become no more than a roommate that he was subsidizing.

Today needed to be the day to end things with her. It wasn't fair to keep the status quo any longer when he knew they didn't have a future together. They would both get a fresh start. Their breakup might even help spur Madison's writing.

Leaving her the brownstone would be his best move. Their lease ended at the beginning of March. She could either renew the lease on her own or find another place to live. Or a job. She had resisted his encouragement to find at least part-time work.

Holden showered and toweled off, wrapping the towel around his waist as he shaved. He had just finished brushing his teeth when his cell rang. Glancing down, he was pleasantly surprised to see Wolf Ramirez calling to FaceTime. The director was only in his mid-thirties and had a stellar reputation in Hollywood, both as a kind man and a professional who delivered strong films. They'd become friends during the filming of *Capitol Crimes* and spoke occasionally.

Picking up his phone, he tapped it. "Hey, Wolf. What's going on with you?"

"Quite a bit since we last spoke, my friend. I'm striking out on my own. I've formed my own production company, Holden."

He went to the den, taking a seat. "That's fantastic, Wolf. Will Ana be a part of running things?"

His friend smiled. "You know my wife is the real brains in our family. With her accounting background, she'll definitely keep the books—and keep my budget requests in line. Ana is also very organized, so she'll share co-producer credits with me on all productions. She'll handle everything from scouting locations to helping with casting to finding the right food trucks. And my brother Rey is a lawyer. He's already set up the company for us and will serve as its general counsel."

"I couldn't be happier for you, Wolf. You won't have to worry about the big boys coming to you in the future. Instead, you can go after the projects which truly interest you."

"Funny you should mention that," Wolf said, a gleam in his eyes. "I haven't seen in the trades where *Hill Country Homicide* has been optioned yet. I'd like to step in and bid on it and make it the first film from WEBA Productions. I've lived in the Hill Country my entire life. I know these people, Holden. I can make this film sing.

"I know you've been well compensated in the past, but after the success of *Capitol Crimes* and the strong sales with book two, Evan has set the bar pretty high as far as bidding goes.

"That's why I'm calling you first and not your agent. No, I can't afford to buy the rights to your novel at the price a large studio could fork over. What I can guarantee, however, is giving you percentage points from the profits."

Holden whistled. "That's an intriguing offer. Especially because the movie version of *Capitol Crimes* did so well."

"I can't promise my film of *Hill Country Homicide* would generate the kind of profit our first effort together did. It's a completely different story. A totally different audience. But to sweeten the pot? I have an idea that I hope you'll go for." Wolf paused. "I want you to write the script for it, Holden."

The director's words took him aback.

"I've never had any experience with screenplays," he blurted out. "The only thing I know about them is that one page of script equals one minute of film. *Homicide* is about three hundred and fifty pages long. I don't know if I'm up to the challenge of trimming it down to a hundred pages or less."

"One thing you are is a master of description, my friend. You set a scene incredibly well. Your readers can see it crystal-clear in their minds. You also describe your characters at length. Visually, a film allows an audience member to see that scene and character, taking it all in within seconds. That alone would help you cut down on pages. You came on set before. You know how things work."

He shook his head. "Seeing how they work and actually *doing* that work? I'm not sure, Wolf. It's way out of my wheelhouse."

They fell silent, and he knew his friend was giving him

a chance to mull over the offer. Holden made an instant decision, one which he hoped he wouldn't regret.

"I've just finished my third novel. Given the last of it to Madison to read. That means I'm between projects. What if we worked on the screenplay together?" he offered.

The director nodded enthusiastically. "You know the characters and story better than anyone. You could take the first pass at it. I could read over and make my tweaks. Yes, that would work." He hesitated. "I don't want this kind of thing happening long distance, though. Yes, it's easy to email back and forth, but I like what we did with our first project."

Wolf referred to the three days they'd spent together, talking about Holden's story and characters, allowing the director to soak up everything firsthand from the author before shooting anything.

"Would you consider coming to Texas? Your murder mystery happens in a small town here. We could talk things over, and then you could write the first draft. You're welcome to stay at the ranch. Ana and the kids would like that."

"I could come for a few days and talk things to death with you, Wolf, but then I'd need to have my own place. I'm better when I have no one around. No distractions."

"Will you bring Madison with you?" the director asked.

"Ironically, you've called on the day I've decided to end things with her. We've been in a rut for a long time. If I clear out of the brownstone and come to Texas, I think it would help it be a clean break."

"I'm sorry things did not work out." Wolf didn't look

sorry at all. "At least you figured that out before you married her. Divorce can be messy, my friend. Especially if children are involved."

Knowing the chance to leave and stay at Meadow Creek Ranch made Holden say, "I'll call Evan now and tell him that I want to sell the rights to you for the price you name. Make it fair, Wolf. I'll also tell him that I'll be writing the screenplay."

"You'll receive a salary for that, as well as what I can give you, point-wise." Wolf smiled. "I look forward to working with you, my friend. Maybe our partnership will yield several films to come."

"Wait to hear from Evan," Holden said. "But from my end? It's a go. I'll let you know when I'm heading to the ranch."

He went and dressed, hanging his towel neatly, ignoring the one Madison had left on the floor. It was only one of a hundred little things she did which bothered him. He knew a part of their problem had been that she came from money, and he hadn't. The Parmalees had maids to pick up towels off the floor and launder them, while his family had barely scraped by. If he hadn't won a scholarship to college, he would most likely be laying bricks or driving a truck now instead of being an author.

Going to his desk, he sat, calling Evan.

"I was just about to call you, Holden," his agent said when he answered. "It's been a good day to represent you. I have four different offers to bring you regarding *Homicide*. Two are preferable, but I always like to let you hear all the players vying for you work and make an informed decision."

"Save your breath, Evan. I've already promised the book to Wolf Ramirez."

"What studio is Wolf attached to? No one pitched him as the director in our negotiations."

"He's striking out on his own and is starting up his own production company. Wolf wants *Hill Country Homicide* to be the first film he directs for it."

"I like Wolf, Holden. You know that. I know the two of you have become friends, but you've got to think with your head and not your heart. He won't have the kind of financial backing that a major studio does."

"I don't care. He's promised me a healthy percentage of the profits if I'll sell the rights to him at a lower price."

Evan was quiet a moment, and Holden could almost hear the agent run the numbers in his head. He knew this was a big ask. Not only would he take a big cut, but Evan would also lose money if they sold the screen rights to Wolf.

"*Homicide* is selling extremely well. I don't think it'll do the box office numbers of *Capitol Crimes*, though. You have to take that into consideration. Points or no points."

"Wolf has also offered me the opportunity to write the screenplay, Evan. I want to do this. Wolf gets me. I know this cutting a deal with him eats away at your percentage, but it's what I want."

"We've already made good money together. I see that continuing in the future. If you were my only client, I might be pissed, but I have other lines out there. Would I have wished to sell it to a big studio and claim a huge payday? Of course. In the long run, though, I want a happy client so that I have a happy life. If writing this screenplay challenges and inspires you, then I'm all for it. I'm definitely into the idea of sharing points. Because we'll be dealing with a fledgling company, I have way more leverage in the negotiations."

"Wolf's brother Reynaldo Ramirez is his attorney. Rey will be hammering out the contracts with you. I suggest you call Wolf and get the ball rolling."

"I'll do that now. I suppose he'll want you down in Texas since he's based there. After you write the screenplay, he's certain to film in Texas, as well, since the book is set there." Evan paused. "How will that go over with Madison? Have you run this by her yet?"

"Madison doesn't figure into my life anymore. We're done. I'm going to tell her today."

"Good luck with that," Evan said. "That is one woman who doesn't like to hear the word no."

Madison had wanted Evan to also represent her, but he had refused to do so, saying he didn't want any conflict of interest, with Holden being whom he'd originally signed. She had begged, wheedled, cajoled, and finally screamed at the agent, demanding he sign her, which had embarrassed and angered Holden. Evan had remained firm, however. Madison had found representation, but she had since gone through three different agents and had no one repping her interests at the moment.

He spent the rest of the day scouring the Internet, reading everything he could about writing a screenplay.

There was no time to enroll in classes. He'd have to learn on the fly.

Taking out his leather-bound copy of the screenplay for *Capitol Crimes* which Wolf had gifted to him, Holden read the first twenty pages of it and compared it to his novel, seeing how his work had been condensed. He would have to really give things some thought. Perhaps use a few composite characters. Already, though, ideas were swirling in his head, and the thought of authoring the screenplay for his novel excited him.

About four, he heard the front door open and knew Madison was home. He went to greet her, seeing her place her messenger bag on the kitchen counter.

"How was your day?" he asked, his gut churning with the news he was about to give her. "Any good pages written today?"

"I really think I'm on to something, Holden," she said brightly. "I've gone through a long dry spell lately, but I got a really interesting idea today and ran with it. I wrote twenty pages. Twenty!"

A great day for Madison was usually five pages, so he nodded enthusiastically. "That's wonderful."

"Did you start anything new yet?" she asked, opening the fridge and removing a sparkling water. She popped the top and took a big swig before setting the can on the counter.

He swallowed. "I've told Evan to sell the film rights of *Hill Country Homicide* to Wolf Ramirez."

She looked at him quizzically. "To Wolf?" Then a

knowing looking crossed her features. "He's started his own production company, hasn't he?"

"He has. We're eager to work together again."

Frowning, she said, "He won't be able to pay you nearly what you deserve. I've been reading the trades, and I know what Evan can get for the rights. No, Holden. Call both of them back. Cancel the deal."

He couldn't believe what she was saying. Looking steadily at her, he told her, "It's my novel, Madison. My decision. I want to work with Wolf. In fact, I'm going to write the screenplay for the film."

Astonishment filled her face. "Are you serious? You have zero experience with writing a script. If you want to torpedo your own reputation and his, that's the fastest way to do so."

Her words let him know he was doing the right thing by splitting with her. Where once, Madison had been supportive, now she was demanding and spiteful. "You don't believe I can do it?"

She looked at him in exasperation. "What I'm saying is you're a fool if you walk away from the kind of money Evan can get you for this book. Stick with what you do best, Holden. Writing novels is your forte."

Her words assured him that he was making the right decision. "It's my book. My choice. And I'll be going to Texas." Holden paused. "It's not working between us, Madison. It hasn't for a while now. With me being in Texas to write the screenplay and staying there during filming, this is the right time for us to end things."

Red blotches of anger stained her cheeks. "You don't

get to decide that. We're getting married, Holden. You're going to keep writing books. You'll make enough for us to leave this dump and move to a nice high rise in Manhattan. We'll—"

"There's no *we* anymore, Madison. Listen to what I'm saying. We're not happy."

"We are," she insisted.

"*I'm* not happy," he said with brutal honesty, trying to get through to her. "We had some good years, but it's over now."

Out of nowhere, she slapped him, so hard that he saw stars.

"You mean I'm not some bestselling novelist. You're embarrassed by me."

"No," he said firmly. "I think you're talented. I hope you'll get a break. And I wouldn't care if you were a trash collector or a plastic surgeon. I'm not breaking up with you because you aren't published, Madison." He hesitated but knew he had to cut all ties. "I simply don't love you anymore."

Holden wasn't sure if he ever had. They'd had writing in common. She had seemed so sophisticated and exciting when they'd first met, but he'd grown bored with the airs she put on. Actually, he'd grown tired of living in New York. The call of home sounded loudly within him. He'd thought leaving Texas was the best thing he'd ever done. Now, he could see it was the place which would always be home.

She huffed, anger sparking in her eyes. "You are nothing but trailer park trash, Holden Scott. You might have made good money from a couple of books, but you'll never fit in with people who have good breeding."

"I agree," he told her. "Your parents have made it perfectly clear that you could do better than me. Go find your kind of people to be with, Madison."

"Get out!" she screamed at him.

"Gladly. Give me ten minutes."

Holden went to pack, filling two suitcases and his backpack. Madison hovered at the doorway to the bedroom, glaring at him as he did so. The brownstone had come furnished, so all he really needed were his clothes and his laptop, along with a few books.

Facing her, he said, "The rent is paid through the end of February. You can renew the lease or move. It's up to you."

He pushed past her as she shouted profanities at him the entire way. When he reached the door, he removed the key from his pocket and tossed it on the table. Without another word, Holden walked through the door, ready to start a new chapter in his life.

1

MEADOW CREEK RANCH--JANUARY

*H*olden rose early, keeping to old habits in the month he had spent at Wolf and Ana's ranch. He dressed in a sweatshirt and jogging pants and went to the kitchen, finding Ana brewing coffee. Where her husband was a night owl, often working until three or four in the morning, Ana was an early bird like Holden, saying she enjoyed being up to greet the day, having it to herself for a little while before the chaos began.

"Coffee?"

"Please," he said, taking a seat on one of the stools at the oversized island.

"Are you making any headway with the script?" she asked, the first time she had brought up business with him.

"Actually, I have the first twenty pages under my belt. Wolf read them yesterday and gave me some great feedback. Overall, though, he approved of the direction I'm taking and said to keep going after I make the tweaks he suggested. I've found my rhythm now. It's going to go faster from here on."

She brought the cup of coffee to him, having already added the one sugar and amount of creamer he liked.

"If Wolf said it's good, it is. He's not one to heap praise where it isn't deserved."

"Thank you," he said, accepting the coffee and taking a sip of it. "I think I'm ready to find a place to live."

Ana clucked her tongue, taking the stool beside him. "You know you're welcome to stay at the ranch as long as you'd like, Holden. We have plenty of room for you. Besides, Eva and Bear adore you."

She referred to the couple's two children. Not having had siblings, Holden hadn't really known much about kids, but the Ramirez children had taken to him the last time he'd visited when he'd come down to Texas to discuss his characters and plot with Wolf before the director begin filming *Capitol Crimes*. He'd found he had really enjoyed being around them and saw what a great mom Ana was. He could now trace the beginnings of his discontent with Madison to the fact that he'd wanted children someday. She hadn't when he'd brought up the topic.

"Your hospitality has been appreciated, Ana, but I'm ready to get a place of my own. Something nearby, so that I can meet with Wolf often, but I just need my own space."

She smiled, taking a sip of her coffee. "You mean you don't have time for tea parties or playing Ninja Turtles?"

"I'll always have time for that when I visit. I work better in total quiet, though."

"Have you heard from Madison?" she asked out of the blue.

A sour taste filled him. "She called me a few times. I let it go to voicemail. She said some pretty nasty things. Then she bombarded me with texts. I finally blocked her without responding."

"Did you save any of those voicemails or texts?" Ana asked, clearly concerned.

He nodded. "I did. My first instinct was to delete them. Get them out of sight and out of mind. But then I thought about an important plot point in *Hill Country Homicide* and decided that would be unwise. I hope I've learned something from a foolish character."

"I think you made a wise decision, cutting ties with her. I only spoke with her briefly on set when she visited. That woman was not for you, Holden." Smiling brightly, Ana added, "Maybe we can find you a good Texas girl."

"No matchmaking. Please," he said lightly, not certain if Ana were teasing or not. "I was with Madison five years. I want to be on my own now and not jump into a new relationship."

"I can understand that." She paused. "Still, don't push away an opportunity if you do meet someone interesting. Simply because things didn't work out between you and Madison, you don't want to turn a blind eye to every woman you meet."

Laughing, he said, "I'll stick to the women in my screenplay for now. Changing topics, do you have an idea where I might be able to rent a place?"

"Boerne is closest to us," she said, referring to the town

ten miles to the south. "About five miles to the east is Parham, but it's little more than a speck on the map. I think you'd have better luck going north to Lost Creek."

The name intrigued him. "How big is Lost Creek?"

She thought a moment. "Probably twenty thousand or so. Big enough to have some conveniences, and yet it still has a small-town feel. They started something really fun last summer, a thing called Harmony & Hues."

"What was it?"

"An event which celebrated artists in the community. Shops on the town square stayed open late on Saturday nights. People could shop or grab a bite to eat. Along the sidewalks, various artwork was displayed. Mostly paintings, but there were also some pieces of sculptures, pottery, and even jewelry which had been hand-crafted by local artisans."

She pushed aside her hair, revealing an earring. "I picked these up there. Once people had time to view the art, the musical portion of the night began, featuring singers and musicians from around the area."

"Ah, a fusion of music and art. I like the idea."

"It was started by the local coffeehouse owner and his girlfriend, who's a painter. Her work is really good. I've read she's going to have a show in New York soon at Clive Crutchfield's gallery in Soho."

He was familiar with the name from having lived in New York. "She must be better than good if Crutchfield is interested in her work."

Bear bounded into the kitchen, running to his mom

and hugging her leg before turning to Holden and reaching out his arms.

He leaned down and scooped up the five-year-old, placing the boy in his lap. "Ready for another day at preschool?" he asked.

"We get to do finger paints today," Bear announced.

"That sounds like a lot of fun. You'll have to tell me about what you paint when you get home this afternoon."

Standing, he kissed Bear's head before placing him on the stool. "I'm going for my morning walk. See you later, buddy."

As he headed into the laundry room and slipped on his jacket, Holden heard Eva's voice asking for pancakes. Bear's older sister was a true girly-girl, liking bows in her hair and polish on her fingernails. He'd grown close to both children in his month at the ranch, and it had reaffirmed that he would definitely choose to be a parent one day.

He was gone for about ninety minutes, thinking about the next scene he would write, playing out the dialogue and then honing it as he spoke into his phone.

As he'd suspected, writing a screenplay was a huge challenge. The writing hinged upon the dialogue, which had to be terse and compelling. Holden had taken to reading Hemingway each night before bed, just to get a feel for how concise language could be. He had also read a minimum of one screenplay a day, getting a feel for how other writers put words on a page. Wolf had been helpful in this, recommending a variety of movies, including a few murder mysteries. He was glad his friend had asked him to write this script.

Returning to the house, he knew he'd made the right decision in leaving New York—and Madison. It had been liberating to come back to Texas, unencumbered with a messy relationship, everything he owned, easy to transport. The open skies and quiet of the country would be conducive to his work. While he'd grown up in Austin, Holden wasn't sure if he'd ever live there again. The city was still full of great restaurants and cultural events, but the one time he'd gone to Austin since his return, the traffic had astounded him.

He had the money to buy something, but he wasn't ready to sink roots anywhere just yet. For now, he would investigate Lost Creek and see if he might find a place to rent while he worked on his script.

The kitchen was empty. Ana would be on her way to drop off the kids at their different schools. Wolf wouldn't be up for another few hours. Holden went to his guest suite and showered and dressed, grabbing his laptop and doing a search on Lost Creek. He brought up the city's website. The photograph on the home page was picturesque, showing the town square Ana had mentioned. He clicked on the various tabs and liked what he saw.

Pictures didn't ever tell the full story, so he'd drive to Lost Creek now and check it out in person. If he liked what he saw, he would go by the local real estate office to see about available rentals.

Wolf had given him use of a truck during his stay, and

he went to the garage now and drove off the property, heading the fifteen minutes north to Lost Creek. On the way, he passed a winery, recalling now that several of the wines Ana had served bore this label. He might have to stop in and do a tasting on his way home. Even purchase a few bottles to bring back to his hostess.

Holden drove around the town, getting a feel for the place, and then found the square and parked. If anything, he loved a good cup of coffee and decided to stop into Java Junction.

Entering the coffeehouse a little before eight-thirty, he saw it was busy this Friday morning. He wondered if it emptied out after the morning rush and might be more conducive to writing.

One of the baristas smiled at him, a tall, lean man who looked to be in his early thirties.

"What can I get you?"

"I'm a coffeeholic," he admitted. "First time here. What do you suggest?"

"I'm a purist myself, so I would start with a pour over or drip brew. It's like when I eat at a new Mexican restaurant. I go with beef enchiladas and a bowl of chicken tortilla soup. If those basics are good, I know the rest of the food will be. I can make you whatever you want, though. The call is yours. And since you're new, it'll be on the house."

"That's generous of you, but I don't want to get you fired for passing out free coffees."

The barista's eyes gleamed, a hint of mischief in them. "Since I'm the owner, I think it'll be okay." He reached his hand over the counter. "Dax Tennyson. Owner of Java Junction."

Taking the offered hand, he shook it, saying, "Holden Scott. Writer, and possible new resident in Lost Creek. If the coffee proves good, that is."

Recognition flickered in the coffeehouse owner's eyes. "*The* Holden Scott? I should've known you from your picture on the jacket." Dax said. "I've read both your books. They're way different, but both are compelling."

"Thank you. It's nice meeting a fan."

"Have a seat, and I'll bring you something special." Dax grinned. "On the house. And I promise not to text my wife to bring me copies of your books so that you can sign them."

"Text away," he said, liking this man. Hoping he might have found a friend, something he could really use.

Holden walked through the coffeehouse, noting the casual placement of comfortable furniture scattered about. A group of men in their seventies and eighties gathered in a back corner. From their laughs, they were obviously enjoying themselves. Different pockets of women in athleisure wear were at various tables, sipping their drinks.

He paused, admiring a painting of a lake. The use of color was extraordinary and drew a person into the scene. Then he found a spot at a table for two that looked out over the square. He noted several places to eat. A diner. A sports bar. And what looked like a place with country cooking. The square also had a few clothing shops. A bakery. An antique store.

Dax approached, setting down a coffee, along with a sausage roll. "Here you go, Holden. Hope you enjoy it. It's a Cortado. Think of it as a beefed-up macchiato. It balances espresso with warm milk for less acidity."

"Would you like to sit a minute? After all, you are the boss."

"Sure." Dax took the seat across from him. "Are you here to do research for another book? I recall your bio said you were from Austin originally."

"I grew up there. Went to college at SMU."

"No kidding. It's a small world. I went to business school there."

"English Lit major for me. I guess our paths never crossed in the classroom."

"Fraternity?" Dax asked.

"Nope. Too poor. Scholarship student."

The coffeehouse owner grinned. "Same. But I went to a ton of frat parties. As the DJ."

He vaguely remembered hearing others talk about a fellow student who DJ'd a lot of Greek parties. "So, how does a DJ slash business major wind up owning a Hill Country coffeehouse?"

"I made good money quickly, thanks to some timely investments, and wanted to get away to a quieter, kinder life. Drove around Texas until I got to Lost Creek. Something in the town called to me, so I stayed."

Holden pointed to the painting of the lake. "Is that your girlfriend's work?"

Dax looked surprised. "You know Ivy?"

"No."

Briefly, he explained how he was staying with Wolf Ramirez and how Ana had mentioned attending Harmony & Hues a few times the previous summer.

"Ivy's my wife now," Dax said, pride evident on his face. "And that's Lost Creek Lake she painted."

"She's talented."

"Very. Ivy really got the ball rolling on Harmony & Hues. I just took my cues from her. We plan to hold it again next summer. In the meantime, Java Junction hosts musical nights every Wednesday and Saturday, spotlighting singers and musicians in the area. You should come tomorrow night. I've got an interesting singer/songwriter performing."

"I might do that," he said. "What time does it start?"

"Seven. Let me know if you decide to drop by. I'll save you a table."

"Could I bring Wolf and Ana?"

Dax smiled. "The more, the merrier. Ivy will be there. Sometimes, her sister and brother-in-law stop by or her teacher friends Finley and Emerson come."

Thinking his coffee had cooled enough to drink, Holden took a sip. "*That* is a great cup of coffee."

"I've got a wide variety of both coffee and tea. Try the sausage roll. It's from The Bake House."

He bit into the roll and chewed a moment. "Outstanding. I'm finding a lot to like about Lost Creek."

"Back to my question. Are you here researching?"

"No, I've agreed to write the screenplay for *Hill Country Homicide*. I've never written one before, but Wolf is starting his own production company. He bought the rights to my book and asked me to try my hand."

"It's a great story. Usually, I can guess who the murderer is halfway through a book or movie, but you kept me guessing up to that final page."

He smiled. "That's a great compliment. Since you live here, can you give me any tips on a place I might be able to rent? Somewhere quiet."

Dax thought a moment. "I have the perfect place. It's a B&B just outside of town."

"No," Holden protested. "I don't want to be in a house with others."

"This is different. The Inn on Lost Creek is a traditional B&B with rooms in the main house, but Jean Bradley also has a couple of cottages on the property. They're close to Lost Creek. The area is wooded. Peaceful. I'll bet you could rent one for a couple of months. They even have a small kitchenette."

Nodding, he said, "That sounds perfect."

Dax gave Holden directions and said, "I'll give Miss Jean a buzz. Tell her you're dropping by."

"Is that part of the small-town service?"

"I had to learn just how tight-knit a small town is when I moved here this time last January. Yes, everyone knows your business, but the residents of Lost Creek are really friendly. After you check out Miss Jean's place, you might want to stop by the local library. They've got some nice nooks you could write in for a change of scenery."

Again, the coffeehouse owner gave Holden directions to the library and then stood.

"I'll let you finish your coffee and sausage roll in peace. I hope you'll decide to stay in Lost Creek, Holden." He paused. "This place changed my life."

"Count on the three of us coming tomorrow night."

Dax smiled broadly. "Sounds good. And I just may have a book or two you could sign for me."

He laughed. "For the free coffee and roll? I think I can give you my John Hancock."

Holden stayed another quarter-hour, observing the patrons in the coffeehouse. He'd always studied people from the time he was young, making up stories in his head about them and their lives. Already, he had a good feeling about Lost Creek and hoped one of the cottages Dax had mentioned would be available. He didn't want to have to do upkeep on a house.

The directions he'd been given were easy to follow, and he was at The Inn on Lost Creek seven minutes after he got into the truck. He went up the stairs and rang the bell.

The door opened, and a woman in her early seventies beamed at him. "You must be Holden. I'm Jean. Dax said you're a writer and looking for a quiet place to work. Let me show you one of my cabins."

They walked about a hundred yards away from the main house, where two cabins faced one another.

Pointing to one, she said, "That's my honeymoon cabin. Even at this time of year, it's booked up most weekends. I think this other one would suit your needs, though."

"Is it available for three months or so? Once I settle in, I wouldn't want to have to move."

That was the deadline he'd given himself for finishing the first draft of the script and then passing through it again, using Wolf's notes.

"Yes, it's free until the end of April. Starting in May, I do have scattered bookings for it, though. Let's go inside and see if it'll work for you."

She unlocked the door and let him enter first. The room was large, furnished with a sofa and chair that turned out to be a rocker, which he loved. A TV graced the wall. A countertop with two stools next to it was the only place to eat. The kitchen was small, but it had a coffeemaker, microwave, and toaster oven, along with a decent size fridge.

The innkeeper went about the room, opening the blinds. "It gets good natural light. I want you to see that. It's a one-bedroom. Let's look at it."

She went first, opening blinds again in the bedroom. A queen-sized bed stood in the middle, two nightstands on either side of it. A dresser completed the room.

"Bathroom through there. No tub. Only a shower."

He grinned. "I haven't taken a bath since I was about six years old. A shower is fine."

Holden went inside the bathroom, seeing it was neat and updated. The cottage appealed to him, and he made the decision to move here.

"When would it be available?"

"You could move in tomorrow morning," she replied. "I'd like to give it a once-over. Sweep and mop. Dust. I can do those things for you once a week. Change the sheets. You'd get fresh towels daily. It's got cable TV with Netflix."

"I'll take it," he said, quickly coming to an agreement for the next three months.

They returned to the house, and Holden gave Miss Jean his credit card, telling her to put the entire three months on it.

"If you're sure," she said. "I don't mind billing you weekly."

"I'm good for it."

As the innkeeper ran his credit card, he was glad he'd never merged finances with Madison, much less given her access to his credit card. With the way she was screaming at him when he left, she probably would've bankrupted him if she'd known his number.

Miss Jean gave him a key, saying she had the other copy. "I'll spruce it up for you this afternoon. I'll clean on Mondays at eleven if you're agreeable to that. You're welcome to come here and use the gathering room to write. Or you might want to go to the local library. With school in session, that place is usually quiet as a tomb unless it's Mommy & Me Storytime. That's on Wednesday mornings at ten."

"I think I'll drop by the library now," he said, wanting to become familiar with the facility. Libraries had always been a friend to him.

Holden thanked Miss Jean again and returned to his truck. Finding the library was easy, and only a handful of vehicles stood in the parking lot. He entered and saw the checkout desk was to his right. To his left, he saw an array of black and white photographs on display and went to view them.

One by one, he studied each image, the black and white a stark contrast. The photo display was of the Lost Creek area, and he drank it in. As a storyteller, he was drawn to art, and these photographs definitely told a story of their own. He felt a burning need to meet the photographer and compliment him or her.

Spying a woman seated at a desk in the center of the library, he headed toward her.

"Excuse me," he began. "I'd like to know—"

"Holden Scott!" she exclaimed, quickly standing. "It really *is* you. Dax Tennyson called and told me you might be stopping by. I'm such a fan, Mr. Scott. I'm Dorothy. Dorothy Prigmore, the head librarian."

Dax was right. A small town was different.

"I'll be staying in Lost Creek for a few months," he explained. "Working on a new project. I thought I'd come by the library and become familiar with your facilities."

"Then let me give you the grand tour," Dorothy said.

It only took a few minutes to see the entire building. Dorothy was warm and welcoming, even showing him the employee break room and offering him the opportunity to stop in for a cup of coffee during the times he might be writing here.

"I appreciate that," he said.

She showed him a small area with furniture that looked out over a beautiful park. "This might be a place you'd like to sit with your laptop and write. Or any of the study carrels. And remember, you can always book time in one of the study rooms if you'd prefer that."

"You've given me a lot of options, Dorothy. Thanks for the tour. One more thing before I go. I was really drawn to the photographs on exhibit as I entered the building. Can you tell me anything about the photographer?"

Dorothy smiled brightly. "They were taken by Finley Farrow. She's a teacher here in town, and she also pursues photography on the side."

Dax had mentioned a Finley being one of his wife's friends who came to listen to music at the coffeehouse. With such an unusual name, he didn't think there would be another Finley in Lost Creek.

Holden looked forward to meeting Finley Farrow and talking with her about her photographs.

2

$\mathcal{F}$inley Farrow circled the classroom as her fifth-grade students began saving and closing their PowerPoints. They had been working in pairs, some creating slideshows elaborating on causes leading up to the Civil War. Others had focused on sharing information about major battles, while the last group focused on creating presentations of outstanding leaders of the era.

"Remember, you'll have time on Monday to finish embedding your research. Presentations will start Tuesday."

She had been teaching for six years now, and she had come to a crossroads. While she enjoyed what she did, her photography pulled at her, demanding more time from her. Finley photographed weddings and other events held at Lost Creek Winery for her close friend Harper Clark, who ran the event center at her family's vineyard. She also had a growing side business, photographing others in the community for milestone events. Engagement and bridal portraits. Senior high school portraits. Newborns' first photo sessions. Photography was bringing far more satisfaction to her than teaching.

It would disappoint her parents if she left education. Sam and Dianne Farrow ran the Bluebonnet Montessori Academy in Lost Creek, and she knew one day they would like her to take over the center. Her brother Ches had spurned the education field totally and operated Hill Country Water Sports with his wife Sally. They had two children whom Finley adored, and Ches had told her he was glad he had stood up to their parents and made his own decision about what he did for a living. Running his own business made him happy.

She, on the other hand, had always been a people pleaser, never wanting to rock the boat in her family, and later being a model student in the classroom. While she had excelled in her elective classes in high school, which had included photography and graphic design, it was assumed that she would major in education in college. Finley had rebelled a bit, choosing elementary ed as her major versus early childhood education, wanting to have her own classroom and gain experience and not immediately step into a role at Bluebonnet Montessori. She wanted to find her own identity, both personally and professionally.

Would she have the guts to leave education totally behind?

"Miss Farrow, my cousin is getting married next month. Are you going to take pictures at her wedding?"

"Will she be getting married at the winery, Lisa?" Finley asked.

Her student nodded enthusiastically. "I get to be a flower girl. Amy said I'm too old to be one, but I don't care. I want to be one."

"It's an honor that your cousin asked you to be in her wedding, Lisa. It doesn't matter what Amy or anyone else says. If you are happy and your cousin is happy, that's all that matters."

She tried to teach more than academics to her students, giving bits of life advice such as this over the course of a year with them. Instilling core values in her students was important to her. An individual not being swayed by the opinion of others was merely one of those lessons. She tried to build up her students so they were confident and caring people, even if they were only ten and eleven years old.

The bell rang, and Finley dismissed her class for the day, wishing them a good weekend. Josh asked if she would be at his soccer game the next morning at ten, and Finley told him she would stop by for a few minutes.

"Remember, Miss Farrow, I'm the goalie for the Tigers. That way you know where to look for me. Field three."

"I'll see you at the game, Josh," she said brightly, turning to see Brian Withers still seated, a sullen expression on his face.

A parent conference had already been scheduled with Brian's parents for after school today. It was meant to discuss his lack of academic progress, but it would be more intense after events which had unfolded today.

"Brian, let's go to the office now. Your parents will be here soon."

He stood, glaring at her, and she ignored the hostile look, escorting him to the main office.

Sheila, the school's secretary, greeted her. "Mr. and Mrs. Withers are already in the conference room, Miss Farrow. I'll keep an eye on Brian for you."

Turning, Finley told the boy, "Wait here, Brian. I'll speak with your parents first, and then we'll have you come and visit with us."

"They won't care what you say," he said belligerently, oozing attitude like a fifteen-year-old.

She stared intently at him, not speaking, until he sat in the chair, staring at the floor. She went down the hall, passing the teacher mailboxes, and tapped lightly on her principal's open door.

Mary Miller glanced up. "Ready for our conference?"

"Thank you for clearing your calendar so you could sit in," she said. "I've met with them before, and they've been... difficult."

"What happened today is very serious. You know I will always have your back, Finley. Hopefully, the Withers will work with us on this situation."

She didn't think Brian's parents would be interested— much less cooperative—but followed Mary to the conference room.

Mr. and Mrs. Withers looked up, wariness in her eyes and hostility exuding from him.

"Good afternoon, Mr. and Mrs. Withers," Mary said. "I

am Mrs. Miller, your son's principal. I know you've already met Miss Farrow."

The two women took a seat, and Mr. Withers said, "I don't know why you've called us back here again. We've already met with this teacher, and nothing's changed. Brian keeps bringing home failing grades."

"You told us you would work with him," Mrs. Withers said accusingly. "Well, that hasn't happened. We haven't seen a lick of improvement."

"I've told you that I'm here every day to tutor Brian, whether he comes in before or after school. He rarely attends tutoring and when he does, he doesn't put forth his best effort."

Finley spoke in her most professional voice, wishing she could say that Brian Withers was lazy, rude, and unwilling to put in the work to learn how to be successful.

"I don't know what you expect from us," Mr. Withers said, glaring at her. "Unless you tell us we're supposed to hire some damn tutor and pay for it out of our own pocket. We pay enough taxes as it is. *You* tutor the boy. *You* make him learn what he's supposed to learn. He's already been held back once."

She defended herself, calmly saying, "I am always here and open to helping Brian, giving him as much support as he needs. He is distracted in class often and even falls asleep at times recently. You might want to work with him on setting an earlier bedtime."

"It's hard to keep him off his phone," Mrs. Withers complained. "And those video games. He's playing them all the time."

"He's twelve," Mr. Withers said. "He knows when to go to bed without us nagging him."

Mary stepped in, gently saying, "Even twelve-year-olds need rules, Mr. Withers. Rules you set, which they must follow. You might want to limit Brian's screen time. Set a bedtime for him so that he gets a reasonable amount of sleep."

The man looked offended. "If you people did your job and made things more interesting, Brian would want to learn."

Mary's look could have frozen over Lost Creek Lake on a hot summer day. "I will have you know that Miss Farrow is one of the most outstanding teachers I've had the pleasure to work with. I have personally sat in her classroom on numerous occasions and seen the creative, engaging lessons she presents to her students. We are at a point in the academic year where Brian needs to start pulling his own weight," the principal said crisply. "He is in fifth grade and should no longer be spoon-fed. He must learn to put in the effort and work to meet with success so that he can move on to the middle school next August. At the rate he is going, Brian will most likely be retained in fifth grade."

Mr. Withers slammed his hands on the table. "You can't hold him back. I told you that already happened a few years ago. Before we moved here. My boy needs to get to the high school so he can play football. He's going to be in the NFL someday."

"Brian may be a talented athlete, Mr. Withers," Finley said, having had this conversation with more than one parent over her teaching career. "While wishing to play professional football is an admirable goal for Brian to have, he is still a boy. He will need a backup plan in case something happens. Sports injuries do occur. His interest in football might wane."

"My boy *is* going to be an NFL linebacker," Mr. Withers reiterated.

Her principal had had enough and said, "That won't happen if Brian is in jail, Mr. Withers."

The father's jaw dropped, and Mrs. Withers leaned forward, asking, "What do you mean by that?"

Mary glanced to Finley. "Brian has been bullying other students. This only came to light today when one of my students came to me."

Mr. Withers snorted. "You mean some tattletale said something about my boy. Well, I don't believe it. Kids lie all the time."

"We talked with several children, and they all spoke about how Brian has bullied them. Physically. Verbally."

"Boys will be boys," Mrs. Withers said, trying to smooth things over. "Yes, they get into arguments and fight a bit."

"It's far beyond that," she said. "Brian's verbal abuse is out of hand. He's also been taking items from other students. We went through his backpack and locker today, and—"

"You searched his things?" Mr. Withers said, his voice raised. "That's a violation of his rights. I'll sue your ass and this entire district's. We'll walk away with millions."

"Unfortunately, Mr. Withers, you are mistaken," Mary

said. "Legally, a student is not an adult and does not have a set guarantee of rights as outlined by our constitution. Schools operate under the basis of *in loco parentis*."

"Don't speak Greek to me," Mr. Withers spat out.

Mary waited a moment before continuing. "It is a Latin phrase which means 'in the place of a parent.' It speaks to the dedication of caring for and educating children in the public schools. We, as educators, take on some of the responsibilities of a parent while your child is in our custody during the school day. We enforce rules such as our dress code. We require students to be at school by a certain time. And students are expected to obey their teachers and not obstruct the learning process."

"Lockers are property of the school district," Finley added. "They are merely loaned to a student for his or her use during the school year. Since we legally own what is on our property, we have every right to open and search a locker at any time."

The principal let this information sink in with the Withers. Finley watched Mrs. Withers began shrinking in her seat. All the fire seemed to have left Mr. Withers now, and he deflated.

Mary elaborated on the items which had been found in Brian's backpack and locker and said that everything not belonging to Brian had been returned to their proper owners.

"This weekend, I will be calling the parents of each student Brian stole from, as well as those he verbally threatened," the principal continued. "I cannot guarantee if they will press charges against Brian or not. I will do my best to ask these parents to be reasonable, especially since what was taken has now been returned, but even if the police are not brought in to investigate, your son still faces consequences here at school."

Mary paused. "I hope Brian will understand how serious his actions are. He will, on Monday, begin serving time in our in-school suspension unit."

"You mean you're sticking him in a room by himself. He's got to teach himself when he can barely read or add?" Mr. Withers demanded, his face having gone beet red.

"A certified teacher will be with Brian at all times," Mary assured the pair. "While our counselor will also meet with Brian to discuss his poor choices and bad behavior toward other students, it might be best if you sought professional counseling, as well. I have a list of resources you can reach out to."

Mr. Withers came to his feet so quickly that he knocked over his chair. "I don't have to put up with this. We're pulling Brian from this crappy school."

Finley came to her feet. "That would be a mistake, Mr. Withers. Brian is still young and impressionable. I believe he can turn things around, with your support and ours."

"No," the man said. "Do whatever you have to do to unenroll him, but don't expect my boy to show up and sit in your jail on Monday. And don't sic the cops on him, either. Nobody got hurt." He stormed from the room, slamming the door behind him.

His wife, whose gaze had dropped during her husband's outburst, finally looked up. Her eyes met Finley's. "I'm sorry. I'll do what I can. But Brian takes his cues from his father. As you can see— he has a temper — and he always thinks he's right."

Mrs. Withers rose. Finley went to the woman, placing an arm about her.

"Do you need any help, Mrs. Withers? We can put you in touch with our school resource officer." She hesitated. "Or even a women's shelter for domestic violence."

The woman flinched. "I'm fine," she said abruptly. "We're fine."

She watched Mrs. Withers leave the room, and her heart sank. She didn't know if Mrs. Withers was physically or verbally abused by her husband— or son —but she now suspected it to be the case.

Turning to Mary, Finley asked, "What are we supposed to do?" Tears of frustration spilled down her cheeks.

Mary nodded sadly. "It's a problem I'm seeing more and more these days. I know your students will most likely feel relief when Brian's seat is empty come Monday. But I worry about that boy. And his mother."

"Should we request a welfare check?"

"We have no proof of anything wrong going on, Finley. Just one loud, obnoxious father and one little boy who will more than likely continue to emulate his father. I believe more than a few of the parents will want to file charges against Brian, and I can't blame them. Most of those would be Class C Misdemeanor Theft since a lot of what he forced students to hand over was under one hundred dollars. But a few of the items would fall into the Class A and B categories."

Mary shook her head sadly. "Brian will most likely be

placed in the juvenile justice system. It might actually be the one thing which saves him." She rose and embraced Finley, saying, "Call me if you need to talk."

"Okay," she said glumly, needing to put today behind her.

Returning to her classroom, Finley readied a few things for Monday's lessons before slipping into her coat and throwing her purse strap over her shoulder. She went to her car. Only two vehicles sat in the parking lot now. The other was Mary's. With it being the start to a weekend, other teachers had quickly cleared out, going home to their families or stopping at Hill Country Hangout for happy hour. Feeling drained, she merely wanted to go home and forget about today.

When she entered her house and hung up her coat, she smelled the sweet scent of a cake, remembering that she and Emerson were due to have dinner with the Clarks and Tennysons. Though she was in no mood to do so, it was probably what she needed to pull her from her doldrums.

Entering the kitchen, she saw Emerson pulling ingredients to make the frosting for the naked cake sitting on the counter.

Mustering a smile, she asked, "What did you make for dessert this evening?"

"I didn't have time to try anything new," her roommate said. "You're getting a regular chocolate cake from me."

"You won't find any of us protesting with chocolate involved," she said, taking a chair at the kitchen table.

Emerson sat next to her. "What's going on, Fin? Is it Brian Withers again?"

Briefly, she told her friend about what had happened today and the Withers' decision to pull their son from school.

"How could I have missed the bullying? Was I so focused on Brian's lack of academic progress that I couldn't see anything else? I've witnessed students being bullied before and addressed it right away, but this time? I didn't have a clue what was going on."

"You have the oldest group of students in the school. My third graders are much more likely to tattle if someone is mean to them or takes something of theirs. Fifth graders close ranks when adults are around. It must have been bad, though, for the dam to break."

"You wouldn't believe the things we found in Brian's locker," Finley said. "Money. Jewelry. Shoes. Books. Two cell phones. A tablet. Being held back a year, Brian always has been physically bigger than his classmates. I'm just upset because my babies were hurting, and I didn't see it."

"No one loves her students more than you do, Fin. Those fifth graders think you walk on water. I see how they treat you at school and how eager they are to come and talk to you whenever we're out in public. They adore you. They don't blame you for what Brian Withers was doing."

Her gaze met Emerson's. "I think I'm ready to quit teaching," she said, her voice barely a whisper.

"The feeling will pass. This incident with Brian will blow over."

Finley shook her head. "I've been thinking about this for almost a year, Emerson," she confessed. "Teaching isn't what I thought it would be. I keep thinking if I left, though, how I'd be disappointing my parents."

"Your parents want you to be happy. Yes, they might feel a little bit disappointed, but they'll support you in whatever you want to do." Emerson paused. "It's photography, isn't it? You want to pursue it full-time."

She nodded. "I find such joy in taking photos of others. Telling their stories in a way no one else can. I think what convinced me wasn't what happened today with Brian and what happened with his parents. It's when I put together that exhibit for the library that just went up."

Finley had taken to driving around the Hill Country with her friend Ivy, who was a painter. Every now and then, Ivy wanted to drive through the area, stopping to take pictures with her phone or even sketch the landscape. Finley had begun tagging along on some of these trips, taking pictures of the land. Mesas. Wildflowers. Valleys. The Guadalupe River.

She had begun experimenting with black and white film. Some of her best wedding and newborn portraits had used black and white film. She had done an entire series of black and white landscapes of the Hill Country and asked Dorothy Prigmore, the city's librarian, if she might place them on display at the library. Dorothy had readily agreed, having seen Finley's work, both when Finley had photographed her current senior in a series of outdoors portraits, as well as her son's wedding last month.

"I find that through photography, I can express myself in ways I never will be able to do in the classroom. I still love teaching and being with my kids." She hesitated. "But I don't think I'm meant to do it for the rest of my life."

She reached and took Emerson's hand. "I'm scared to death. I don't know if I can make a living from my photography. Sure, it's a great side business now and brings in quite a bit of extra income, but I don't know if it's enough to live on."

"I've got the rent covered, Fin," her longtime friend assured her. "Don't worry about paying it."

"I won't live off your charity, Em."

"Follow your heart. That's my advice. You won't be happy otherwise."

She would finish out this school year. She owed that much to her students and Mary. It was only the end of January, so she had a few months before she needed confirm her decision and turn in her resignation to Mary.

In her heart, though, Finley knew the decision had already been made.

3

inley looked around the crowded table as Emerson passed out slices of the chocolate cake she'd baked.

"Please tell me that's your famous buttercream frosting with caramel sauce," Dax said, dragging his finger through the top of his piece of cake and slipping his finger into his mouth.

"From the satisfied look on your face, I'd say you guessed right," Braden said, taking a bite of the dessert and sighing. "You never make a bad cake, Emerson."

Emerson's brows shot up haughtily. "Well, I am *the* exclusive baker for Weddings with Hart."

"Best hire I ever made," Harper said, then glanced to Finley. "Or maybe I should say it's a tie. Your photos take the cake, Finley."

Everyone laughed, and Finley was glad she had forced herself to come to dinner tonight. This would be the last time they were able to walk down a few doors to eat dinner with Braden and Harper. The couple, who had wed in October, had recently purchased their first house. It was just outside of Lost Creek and about seven minutes from the winery, where Braden was the head winemaker.

"When is moving day?" she asked.

"For which one of us?" Ivy said.

"You're moving, too?" Emerson asked.

Ivy nodded. "Dax and I are pretty cramped in his apartment. While it's convenient for him to trot downstairs to Java Junction and me to walk across the square to my art studio, we need more space."

"For now, Ivy and I are moving into Braden and Harper's rental," Dax shared. "We'll sublet it through April. Hopefully, we'll have found a place of our own by then."

"Moving day for us is Sunday," Harper said. "We thought it would make sense for us to totally be out of the house, and then Ivy and Dax will move in on Monday."

"Thank goodness your rental is furnished," Ivy said. "It'll be easy to move into your old place and hopefully give us time to find something of our own."

"You'll need to sweet talk Finley into helping you when you do find a house. She's helped us furnish our new place," Harper said, smiling at her friend. "You've made things really easy. You have a great eye and flair for what works in a room. Maybe you should ditch teaching and go into interior design work."

She wanted to share with her friends what her future plans held, but she wasn't ready to open up about leaving teaching just yet. Finley still wanted to give it some thought, making certain she was making the right career move. It would be important to also talk things over with her parents and let them know before word got out. She did owe it to Mary to let her know as soon as possible so that the principal could hire Finley's replacement.

"It's what makes you a great photographer," Ivy said. "You have a way of seamlessly blending art with emotion in every picture you take."

Blushing, she said, "That's high praise coming from the painter who has a big, fancy art show coming up in New York."

Ivy waved her away. "That's not anytime soon. Fortunately, Clive Crutchfield is not pushing for me to race through canvases. I don't mind working at a steady pace, but I'm relieved that my exhibition won't be until September."

"Do you need any help moving?" Finley asked.

"No," Harper said. "I think we've got everything under control. You've already placed so much furniture in the new house as it is. I want to give it a few weeks, and then maybe we can go into San Antonio again to work on completing the rest of the house."

Finley had a suspicion that in a few months, the couple would need to look for nursery furniture. She knew her friends were already trying for a baby.

"I'm happy to accompany you anytime. Especially if we stop by Mi Tierra," she said, referring to the famous bakery.

"I'm assuming you have an event scheduled for tomorrow night," Dax said, his dessert plate now empty.

"Yes. Not a wedding but a fiftieth anniversary party for a couple. Their kids and grandkids have been really involved in the planning. They're not using any catering. Everyone is bringing favorite family recipes from over the last several decades. One of the grandsons has a band, so they'll be playing. Another is a photographer, which means Finley is off the hook for the evening."

Dax looked to Emerson and her. "Then will either of you be able to make it to Java Junction tomorrow night and keep Ivy company since I'm performing?"

"I can't," Emerson said. "I'm actually going to a wedding in Austin tomorrow afternoon. A friend from the bakery I used to work at in college is getting married. After the reception, several of us are going to hang out. Have dinner. I'll wait and come back Sunday morning."

"I can go," Finley said. "You know I love your music, Dax. Besides, I could probably take a few new pictures of you performing and let Ivy update the website some."

"You're just hoping I'll comp your drinks if you're working," he teased. "Hey, I invited someone new to stop by tomorrow night."

"Oh, that's right," Ivy said. "You'll never guess who came into Java Junction? Holden Scott."

Finley perked up. "*Capitol Crimes* Holden Scott?" she asked, immediately recognizing the name.

"Yes, the author himself," Dax confirmed. "He's a really decent guy."

"Why was he in Lost Creek?" asked Harper. "Researching a new book?"

"He told me he was writing the screenplay for his latest

bestseller," Dax told the group. "Actually, he seemed pretty nervous about it. Said he's never written a screenplay before. He's originally from Austin. I guess he wanted to come back to the Hill Country to work. Maybe soak up the atmosphere of the place and be inspired as he writes."

"Dax asked Holden to stop by tomorrow night. He said he would," Ivy added. "He's bringing the director who did his first movie and his wife."

"I'm definitely in," Finley declared. "I loved everything about *Capitol Crimes*, both the book and the movie. I haven't had time to read his latest one yet, though."

"Because my wife keeps you busy photographing weddings," Braden said, slipping an arm around Harper's shoulders and kissing her.

"Here they go again," Emerson said, laughing. "All right, people. I've got to go home and get some sleep. It's almost ten o'clock and this week at school wore me out. Foolish or not, I promised Ethel I'd pull a shift until noon at The Bake House tomorrow since she's going to Houston for a few days."

Emerson had worked a second, weekend job at the town's bakery until recently, when she'd decided to work for Weddings with Hart. Her roommate often left school and went to the event center, where Harper had put in a gourmet kitchen for Emerson to use in order to bake cakes for scheduled events on the premises.

"We should go home and pack," Harper said.

"Yeah. Pack," Braden replied, giving his wife a hungry look, which had them all laughing again.

"We're actually the newlyweds," Dax pointed out.

"We've only been married a little over two months to your three months."

Ivy wrapped her arms about her husband's neck. "Then let's go home and do some packing of our own," she purred.

"Okay, the new code word for having hot sex is packing," Finley joked. "Not that I've done any packing in quite a while."

"I like it," Emerson said. "Packing. Okay, I'm leaving the cake here. Dax, you and Braden can fight over it."

She and Emerson slipped into their jackets and walked home.

"I'm beat," her friend said. "And I'll have to be at the bakery by three tomorrow morning. Goodnight." Emerson headed to her bedroom.

Finley was too restless to sleep, though. She found her Kindle and called up *Capitol Crimes*, re-reading the prologue. The book was a true thriller, and she had raced through it the first time.

Curious, she went to Amazon and searched for Holden Scott's latest novel and bought it, downloading it to her Kindle and opening it up. Once she began reading, she couldn't stop. It was very different in style and content from Scott's first effort, but it was gripping, nonetheless. It was obvious to her, having lived in the Hill Country her entire life, that the author knew the area well and the people who lived here.

When she reached the last page, she gasped aloud. The reveal of the killer totally blindsided her. Finley closed her Kindle, sitting in shock.

"Are you still up?" a voice asked, startling her.

She saw it was Emerson, her hair swept back in a high ponytail, wearing her a shirt with *The Bake House* scrolled above the pocket.

"Yes," she said. "I started reading the new Holden Scott book. I couldn't stop. It's that good. I just finished it."

"Go to bed, Fin," her roommate encouraged. "I'll see you when I get home on Sunday."

She locked the door behind Emerson and washed the makeup from her face and brushed and flossed. Putting her cell on the charger, she fell into bed. At first, she kept seeing images of the people in Scott's murder mystery, ones she'd created in her head as she'd read.

Then she woke up. Her bedroom was filled with light. Finley realized she'd actually gotten some sleep.

Picking up her cell, she saw it was just past eight-thirty, the latest she'd slept in months. Then again, she hadn't gone to bed until a quarter to three. Though she should feel tired, she never needed more than five or six hours of sleep. She made herself a cup of tea and then jumped in the shower. By the time she got out, her tea had steeped and was the perfect temperature. As she drank it, she put on light makeup and did her hair before dressing in jeans and a sweater.

Josh's game would be starting soon. She decided to head to the city soccer fields and watch a few minutes before running her errands. It took several minutes to find a parking place, but once she did, it only took her five minutes to reach the field the Dragons were playing on.

Spying Josh's parents, she climbed into the bleachers

and sat with them a few minutes. She knew the couple well since they served as room parents and helped her in planning parties, as well as chaperoning field trips.

Josh leaped into the air as the soccer ball was kicked toward the goal by the opposing team. He blocked it, and a cheer went up from their side of the bleachers. Immediately, the boy looked into the stands and waved at his parents and her.

"He'll be thrilled you saw that save," the mom said. "Don't feel like you have to stay longer, Finley. I know you have a lot going on."

She decided to slip out and run a few errands before her afternoon photo shoot, stopping at the dry cleaners, filling her tank with gas, and picking up a few groceries. By then, it was noon, so she ate a peanut butter and jelly sandwich before grabbing her camera equipment and heading to Sylvia Torres' house. They had gone to high school together, though Sylvia was a year behind Finley. Sylvia had recently had a baby girl and wanted newborn portraits taken.

Finley knocked on the door instead of ringing the doorbell. She'd learned early not to make that mistake and have a crying baby.

Sylvia answered, Jessica in her arms. "Come in."

"Oh, she's precious. We're going to get some great pictures, Sylvia. Let me set these things down. I have a few more props."

Soon, Finley was photographing the sleeping Jessica, focusing on tiny toes and her sleepy grin. She placed the baby inside one of the baskets she used, draping material over her. Then she pulled out one of her Flokati rugs and created a dip, setting the baby inside it.

"We'll do a womb pose, then get her with her hand under her chin."

After several more shots, she said, "Okay, Mom. Time for you. Hold her. Look down at her. Good. Now smile at her. Nice. Kiss her forehead."

Sylvia had placed a headband with a bow around the baby's head, but for a different look, Finley replaced it with another one and then totally left it off.

"Dad's turn," she said brightly, walking him through various poses.

"Oh, I love that one," Sylvia said, tearing up, as her husband held the baby, cradling Jessica's head in one hand, smiling down at her with love.

"Let's get a few family shots," Finley suggested.

By now, Jessica was stirring, so Finley worked fast. Sleeping babies made for better pictures than hungry babies who woke up fussy. Sure enough, after rolling off several shots, a few with Jessica's eyes open, the baby began to cry.

"I think I got everything I needed," she told the parents. "I'll put together several poses and packages and email them to you."

"Thank you so much, Finley," Sylvia said, still weepy. "Jessica is already changing so much. We've only been home from the hospital two weeks, and she's already gained a pound and has different expressions."

"That's why it's smart to capture what she looks like

now." Finley smiled. "Congrats to you both. I know you'll be terrific parents."

It didn't take long for her to pull the best pictures of the baby. Newborn shoots were some of her favorites to work. She took a break, though, heating up some leftover spaghetti and meatballs for dinner. She went back to sorting photographs, keeping her eye on the clock because she needed to leave soon for Java Junction.

Finley loved the musical nights held there. Tonight would be a great one since Dax would be performing. He only did so about once a month, giving other singers and musicians in the area a chance to have time to shine.

She decided even though it was cold, she would walk the three blocks to the square. It wasn't windy, and she actually preferred cold weather over hot. Entering the coffeehouse, she saw it was already three-quarters full.

"Finley!"

Ivy was waving at her, seated at her usual table in the center of the room. As she drew near, Finley saw another couple seated with her. The man was handsome, with warm brown eyes and a mustache. The woman was gorgeous, wearing a purple, form-fitting sweater and lots of bangles on one arm.

They both rose as she arrived, Ivy saying, "This is my friend I told you about. Finley Farrow, meet Wolf and Ana Ramirez."

"I'm pleased to meet you," she said, offering both her hand. "I loved *Renegade*. And *Capitol Crimes*, too."

Wolf looked pleased. "Thank you for the compliment, Finley. Ivy says you're a teacher and photographer."

They sat and she said, "Yes, I juggle both."

"I've created my own production company and have a cinematographer I work with," Wolf said. "But I've always used the photographer of whichever studio I'm working with for stills. Maybe you could show me some of your work and I could see if your talents might be suited to the film industry."

"Finley has a gift," a voice said. "You'll love her unique perspective, Wolf."

She turned, gazing up at the tall man with the low, rumbling voice who stood next to her. He had dark hair and moss green eyes which drew her in. The wire-framed glasses he wore only emphasized their unusual color. He was lean but looked strong and looked vaguely familiar.

He also took her breath away.

Setting down the tray of drinks he carried, he pulled out the chair next to her and held out a hand. Finley took it, her heart racing.

"I'm Holden Scott," he said. "I've been wanting to meet you—because your photographs spoke to my soul."

4

*H*olden was at the barista bar with Dax when the blonde entered Java Junction. Something about her drew his eye. He watched as she made her way to the center of the coffeehouse and greeted Ivy Tennyson, who introduced her to Wolf and Ana.

This had to be Finley Farrow.

"I'm glad things worked out for you to stay at Jean Bradley's place," Dax said.

He had to force his attention away from Finley, and he looked back at Dax.

"Yes, it's the perfect size, especially since it's only me. It's got some pretty trails nearby, so I can take a break and clear my head if I need to. Do a bit of hiking."

"Java Junction might also be a good place to come in and write if you need a change of scenery from the cottage," his new friend continued. "It's pretty quiet from around ten until three each day. My old geezers leave by ten, and the moms who've driven carpools scatter. We get the occasional drop-ins during lunch. Then things pick up once the high school lets out for the day."

"I'll keep that in mind. I've never written in a public place before. I've thought it would be too distracting."

"That nook in the back?" Dax asked. "It's got your name written all over it. You can also run a monthly tab if you choose. I only offer that to my regulars."

Holden grinned. "So that's how you suck people in. Offer a free drink the first time—and then a house tab."

"You got me. No, seriously, you're welcome to come in and write without drinking a thing, Holden. Java Junction's doors are open to everyone, whether you order something or not."

He glanced back to the table at the center of the room.

"Oh, good. Finley made it. You'll like her. She grew up in Lost Creek. Her parents run a Montessori preschool, and her brother and sister-in-law operate a water sports rental place at the lake. I know now isn't the optimum time of year, but you can rent canoes, paddleboats, and kayaks from them if you decide to stay around for warmer weather."

"I may need to buy one of your wife's paintings," Holden said, glancing to the one Ivy had done of Lost Creek Lake.

Dax beamed with pride. "You'll have to wait a while on that. Ivy's working on paintings for a show next fall in New York. It takes a long time to produce enough pieces to put together an exhibition."

"Ready for you, Holden," Scott Bartlett said, handing

over a tray of drinks to his boss. "I saw Finley come in," the barista added. "I'll make her usual and bring it over."

"You're busy," Holden said. "I'll take the drinks over for everyone. I'm looking forward to this evening, Dax. Thanks for inviting me."

Holden weaved his way between tables and as he reached the center, he heard Wolf say, "Maybe you could show me some of your work, and I could see if your talents might be suited to the film industry."

"Finley Farrow has a gift. You'll love her unique perspective, Wolf," he said, placing the tray on the table.

The blonde looked up at him with piercing, aquamarine eyes. She had an unconventional beauty, with all the parts coming together in a way which drew him in. Those eyes mesmerized him, and Holden knew he could be lost in them.

He took the chair next to her and offered his hand. "I'm Holden Scott. I've been wanting to meet you because your photographs spoke to my soul."

Her eyes widened, and he added, "As you can guess, I saw your exhibit at the library."

A blush tinged her cheeks. "It just went up last weekend," she told him.

"I was just telling Finley that I don't have a photographer on the payroll for WEBA Productions. I'll have to stop in and see your work."

"What is WEBA?" Ivy asked.

Ana smiled. "It's an acronym for the four of us. We have two children, Eva and Bear, hence WEBA."

Scott appeared at their table. "Here you go, Finley," he said easily.

Looking up, she said, "Thanks for taking care of me, Scott," and took a sip of her drink.

All Holden could think of was drinking from her lips.

He told himself this was crazy. He'd never been smitten instantly by any woman, and he certainly wasn't ready to become involved with someone else, not with a screenplay to write. He needed Madison to be a distant speck in his rear-view mirror before he considered spending any time with another woman. Still, Finley's photographs intrigued him.

"Where did you go to shoot your series?" he asked.

"Most of those photographs are within ten miles of Lost Creek," she informed him. "Ivy likes to go driving, looking for inspiration for her art. I've started tagging along, shooting photos."

He forced himself to turn from Finley to Ivy. "I know you painted that picture of Lost Creek Lake up there. I would love to see some of your other work."

"I'm not in the habit of showing it off, but you're a fellow artist. Just as Finley paints a story with her camera, you do the same with your words." Ivy looked to Wolf. "And Wolf also is a storyteller."

"I wish I could say I wrote my own scripts and filmed them, but I find it easier to take the words others have crafted and bring them alive on screen," the director said. He smiled at his friend. "I'm really pleased that Holden agreed to write the screenplay for *Hill Country Homicide*."

"I just read it last night," Finley said, drawing Holden's

attention again. "I'd read *Capitol Crimes* when it came out and thought it was terrific. When Dax said you were coming to Java Junction this evening, I decided to start *Hill Country Homicide*."

She chuckled, a deep, throaty laugh that caused desire to race through him. "I read it in one sitting, Holden. I think that's probably the biggest compliment I could give an author. That ending had me flummoxed. I never would have guessed who the killer was."

"That's what I liked about the book," Ana commented. "Holden gave us an advanced copy, and I was curious to see what his follow-up to *Capitol Crimes* would be like. I was startled by the reveal of the killer. No, dumbfounded," she corrected. "Then I went back through the book again, re-reading certain passages, and guess what? Holden had dropped subtle breadcrumbs throughout the novel. The answer was there all the time, right under a reader's nose."

Finley looked at him with those amazing aquamarine eyes and asked, "What's the difference between writing a novel and a screenplay?"

He laughed. "I'm learning on the fly. Wolf thought I'd be the ideal person to adapt my novel for screen since I'm intimately familiar with the plot and characters. It's a very different kind of writing than I'm used to, though. Dialogue is everything. I'm having to shave about two-thirds of the pages in the novel to be a manageable size for screen."

Wolf jumped in. "Most films run between ninety and a hundred and twenty minutes. That's as long as movie theaters want. If you go longer, it cuts down on a showing a day for them, and that's not something they like."

"I can't imagine having to edit out so much," Ivy said. "That's like viewing one of my canvases and two-thirds of it being empty."

"The tricky thing," Holden continued, "is that you must get the entire story in. A very condensed version, that is. You can't simply film the first third— or the last third —of a novel. It has to be pared in a way where you have a complete story. Intro. Rising action. Climax. And a satisfying conclusion. And that's not to mention character development. I'm having to create a few composite characters, blending two or three from the novel together and allowing them to serve a single purpose. Film is a visual medium, though. What it takes me to describe in a page, a moviegoer can see and assess within a couple of seconds. That's definitely helping trim things."

Holden saw that Dax took the stage, and the coffeehouse began to quieten. He had a guitar in hand and slipped the strap over his head, taking a seat on a stool.

"Thanks for turning out tonight," he said. "I haven't been up here for a while. I've written a few new songs to share with you, along with some of the older ones you've heard before."

"*Forever's Embrace*," called out a woman two tables away.

Grinning, Dax said, "I'll always play that one. For my one true love."

Dax looked at Ivy with such tenderness in his eyes that Holden was moved. He glanced to the painter, seeing love reflected in her eyes for her husband. It seemed in that moment as if the two were one.

Holden had only witnessed that kind of love between Wolf and Ana. He certainly had never looked at Madison that way. Part of him regretted the years he had spent with her. Their relationship had never moved forward, remaining stagnant, and he should have been more aware of that instead of letting things slide along.

He wanted more in his life than a status quo.

Holden realized he yearned for love.

By now, Dax had begun to play. Holden sipped his drink, aware of Finley sitting nearby. Closing his eyes, he caught the faint scent of strawberries and knew it wafted from her skin.

Dax played for close to an hour, mesmerizing the coffeehouse's crowd. Then he said he was ready to play his final number and began.

Holden listened carefully to the words, knowing they had been written for Ivy. He wondered if he would ever write a novel for a woman he loved.

Glancing at Wolf, he saw the director held hands with his wife, and they both stared wordlessly into one another's eyes, lost in the moment.

The last note ended, and applause erupted throughout the crowded coffeehouse.

"Thanks for turning out tonight," Dax told the audience. "We'll be closing in the next fifteen minutes. Hope to see you next time. Or tomorrow morning."

Everyone laughed as Dax left his guitar on the stool

he'd occupied and returned to their table. Holden rose, offering his hand.

"And here I thought you were just some hack who made coffee," he joked. "You're talented, Dax."

Ana said, "We enjoyed hearing you play so much, Dax. Of course, Wolf and I heard you play a few songs at one of the Harmony & Hues we attended last summer. Will you be holding the fusion nights again?"

"Ivy and I have talked it over, and we want to do it for the Lost Creek community again. We're even considering opening up other Java Junctions throughout small towns in the Hill Country and starting Harmony & Hues nights in them, as well."

Wolf's eyes lit up. "This would make for a fantastic documentary, Dax. Even if I just filmed Lost Creek's Harmony & Hues nights next summer, that would be compelling enough. Could we get together and talk about it?"

"Do you have time right now?" Dax asked.

"Of course," Wolf and Ana said in unison, causing the others to laugh.

"I'll be going," Finley said. "It was so nice meeting you Ana, Wolf."

"We do want to see your photo series, Finley," Wolf told her. "Would you mind showing them to us? I'd like to ask questions of you when we view it."

"The Lost Creek Library opens at one on Sundays," she said. "If you could come tomorrow, that is. During the week, I teach fifth graders, so I'd have to meet you after school if you choose a weekday."

"Tomorrow is good for us," Ana said. "We'll bring Eva and Bear along." She turned to Holden. "Eva wants to see where Uncle Holden is living now. She said she was going to come spend the night with you so you could have a tea party and watch Disney movies together."

"Why don't we get together for lunch?" Finley suggested. "We could meet at noon and then head to the library afterward."

"What's good in Lost Creek?" Wolf asked.

"Blackwood BBQ is the best place in town. It's on Main Street, just a few minutes from the square."

She glanced at Holden. "You're welcome to join us. If you'd like, that is."

He had been trying to figure out how to weasel an invitation to tomorrow and smiled at her. "I'd be happy to see your photos again, Finley. Especially if you will be giving insight into them."

She stood. "Then I'll see you at noon. Ivy, you and Dax are welcome to come if you can."

Ivy shook her head. "I've got my Sunday shift at the tasting room."

"You paint and talk about wines?" Wolf asked.

"My family owns Lost Creek Vineyards. My sister runs the event center, and her husband is our chief winemaker. Dad is in charge of marketing and advertising, and Mom keeps the books— and keeps Dad in line."

"Sundays are super-busy at Java Junction," Dax said. "Besides, Ivy and I have seen all the photos in this series. Feel free to stop in for a coffee after the library, though."

Holden stood, offering Dax his hand and they shook.

"Thanks again for the invitation tonight." Looking to Finley, he asked, "May I walk you to your car?"

She nodded, slipping into her coat. He placed his hand on the small of her back, guiding her through the coffee-house. Even through the layers she wore, the touch was electrifying.

Outside, he asked, "Which way to your car?"

"Actually, I walked to Java Junction. The square is always crowded on nights someone plays. I only live three blocks away. I can walk home."

"I'll drive you," he insisted.

"You don't have to do that."

"I know," he said softly. "But I want to."

He led her to Wolf's borrowed truck, thinking it was time he bought transportation of his own. He didn't see himself returning permanently to New York. The past month in Texas had told him that his heart was in the Hill Country.

He'd never leave it again.

Finley gave him brief instructions, and he pulled into her driveway less than two minutes later. They sat for a moment in silence, and Holden wondered if she might be as reluctant to part from him as he was from her.

"Would you... would you like to come in for a cupcake? My roommate brought a couple home from the bakery today."

His gaze met hers. "I'd like that. Very much."

---

5

*N*erves rattled through Finley as she climbed from the truck and moved toward her front door. She hadn't brought a guy home in… forever.

Holden Scott wasn't just any guy, though. He was a famous novelist. He traveled in circles she read about in *People*. No way was he interested in her. She doubted he'd felt the same spark she had when they'd shaken hands. And when he'd guided her through the coffeehouse, his hand at the small of her back, she'd almost passed out.

"Get a grip," she muttered under her breath as she dug in her purse for her keys.

"I'm sorry?" he asked, once again resting his hand on her back as she produced her key ring.

"Nothing. Just talking to myself," she said, shrugging, embarrassed.

He smiled. An achingly beautiful, wonderful, impossible smile. "And here I thought only writers did that kind of thing. Maybe it's all creative people who do so."

Inserting the key into the lock, Finley said, "I wouldn't put myself in that category."

She started through the door, but he grabbed her elbow, impeding her progress. It caused her to look up at him. His gaze pierced her, seeming as if he saw into her soul.

"You have talent. Don't ever doubt yourself, Finley."

He released his hold on her. Shakily, she turned back to the door, stepping in and slipping off her coat. She hung it on the coat tree.

"Can I take yours?" she asked as he shrugged out of his.

He handed it to her, their fingers brushing.

Fire...

She sucked in a quick breath. He did the same. Their eyes met, and Finley quickly looked away.

"Come into the kitchen," she said, walking briskly, trying to put distance between them.

Because she didn't trust herself.

Flipping on the kitchen light, she went to the cupboard and removed two dessert plates.

"Would you like something to drink?"

"I noticed you drank tea tonight."

"Ah, the observant writer," she said lightly. "I don't do caffeine after noon. If I did, I'd be wide awake at three in the morning. I've got herbal teas I can offer you. Regular and decaf coffee pods. Bottled water."

"I'll take tea. That sounds good with a cupcake."

Glad she had something to do, she filled two mugs and

placed them in the microwave. Seeing he still stood, Finley said, "Please. Sit. I'll get my tea caddy."

She brought the caddy to the table. "I've got orange spice. Raspberry. Chamomile. Peach. Apple cinnamon. Decaf Earl Grey."

"Peach for me."

She opened two packets. "I don't have sugar. Emerson and I use stevia in our drinks." She chuckled. "We get enough sugar when she bakes."

"You mentioned the bakery. Does she work there?"

The microwave dinged. Finley retrieved the cups and placed them on the table, dipping both teabags into them before taking a seat.

"She used to. Emerson and I teach together. We met at UT in Austin. Roomed together our first year and stayed friends. She did weekend shifts at The Bake House until recently. Harper— Ivy's sister —started Weddings with Hart. Emerson bakes wedding and groom's cakes for receptions held at the winery. She also does other desserts for different events. Anniversary parties. That kind of thing. I'm Harper's photographer."

Holden dunked his teabag a couple of times. "That's interesting. You have both people and landscapes as your subjects."

She stood again, returning with the bakery box and plates. Opening it, she placed one of the German chocolate cupcakes on a plate and pushed it toward him, seeing his eyes light up.

"You didn't tell me I'd be getting German chocolate. I can't remember the last time I had it."

"Emerson is a master baker, but she really excels with anything having to do with chocolate. These are my favorites." She plated a cupcake for herself and took a bite, sighing.

"When did you start pursuing photography?"

"High school. I took a class. Served as a photographer for the newspaper and yearbook staffs. My specialty was sports. Actions shots can be tricky. You have to capture a certain moment before it vanishes. A forward springing into the air, dunking a basketball. A runner leaning, trying to cross the tape first. A golfer in mid-swing."

He smiled, making her heart skip a beat. "You have a true passion for it."

"I photographed a lot of events for my sorority in college," she continued. "I'm also the unofficial photographer for my elementary school. And I have a side business, beyond what I do for Harper and Weddings with Hart."

"Is that where your landscapes come in?"

"Oddly, no. What you saw at the library is my first attempt at that. Up until now, I've focused on people."

She went on, explaining how she did engagement and bridal portraits and told him about the newborn shoot she'd completed yesterday.

"Could I see some of those shots?" he asked, genuine curiosity on his face.

"Sure. Work on your cupcake while I'll get my camera."

As she left the kitchen, he said, "You better move fast, or I'll finish yours, too."

Finley laughed, feeling excited and yet relaxed in Holden's company. She claimed her camera and went through the series of pictures with him, explaining about the different props she used with the baby.

"These are fantastic," he praised. "I like the black and white ones the most."

"I'm partial to those myself. I love the play of shadows and the contrast in shades. I've started offering packages with color and black and white, even with my senior portraits."

He cocked his head. "Seniors as in old people, or seniors in high school?"

She laughed. "Teenagers. I do some of the up close, cap and gown pictures since parents always seem to want those, but my favorites are taking the kids outside. Lost Creek has so many pretty places to use as backgrounds. The hills. The lake. Several bridges which cross the actual creek. Even the gazebo in the town square."

"They wear mortarboards in those?"

"No," she said, laughing. "I pull in what's important to them. They can bring a few changes of clothes. I'll do action shots on the football or baseball fields, with players wearing their uniforms. But I'll also take kids into nature and shoot them there, wearing their band or drill team uniform. Here, I'll show you."

She flipped through her camera, letting Holden see a cheerleader with her pompoms, jumping high off the ground, Lost Creek Rock in the background.

"We talk about their passions before I plan the shoot. I've captured seniors who enjoy art sketching." She showed a girl sitting atop a rock, sketchpad in her lap, drawing a cactus.

"These are really good, Finley. I'm not blowing smoke either."

"I enjoy working with seniors. Here's the captain of the soccer team, holding a ball. That's Lost Creek in the background. This is a kid who's had a starring role in drama productions. I had Ivy create this movie poster with the girl's name on it and placed it in the glass case in front of the theater. Who knows? She might really be famous someday."

"You really have a way of capturing a piece of a person on film." He shook his head. "And these are so different from what I saw at the library. Relating it to my world, it's the difference in writing a thriller versus writing someone's biography. Or a novelist trying to write poetry." He grinned. "Or a screenplay."

"I'm just beginning to experiment with non-people subjects. The Hill Country is full of so many amazing landforms. Full of variety. I hope to do more."

"How do you have time to teach and work at another job? Writing consumes a lot of my waking hours. I can't imagine having to do something else alongside it."

Finley paused. "I'm going to treat you like a stranger on a plane. Someone I'll never see again."

He reached and took her hand, surprising her. "I hope I do see you again," he said huskily.

She swallowed. "Maybe that wasn't exactly what I meant. What I'm trying to say is that we don't really know one another. And how in some situations, you might share things with a person you've just met. Simply to get their perspective."

His eyes lit with understanding. "You want to leave teaching, don't you?"

Holden's thumb caressed the back of her hand, making rational thought barely possible.

"Yes," she whispered. "I've talked to Emerson about it. She gets it. I… I think I've done all I can in teaching. Even though I thought I'd spend my entire adult life in education, I'm finding my passion for photography is pushing everything aside."

"I taught high school for two years," he told her. "I had applied to get into the University of Iowa's Writers' Workshop after I graduated from college. The workshop is a two-year program where you earn your MA in Fine Art and come out with a finished product. In my case, it was *Capitol Crimes*. I liked teaching. I think I was pretty good at it. But I had a burning desire to write. To tell stories. To challenge myself and entertain readers."

He squeezed her hand and then released it, leaving her bereft. "I don't regret the two years I taught. I learned a lot about myself as a person." He grinned. "And had to learn how to exercise patience I never knew I had. But when the opportunity presented itself, I made a beeline to Iowa and never looked back. What I'm saying is you need to follow your heart."

"That's what Emerson told me," she said softly.

"Then I already like her. She's right. Obviously, she's known you far longer than I have, but I feel we're kindred spirits."

Holden looked deeply into her eyes. "I saw something in your photographs, Finley. Something magical. Your art spoke to my soul. Anyone can take a picture. You capture an image. A snapshot of a moment in time. Those images tell a story that move others. If you don't chase this dream — if you keep teaching —you'll slowly shrivel inside. You might be a great teacher, but staying in the classroom when you want to be challenged and fulfilled in other ways will eventually suck your soul dry until nothing is left. Let instinct guide you. Try making photography your profession and not your hobby.

"Believe in yourself."

Finley slowly nodded. "You're right. If I don't do this, I'll always regret not stepping outside my very comfortable box. If I find I can't support myself or I realize I'm not as good as I'd like to be, I can always go back to the classroom. That's the beauty of teaching. With education, I'm not making my way up some corporate ladder and will lose out if I step away for a year or two."

"You're talented," he said firmly. "I don't think you'll need to teach again."

"I'll definitely finish out this school year," she told him. "I owe it to my students. And myself. I'm invested in them, and I know they are in me, too. But you've inspired me, Holden. I'm going to speak to my principal on Monday and tell her that I'll be resigning at the end of the school year."

She stood, ready to take her camera back to her room. Holden stood, too, taking her wrist. He slipped the camera from her hand and set in on the kitchen table.

The air between them was so electric, Finley thought if she lit a match, they might go up in flames.

His thumb caressed her wrist. "I need to kiss you, Finley. Can I do that?"

No man had ever asked her that question. She liked being given a choice. Having control. Being able to say yes or no.

But there was only one answer.

"Yes," she told him, resolve in her voice. Just as her gut knew it was right to give photography a chance, it also told her to explore whatever was between Holden and her.

He slipped off his glasses and cradled her cheek with one hand, his other still holding her wrist. Then slowly, he lowered his lips to hers.

Magic...

From the moment his mouth touched hers, Finley knew this was different. *He* was different.

Holden didn't rush things. Slowly, he brushed his lips against hers, lips which were soft yet still firm. Then he pressed his mouth to hers for a light kiss. Once. Twice. Three times. His hand released her wrist, and his arm went about her waist. He stepped closer to her, their bodies brushing. Her heart raced as she caught his clean, masculine scent. No cologne. Just a fresh male scent that made her knees weak and her blood sing.

Finley slipped her arms around him, feeling the muscles in his back. He tilted his head to the right, the pressure increasing. He continued kissing her, each kiss lingering a bit longer than the one before, causing her to cling tighter to him. She felt his smile against her mouth as he kissed her again, this time much longer than before.

Desire flickered through her, and she experienced an emotional intimacy as never before because he didn't rush things between them.

Then his kiss grew more intense as he deepened it, the pressure greater, the urgency ramped up now. She had never been more turned on by a kiss— and they were still kissing with closed mouths. Her senses were on high alert, a prickling awareness of him coursing through her. She moved her hands from his back, pushing them into his hair, tightening her fingers in the thick locks as she held him close.

He broke the kiss, his lips trailing across her cheek. Along her jaw. Down her throat. He licked her pulse point, beating in overtime now. Finley whimpered.

Holden's mouth returned to hers, and the long, drugging kisses continued. She could have kissed this man all night— but he pulled away, his lips hovering just above hers, their breath intermingling.

"Thank you," he rumbled.

"Thank you," she echoed. "That was... memorable."

He cradled her face, his hands warm. "Memorable?" he asked, a hint of amusement in his voice.

"I was going to say nice. But nice didn't cover it. It seemed... lame. And there was nothing lame about kissing you, Holden," she said, her breath still uneven, her voice shaking.

He leaned in again, kissing her softly. Briefly. "Memorable, it is. Maybe we can go for earth-shattering next time. That is, if there's a next time." Holden paused. "The ball's in your court, Finley."

6

When Wolf Ramirez had signed on to direct *Capitol Crimes*, he had asked Holden to come to his Texas ranch, where they spent three days dissecting Holden's novel. They had delved deeply into character and minute plot details which Wolf thought could be important in his film. Wolf had also allowed Holden to read the script which had been written. He'd made a few suggestions and had noticed when he saw the film version, that those suggestions had been woven in to the finished product.

Not once during his time in Texas had he missed Madison Parmalee.

That alone should have been a wake-up call for him, but Holden hadn't had much experience in dating. Looking back, he realized how immature he had been emotionally, going into his relationship with Madison.

During the filming, a good deal of which occurred in

Washington, D.C., Holden had been invited to the set by Wolf to see his novel come to life. Once more, he never missed Madison during the week they were apart. He had asked her to join him, though, for a couple of days at the end of that week, and they hadn't spent much time together. Instead, his girlfriend had followed various cast members around the set, enthralled by the actors and the experience.

Holden had been apart from Finley twelve hours now, and she was *all* he had thought about. He lay awake last night, replaying their conversation. And kisses. He had dreamed of her and upon awakening, Finley had been his first thought. He didn't believe in love at first sight. This was more than lust in first sight, though. Yes, he was very attractive to her, but instinct told him it ran deeper than that. He wanted to get to know everything about her.

Pulling up to the front of her house now, Holden saw a car in the driveway and thought it might belong to Emerson, the roommate she had mentioned. He got out of the borrowed truck and went to the front door, ringing the doorbell. An attractive woman with dark hair and gray eyes opened the door.

"Hi. You must be Holden. I'm Emerson. Come on in."

"Thank you," he said, stepping into the small house.

"Finley will be here in just a minute. She got a phone call and is booking a photo shoot. She told me that you're a writer."

"Yes," he confirmed. "I've published two novels and recently finished the first draft of my third. While I let it sit a bit, I've taken on a new project, writing the screen-play for the second novel."

"I wish I had time to read," she said wistfully. "I encourage my students to do so all the time, but I stay too busy to read."

"If you made the cupcake I devoured last night, you're quite the baker."

She smiled. "I did make them. I bake cakes for Weddings with Hart, which operates out of Lost Creek Winery. The Harts built an event center on the property last year, and I provide cakes for weddings and other parties held there. You'll have to join us sometime for our weekly dinners with friends. I always try to bake some-thing new and special for them."

Finley entered the room. "Yes, you need to eat with us. Emerson uses a group of us as her guinea pigs, testing all kinds of desserts on us."

He laughed. "I can't think of a job I'd like better than to be a dessert taste tester."

She looked to Emerson. "What night are we meeting this week?"

"Wednesday," her roommate confirmed. "Harper wants to host since they'll be in their new house."

"That's right," Finley said. "They're moving in today. Hopefully, they'll be somewhat settled by Wednesday." She turned to him. "If you're free this Wednesday, we eat at six. Braden and I take turns with the cooking. We also like to experiment and try out new recipes."

"You need to say yes, Holden," Emerson encouraged. "Finley and Braden are terrific cooks."

"You're talking to a bachelor who lives in a cottage with a miniscule kitchen and zero cooking skills. One of my biggest talents was phoning for takeout in New York. I'll be there."

"I can teach you how to cook," Finley told him. "A few simple things to help you get by. Spaghetti. Pad Thai. That kind of thing."

"I don't see how you'd have time. Not with teaching and your photography."

Her gaze met his. "I can make the time— if you're willing."

To be able to spend more time in this lovely creature's company was a no-brainer.

"I'll work around your schedule then. That's the beauty of being a writer. I can write at six in the morning or ten at night."

"We better get going," she said. "It's almost noon now."

"Take your tablet," he suggested. "I want you to show Wolf and Ana some of the portraits you've done before they see your landscapes of the area."

Finley grabbed it from the coffee table, and he drove them to the diner.

"I've always loved a diner," he said, easing into a parking place. "I'll probably pick up dinner here a few nights a week."

"Nope. Lone Star Diner is only open from six in the morning until three in the afternoon. You could always do takeout at lunch. Otherwise, I'd suggest trying The Country Hearth. It's home cooking at its finest. And they're open until eight most nights. We also have some other good restaurants in the area, as well. Mexican. Italian."

"Then I'll let you be my guide to all things Lost Creek," he told her, coming around and opening her door and escorting her inside the diner.

Finley introduced him to Shelly Blackwood, the diner's owner and wife of Shy, who owned and operated the barbeque joint he'd eaten at the previous evening with Wolf and Ana.

"Nice to meet you, Holden. I've already seated your friends," Shelly said.

They made their way to the table, and Eva spotted him, running to meet him halfway. He swung her high in the air, and the little girl squealed with glee.

"I've missed you, Uncle Holden," she said.

"I only left the ranch yesterday, Eva."

"Bear missed you, too. And the chickens."

He set her on the ground and said, "This is Miss Finley, Eva."

The little girl pursed her lips as she studied Finley. "Is she your friend?"

"Yes, she is," he replied, hoping he and Finley would leave the friend zone soon and move on to something else. If last night's kisses had any sway, they were already entering uncharted territory.

They joined Wolf and Ana, and Holden introduced Finley to Bear.

"I like to kick soccer balls," Bear announced. "And Papa is teaching me to ride a horse. I'm five."

"I love to ride horses," Finley told the little boy.

"You can come visit us and take me riding," Bear told her.

He and Eva returned to their coloring, and Ana asked, "What's good here?"

Finley chuckled. "What isn't good? Really, anything you order won't let you down. For me, I'm getting breakfast. That's something Shelly serves all day. I eat pretty light in the mornings before I leave for school, so things such as pancakes, eggs, and bacon are a real treat for me."

"I'm always in search of the perfect meatloaf," Wolf revealed. "That's what I'm having."

Their server took their order. Holden encouraged Finley to show his friends some of her portraits. She handed over her tablet, and Ana scrolled through, Wolf leaning close so he could see.

"I do formal bridal and engagement portraits, and I also shoot events at the winery," Finley explained. "A busy part of the year for me is the month before students return to school."

She told the couple how she took senior portraits, allowing her subjects to bring props to incorporate into their photo sessions, as well as wearing their extra-curricular uniforms.

"Show them the newborn pictures from yesterday," Holden said.

Ana handed Finley the tablet, and she brought up the photo shoot. Soon, Ana had tears in her eyes.

"These are simply marvelous. I wish we would have thought to have something like this done when our kids were this age. They change so fast. I would have had ten babies if I could have, but I had some complications with Bear. He'll be our last one."

"You capture the essence of people," Wolf told Finley. "I feel by seeing your portraits, I know these people. Would you consider coming to the ranch and photographing our children?"

"I'd be happy to do so. They both have such personality. My schedule can get pretty booked, but I actually have this afternoon free. Would you like me to come today after we visit the library?"

"Yes," Ana gushed. "That would be fantastic."

"I'd like to get some pictures of them out on the ranch. With the horses. Riding. If you have any other animals, that would be a fun interaction to capture, as well. "

Their food arrived, and it was as good as Finley had said it would be. Wolf generously picked up the check for their entire party, and they left the diner for the library.

When they arrived, Dorothy Prigmore was just unlocking the doors.

"Hello, Finley. And Holden. I see you found her after viewing her exhibition."

"I was so taken with Finley's work, I told some friends they also had to come see it."

Wolf and his family joined them, and Holden introduced the librarian to them.

Dorothy said to the children, "We have a wonderful children's area. It has a play kitchen. A puppet theater. Would you like to go see it with me?"

"Yes!" chimed the kids in unison.

Dorothy looked to Ana. "I'll keep my eye on them so that you can give Finley's work your full attention."

"Thank you," Ana said. She bent and made eye contact with the children. "You go with Miss Dorothy now and play and read. If you pull a book off the shelf, remember to put it back. Papa and I will be looking at some of Miss Finley's pictures. We'll come find you soon."

"Okay, Mama," Eva said brightly, taking Bear's hand and the librarian's.

The four adults moved further into the library, and Finley said, "Here are my photographs. I'll let you study them a few minutes and then if you have any questions, I'm happy to talk to you about them."

She went and sat on a nearby bench while Holden, Wolf, and Ana moved slowly from one photograph to the next.

He had been impressed the first time he had viewed the exhibit, but he picked up on new things this second time around. The photographs spoke to him as before, perhaps more now because he'd met Finley.

Holden glanced to Wolf and Ana. Both remained silent, intently looking at the photographs. He continued down the line until he reached the end of the series. Finley joined him.

"They haven't said a word." Her brow knit together in worry.

"Wolf and Ana both like to mull things over."

"Their kids are adorable. I like your friends, Holden. You're lucky to be working with them."

"I'm nervous as hell," he admitted. "I've told you that

I've got no experience in screenwriting. Wolf plans to make *Homicide* the first movie his production company releases. If it flops, the entire company might go bankrupt. That's a lot riding on my shoulders."

She placed her hand on his forearm and squeezed it. "That won't happen. You've written a crazy-good mystery. You'll know instinctively what needs to go into your script and what can be left out. I've seen two of Wolf's movies. You can trust him to bring your vision and the story to life. And Ana seems as if she'll run a tight ship."

Finley's hand fell away, turning as the other couple joined them.

Excitement lit the director's eyes. "As good as your portraits are, Finley, you have a career beyond them. You've captured the rugged charm of the place I love. The majesty. The stark beauty. The lushness. Holden was right. He told me that each of your photographs tells a story. That's a gift."

"I don't know much about art or photography," Ana said. "My gut tells me what I like." Beaming, she said, "I love your work, Finley. It moves me."

"Thank you so much," Finley said. "I'm humbled by the praise you're heaping on me. I'm truly a novice when it comes to shooting anything other than people, though. My subjects have always been people. I know— just as Holden as he writes his screenplay —that I'll be learning as I go along."

"You have talent," Wolf declared. "You photograph things from a place deep within you. It's innate." The director paused. "I want to offer you the chance to be WEBA's official photographer."

Startled, she asked, "What would that even involve, Wolf? I know next to nothing about the movie business."

"You'd need to be on set for some of the shoot," he explained. "I like various stills taken when I film a movie. Those would be used for publicity purposes. I'd also want you to work with me in designing the concept for the movie's poster. I think I would even like your input when I cut the trailer because you have a such a good eye."

"Wow," Finley said. "I'm a bit overwhelmed."

"I know you're teaching. I don't want to disrupt your job in any way. I'm hoping to begin filming this summer. June at the earliest. First of July at the latest. While Holden's writing the script, Ana and I will be scouting locations. We'll even start casting. Hopefully, we'll have a completed script by the beginning of April. You could join us on set once school lets out."

Determination filled Finley's face, and Holden knew what was coming.

"I'm going to throw caution to the wind and turn in my resignation. Holden has convinced me that I need to give photography a try full-time. If I don't, I'll regret not doing so." She brightened. "As to your offer, Wolf? Yes, I'll be available this summer— during the week only since I'm still committed to photographing events planned by my friend Harper on weekends. If you can agree to that, I would be thrilled for you to take a chance on me and make me your WEBA Productions' photographer."

inley accompanied Holden to his truck, her legs wobbly. She was astonished that Wolf Ramirez found her work so good that he'd offered her a job with his production company.

"Careful," Holden said as she stumbled on a bump in the sidewalk, catching hold of her elbow and keeping his fingers firmly around it as he walked her the rest of the way to his truck.

He opened the door, and she got in. He didn't close it, though.

"Breathe," he said, taking her hands in his and breathing in slowly.

She imitated him, releasing a long breath as he did. Taking another deep one and once again letting it out. After three breaths, she nodded.

"I'm okay," she assured him. "Well, maybe a little thunderstruck by how quickly things are moving."

"We can talk about it on the way to the ranch." He squeezed her fingers and then closed the door, returning to the driver's seat.

"You don't have to drive me there. I don't want to take up anymore of your time. You've got a screenplay to write."

"Didn't I tell you I can write anytime? I put in some good pages yesterday. It's Sunday. I need to take some time off." He grinned. "Or I'll become like Jack Nicholson in *The Shining* and keep typing *'All work and no play makes Holden a dull boy.'*"

Finley laughed, the humor being exactly what she needed to relax her.

"Okay, you can chauffeur me to the Ramirez ranch. Is it far?"

"Not really," he told her, pulling out of the library's parking lot. "It's about ten minutes north of Boerne. I made it from the ranch to Lost Creek in about fifteen minutes yesterday. I wanted to find a place close so that I could meet with Wolf on short notice without too long a drive. Ana suggested a couple of towns, and Lost Creek felt like the right fit."

She shook her head in wonder. "And if you hadn't come here and seen my black and white series at the library, then none of this would be happening now."

"It's fate," he told her.

As he turned onto the highway, leaving Lost Creek and heading south toward Boerne, he said, "You also have to thank my love of coffee. I stopped at Java Junction and talked to Dax as I was driving around. He's the one who mentioned renting a cottage from Jean Bradley. He also suggested I stop by the library, saying it might be a good place for me to write. If I hadn't stopped in the library, I never would have seen your work."

"And neither would Wolf," she said, seeing how everything had been so connected. She hesitated a moment. "You know how you said you're scared about writing this script? I'm the same about quitting my teaching position. I'm good at my job. I have a real connection with my students."

He glanced briefly at her before turning his eyes back to the road. "Remember, you can always go back to teaching. You need to give photography a chance. Wolf will pay you a fair amount. You'll continue doing your portrait sittings and covering events at the winery. Not clocking in at school every day, though, will give you time to explore your craft more. Experiment. See what works and what doesn't. This could be a real eye-opening year for you, Finley.

"And I'd like to be a part of it."

His words jolted her further. Yes, she was incredibly attracted to Holden Scott. He was smart and funny. Easy on the eye. But she didn't know how long he'd be around.

"What, no response?" he asked, glancing at her again.

She bit her lip. "I'm bad at relationships."

"Why do you say that?"

It wasn't the question he asked. It was his tone. The way he said it, which caused Finley to tear up. She turned, facing away and looking out at the passing scenery, brushing her fingers beneath her eyes.

Holden Scott was famous. He might be renting a place in Lost Creek now, but he wouldn't stay in town forever.

And she had never wanted to live anywhere *but* Lost Creek.

"Finley?" he asked, reaching for her hand and threading their fingers together. "Talk to me."

"I thought I would marry my college boyfriend. We'd dated for three years, since we were sophomores. After graduation, he headed to Wharton to work on his MBA. I got so tired of hearing about Wharton this, Wharton that, and their elevate, innovate, collaborate. I tried to be a good long-distance girlfriend. I texted him every day. Sent him boxes of homemade cookies and long letters. Even went up to Penn twice so I could accompany him to a few important events."

She swallowed. "On his end, communication became sporadic. Then almost non-existent. Finally, he told me I just wasn't ambitious enough. I was too small-town for him. He needed someone more dynamic. A woman with more flair who knew how to dress and how to act in social situations. He told me he needed a partner who could run in the big leagues with him, not someone who wanted to talk about a fifth-grade talent show or field day."

"You think that makes you bad at relationships?" He smiled wryly at her. "Well, I suppose it does if all you dated was an asshole like him."

Finley snorted. "He really was, wasn't he?"

"He really was," Holden agreed cheerfully.

"I've dated a little since I've lived in Lost Creek. A fireman. A plumber. A coach at the high school. The fireman was sweet but without much upstairs. The plumber was divorced and still hung up on his ex-wife. In fact, they actually got back together last year. As for the football coach? He was a real player— and I'm not into games." She sighed. "I just don't know how to date."

"And you think I do?"

"Well, yes," she told him. "I'm mean, look at you. You've got cheekbones that would slice glass. Rugged good looks. The intellectual thing going on, with those GQ glasses."

He burst out laughing.

"What? What did I say? I'm complimenting you, Holden. You're a fit, hot guy."

"Who's crap at relationships myself." He sighed. "I've only had one long-term girlfriend, Finley. I met her at the writers' workshop in Iowa. We moved to New York and lived together. For five years. And you know what? After five years, I still didn't really know who she was. What she liked. What she thought. We had good sex for the first part of those years and then hardly any. And less than zero communication. I don't think either of us loved one another. We merely stayed together out of... habit, I suppose."

He put on his turn signal and made a right, going through the open gates of sign proclaiming Meadow Creek Ranch.

"Besides Madison, I only dated sporadically. I grew up poor so I couldn't afford to take girls out in high school. Every dime I made went toward college, and I kept to myself there. I taught high school English for two years and never asked a single woman out that entire time. So I have one, long-term, failed relationship behind me. I'm not looking backward, though. I'm living in the present—and have eyes on the future."

Holden slowed the truck and then put it in park. "I sense something between us, Finley. I can't promise what'll come of it, but I'd like to pursue this connection. So, I'll ask again."

His gaze pinned hers "I'd like to be a part of your life, Finley. No promises. No guarantees. Just a take it day-by-day and see where things lead. Are you game?"

Her thoughts swirled. It sounded as if he'd recently ended things with this Madison. That alone made him suspect. Finley had no intention of being Holden Scott's rebound fling.

Then she thought about the regret that would fill her if she told him she wasn't interested in seeing him. He had encouraged her to chase a dream that she had thought was too far-fetched. No, Finley had decided to do that very thing. Shouldn't she give Holden a chance, too?

"All right. We can try. I'll admit that I'm a little leery because you're coming off a live-together relationship."

"Don't be. In the last twenty-four hours, I've found more to talk about with you and found you more interesting than the entire time I spent with Madison."

"Is she a writer, too? You said you met her at your writing workshop?"

"She's trying to be. I've always let her read my work, but she stopped letting me see hers a couple of years ago. I paid all the bills. She didn't even bother to get a part-time job.

Madison comes from money, and I don't think she ever really thought about contributing financially to anything. I do know her dad gave her money. How much, I never asked. But I don't want you to worry about her, Finley. Madison is my past. I hope I've learned something about how *not* to be. I hope I'm a better person— and better potential boyfriend —because of what I learned being with her."

His words put her fears to rest. "We can start seeing each other. But I want to take things slowly."

He took her hand and lifted it to his lips, kissing it tenderly. "I tried my best to do that last night when I was kissing you."

"I appreciate that," she told him, wishing she could kiss him now.

He glanced in the rearview mirror. "Looks like Wolf is behind us."

Holden let his friend's truck pass them and then fell in line behind it, following it all the way to a large, two-story farmhouse.

They got out and Ana asked, "Is everything okay?"

"Finley thought she'd lost her earring," Holden said easily. "We stopped to look for it. She found it."

They followed the Ramirez family inside, Finley toting her camera, and she whispered, "Why did you tell Ana that?"

"Was I supposed to tell her we were having a discussion about relationships and how we'd decided to start one? Or how I pulled over, wanting to make out with you like two high schoolers after a school dance?"

She felt her face flame. "Just stick to the facts in the future."

Ana had gone into the kitchen, preparing a snack for her children. As they ate, she asked Finley, "What clothes should they wear?"

"I like the colorful top and dark pants that Eva is wearing. They'll photograph nicely. Bear's shirt is a little pale, though. Does he have anything in navy? Or a deep red? Either would look good on him."

"Both. I'll have him change once they're done with their bananas and goldfish."

"How about I get some candids of you and Wolf with them?"

Ana touched her hair. "Maybe I should go do something to my makeup and hair."

"No. You look perfect. Natural. If you like what I take today, we can talk about something more formal."

"You don't mind denim and boots?" Ana asked, glancing down at her emerald tunic sweater and faded jeans.

"It's you. That's what photographs should be all about, capturing who a person is. Not someone they're pretending to be when they dress up."

"Okay. But Wolf should shave."

"No," she said, laughing. "I like his stubble. It actually brings out the color of his eyes better."

Ana relented. "Well, he does look pretty sexy with it."

Once the kids finished eating, their mother had them brush their teeth. She pulled a crew neck sweater over

Bear's head and combed his hair, but he still had an adorable cowlick sticking up.

When Ana tried to smooth it down, Finley shook her head. "No. It's him. It's how you'll want to remember him at this age. He'll be a teenager before you know it, using product to hold it down. Let him be a little boy today."

She took some pictures of Bear playing in his rooms, first with Legos and then dump trucks. Holden joined in the fun, going to a tea party with Eva. She made certain he was in a few of the shots, but for the most part, Finley took close-ups of Eva. She also had Eva play with her stuffed animals and dolls, and then she had the two children sit on the floor together, with Eva reading to Bear. Flipping through what she had taken, Finley already knew she had gotten some great shots and hoped the parents would be pleased.

The children took her outside and introduced her to their horses. She took photographs of them petting their horses. Hugging them. Grooming them. Then Wolf set them atop each pony, and she was able to get some incredible action shots.

Once they finished with the horses, Bear wanted pictures of him feeding the pigs. Finley got those and others of Eva scattering feed for the chickens. She made certain that Ana and Wolf had been in several of these pictures with the animals.

"Okay. We need to get some shots of you walking. Hold hands, everyone. Turn your backs and walk away from me. Good. Keep going. Now, look over your shoulder. Nice. Okay, turn around and start toward me."

They walked a moment, and then Bear took off running, laughing. Wolf chased him, picking up his son, tossing him in the air. Finley knew those would make for wonderful candids.

Ana smoothed Eva's hair, and again she snapped away, having them walk. Sit. Stand. She motioned them to the corral and had the four sit on the fence side-by-side before having the parents stand as their children continued sitting. Bear wanted to ride Wolf's shoulders, and she took those shots, with Eva trading and also being carried around.

Finally, Finley took a few of Wolf and Ana alone, walking with their arms about one another as they headed toward the house.

Holden joined her as they followed the couple. "It looked like you got some nice shots. Playful. Serious. A good mix."

She nodded. "I think they'll be pleased."

Inside the kitchen, she said, "I'll work on these tonight and send a few preview shots to you."

They traded cell numbers, and she asked for them to text her the email address to send the photos to.

"This was fun," Bear told Finley, hugging her leg. "I like having my picture made."

Wolf ruffled his son's hair. "Says the boy who made terrible faces in his preschool pictures this year."

"Bear crossed his eyes and stuck out his tongue," Eva tattled. "He looked terrible."

"Well, I'll bet I got a few that your mom and dad won't mind putting up," Finley told the girl. She looked to

Holden. "I need to get back if I'm going to work on this tonight and get some papers graded."

Ana embraced her. "Thank you so much, Finley. I enjoyed seeing your work at the library." She smiled. "And I hope I have made a friend."

The couple walked them out to Holden's truck, where he said, "I appreciate the loan of the truck, Wolf. I'm planning to buy something of my own soon." He paused, looking in her direction. "I think I'll be staying in the Hill Country."

8

*H*olden finished reading the pages he had written yesterday. A deep satisfaction filled him.

Maybe he wasn't so bad at this screenwriting after all.

He hadn't seen Finley on Monday. He'd made it clear when he dropped her off Sunday after their time at the ranch that he didn't expect them to spend time together every day. He knew she was busy. So was he. He reminded her that his schedule was much more flexible than hers, telling her to text him when she'd like to get together again.

They would see one another tomorrow night when he went to dinner at Braden and Harper Clark's house. Finley had told him the group of friends had met for dinner weekly for almost a year now. He hoped he wouldn't feel like the odd man out in the tight-knit group and hoped he might fit in. He already felt comfortable with Dax Tennyson and liked his wife Ivy quite a bit. The short time he'd been in Emerson's company had been pleasant.

He had received a text from an unknown sender last night. Upon reading it, he figured it came from Braden Clark, who told Holden he was looking forward to meeting him and hoped he liked fajitas, since that was what would be served. The text also gave the Clarks' address. Holden had replied he was eager to meet them and asked if he could bring anything. The response had been a healthy appetite, which had made him laugh.

Standing, he paced the small cottage, restless after all the tweaking he'd done, thinking he might drive into town and stop at Java Junction, seeing if the coffeehouse was conducive to writing new pages today.

When he arrived, he saw it was as Dax had told him. A few scattered patrons, all of them engrossed in laptops or tablets. Quiet blanketed the place, and he knew this would be an option when he wanted to write in peace.

Placing an order with the barista, he asked her about Dax's whereabouts.

"He usually works the morning rush and then takes off between ten and four," she told Holden. "That's when things pick up again. Can I give him a message for you?"

"No. I'm new in town, and Dax had told me Java Junction might be a place I could get some writing done. I just wanted to say hello if he might be here."

"Oh, you must be Holden. Dax mentioned to Sean and me that you might be coming in and to take good care of you. I'm Jeanine. It's nice to have you in Lost Creek. Go have a seat. I'll bring your coffee to you as soon as it's ready."

He retreated to the back corner and opened his laptop, calling up his document. By the time he had done so, Jeanine headed his way.

"Here you go, Holden. If you need anything else, you just let me know. Hope you get a lot written today."

He worked for a solid two hours, feeling good about the pages he completed. Occasionally, he referred to his chapter summary of *Hill Country Homicide*, something he wrote up at the end of each novel when he read through it a final time, looking for misspelled words or inconsistencies. Having written the source material, though, he was familiar with the turn of events and was learning quickly how to incorporate them into the specialized writing of a script.

Some of the dialogue for the screenplay he pulled straight from his novel. Dialogue was his favorite thing to write, so he spent loads of time honing it, making each sentence as perfect as possible. Since a screenplay consisted of a majority of dialogue, that was probably why he was writing faster than he'd originally expected. Still, he was learning to be brutal, omitting some of the language he was in love with, streamlining conversations to get the point across quickly and keep things crisp and fresh. He thought it would be easier to write a screenplay from scratch than having to eliminate so much of a novel. If the filmed version of *Hill Country Homicide* saw success, Holden wondered if he might balance both kinds of writing, continuing to write novels and yet keeping the door open to the possibility of writing future screenplays.

It helped that Wolf had already read and liked the pages Holden had completed, tweaking them only slightly. Based upon the director's adjustments, Holden had a better idea of what was required in a scene. It wasn't that he'd ridden this particular bike before, but he had an innate feel for what needed to go on the page. Though he'd worried he'd be tearing his hair out, agonizing as he wrote each line of the script, he now was getting into the rhythm and thought he would finish his first draft far earlier than he'd imagined.

Wolf would take a pass through it then, adding his own spin to things, and then return it to Holden for a final touch-up. The faster this process occurred, the better. Holden knew it was the rare actor who would agree to a role without having read a finished script. While some actors would take a part simply to work with Wolf, who had gone from up and coming to established, the leads cast in *Homicide* would definitely want to see the completed screenplay. He wanted to do all he could to contribute to the success of Wolf's first film helmed under his own production company.

He worked another half-hour and then decided to stop for the day, saving his document and closing it before powering down his laptop. Picking up his cell, which he deliberately kept face down when he worked so notifications wouldn't disturb him, he turned the ringer back on and saw he had a text from Finley just two minutes ago.

> Ready for your first cooking lesson? If you
> can come over around four-thirty, I'm
> happy to give you a shot at spaghetti and
> meat sauce.

Quickly, he texted back.

> You are speaking my language when you
> talk pasta. What can I bring?

He waited for her reply, feeling almost giddy that she'd reached out, knowing they would see each other tomorrow night.

> Not a thing. See you soon!

Holden had an hour before he needed to be at her place. He spent the time going through his emails and skimming some news and entertainment sites. He'd always been a news junkie and kept up with entertainment news—especially book and movie notices—after he became published. He read the most recent list of books bought by publishing houses, seeing the name of one of his fellow Iowa workshop authors. Tad had been quiet, but Holden had liked him.

When he saw it was the first novel of Tad's to be published, and a three-book deal, he decided to touch base. He still had Tad's email address, and so he wrote a brief email, saying he'd seen the recent sale in the trades and congratulated Tad, telling him he couldn't wait to read it when it came out. Holden included his cell number in case Tad might like to contact him that way. He would be happy to answer any questions Tad had about navigating the publishing industry and only wished he'd had known someone who could have helped him do the same. While Evan was a terrific agent, he was not a hand-holder. Of course, now that Holden was Evan's leading client, the agent did take more time with him than when he was a new graduate from the Iowa workshop.

By now, it was time to head over to Finley's house. He got in the truck and popped a breath mint, hoping to rid himself of the strong coffee taste that lingered. He didn't know if the cooking lesson would involve any kissing, but he wanted to be ready, just in case.

Then he changed his mind, heading to the other side of the square and parking again in front of a florist. He popped in, selecting a mix of flowers, not knowing what they were. Hoping Finley would like them.

When he reached her house, he parked at the curb again, not wanting to block the driveway since he didn't see Emerson's car and figured she must still be at school.

He rang the doorbell, and Finley answered, her eyes widening when she saw the bouquet.

"You didn't have to bring me flowers, Holden." Still, her eyes lit up when he handed them to her.

"I wanted to add a little sunshine to your day."

"They're beautiful. Come on in. Let me put them in some water."

He followed her into the kitchen, watching her unwrap the tissue paper and clip the stems before filling a tall vase with water. It surprised him when she opened a bottle of aspirin and dropped in a tablet, swishing the water and then setting the flowers inside.

"Flowers get headaches?" he teased.

"It's just one of those tricks my mom taught me. I'm not sure about the science behind it, but it helps an arrangement stay fresher longer."

She fiddled with the flowers a moment, pulling one out and slipping the stem in another place until she was satisfied.

Pulling her phone from her pocket, she said, "I need a picture of these. The first flowers I've ever received from a man. Mums for high school homecoming games don't count."

Her words surprised him, especially since she'd talked about her long-term boyfriend, one it seemed that she thought she would marry. The guy definitely had been an asshole, not to buy a woman like Finley flowers. And a stupid asshole at that because he'd let this wonderful woman go.

He slipped his arms around her, pulling her toward him. "I hope we'll have a lot of firsts together, Finley," he said quietly, lowering his mouth to hers for a sweet, lingering kiss.

Holden released her and stepped back, wanting more, but knowing it was important not to rush things between them.

"What's our first step? Pasta or meat," he added to clarify he was talking about cooking after he saw the look in her eyes, pleased that she had wanted more than a kiss.

"Meat first. Usually, I like a sauce to simmer a good ninety minutes or longer. Today, we'll aim for an hour."

She removed a package of ground beef from the fridge, telling him, "Beef is a good starting point. If you pass today's course and advance further to meatballs, I like a combination of beef and ground pork."

"I've always been a fast learner. Plan for me to pass with flying colors today and graduate to meatballs. And don't think you have to take things easy on me."

Finley got out a cast iron skillet and put it on the stovetop before taking out a few other items, along with a knife and cutting board.

"Open the package and spread the meat evenly in the skillet with this wooden spoon. No lumps. Lumps are bad news."

He did as she asked and then, under her direction, cut up an onion and bell pepper and minced some garlic cloves.

"I've never even known this is how garlic comes," he said.

"You *are* a novice," she teased, turning the burner to medium. "Okay, place everything you've cut up on top of the meat, and then you'll stir thoroughly until it's all mixed well."

As he did, she began removing jars from a spice rack hanging on the wall, as well as opening a few cans.

"Keep stirring. I want the meat brown and crumbly and the veggies tender."

"How long?"

"Between five to seven minutes. You have to eyeball it. Not pink in the meat, but I don't want it to burn."

He kept an eye out as he steadily stirred. "I think it's ready."

"Then drain the grease." She handed him a lid. "Drain in the trash can and never down the sink."

Holden did as she asked, returning the skillet to the cooktop. After she'd inspected the cooked meat and had him drain the grease from it, she instructed Holden to add a can of diced tomatoes, a large one of tomato sauce, and another of tomato paste to the mix, blending thoroughly.

"Most people just use a jar of spaghetti sauce. I'll admit when you're in a time crunch, it's fast and easy. I prefer a sauce which has been simmered, though, letting the flavors come together."

Finley had him add salt and pepper, along with oregano and basil. More stirring was required.

"Cooking is part art, part science," she told him. "Baking is definitely more scientific. You have to measure correctly. That's where Emerson shines. But she also has a tremendous artistic side to her, which is evident in the way she ices and decorates her cakes."

"It smells good," he said.

"Sample it," she urged. "Tell me what you taste and what you think it needs."

He dipped the wooden spoon into the sauce and tasted it. "Pretty darn good. I don't think I'd add anything."

Dipping the spoon in again, he brought it to her lips, giving her a taste.

"You're right. I like it. Stir it well again. It can simmer

now for an hour. Most purists prefer to keep sauce and meat apart, in separate pans, but I like to let the two join. I think it enhances the flavor.

"Lower the heat now," she instructed. "That low simmer will keep it from burning."

Moving to the cupboard, she retrieved a large pot and filled it about two-thirds full of water.

"We have a while before we need to put the spaghetti on to boil." Smiling, she added, "Be glad I'm not having you make pasta from scratch."

"As long as you treat me like a kindergartener and use small words and easy instructions, I'll excel."

She laughed. It surprised him how much he loved that rich sound. He noticed everything about her, from the timbre in her voice when she spoke to the length of her eyelashes. He'd never paid attention to those details regarding Madison. That was surprising because he was a writer. He was supposed to notice everything. Once more, he regretted being immature and not fully giving himself to that relationship.

Then again, Madison had always kept her distance, too. He supposed, in a way, they had used one another, becoming too comfortable too quickly with each other, not putting the effort into the relationship that it had needed to thrive.

He wouldn't make that mistake with Finley Farrow.

She opened a bottle of wine and poured each of them a glass.

"This is from Lost Creek Vineyards. They produce both red and white wines, but they are really becoming known for their red blends. This one is heavy on Cab, with some Merlot and Pinot Noir mixed in."

Holden picked up the wineglass, taking a sip. Immediately, Finley clucked her tongue.

"You better be glad that Ivy isn't here now. She's the manager of the tasting room at Lost Creek Winery and walks people through tastings. She would have a noose around your neck for simply picking up a glass and drinking."

"Oh. I guess I'm supposed to swirl and sniff like a proper snob."

"Exactly. If you're interested, we can go to the tasting room and have Ivy walk you through some wines. Do you prefer red or white?"

He shrugged. "To be honest, I'm more of a beer drinker. Or vodka. It might be fun to learn more about wine, though, especially since there are so many wineries in the Hill Country."

"Then Ivy is definitely the person to teach you. We can talk to her tomorrow night about it."

She had him stir the meat sauce before she told him to add a generous amount of salt to the pasta water and set it to a boil. Finley taught him how to measure a portion of dried spaghetti, and he added four servings to the pot once the water began to boil.

"Emerson had a cake tasting with a bride and groom after school today. She also is going to start some prep work for wedding and groom cakes for this coming Saturday. She told me she'd also bake a dessert for tomorrow night while she was at it."

"Where does she prepare her cakes?"

"Harper put in a first-class kitchen at the events center, getting input from Emerson, Usually, she contracts with various vendors in the area to cater dinners for weddings. You're familiar with Blackwood BBQ. They are her most frequently used caterer. After all, a Hill Country wedding deserves some great barbeque."

When the water reached a rolling boil, Finley taught him to set a timer for seven minutes, saying spaghetti could take up to ten to cook properly.

When the timer went off, she told him, "Use a fork and pull out a couple of strands after seven minutes. Blow on it so you don't burn your mouth. Then chew. You don't want it to have any crunch. It should be a little springy but not hard. It's a little trial and error."

Holden tasted and shook his head. "Nope. I'll give it another minute."

He waited, testing it again. "Perfect."

"Use the colander I set in the sink to drain the water."

She then told him how to plate it, providing pasta bowls like he'd seen in Italian restaurants. Once the spaghetti was arranged in the bowls, he ladled the meat sauce over it. Finley pulled a small block of cheese from the fridge, telling him it was parmesan, and wanting him to grate a bit atop each of their bowls. He did so, and she took a picture of it, texting it to him.

"Your first meal. Nice job," she praised. "Of course, once you get this down, we can work in tossing a salad, testing out some different dressings, and even toasting bread. I wanted to make things simple for you tonight."

"KISS," he said.

"Now?" she asked, carrying their wine glasses to the small café table in the corner of the kitchen while he brought the pasta bowls.

"Keep it simple, stupid," he said. "An acronym which has benefited me through the years, especially when it comes to writing. I've learned not to get too fancy. Neat and clean is better than fussy. That goes for writing. And other things, too."

He pulled her chair out, seating her, and then took a seat himself. Reaching for his wineglass, he held it high, in a toast.

"To the first dinner we cooked together. I hope many will follow."

She tapped her glass against his, smiling at him.

"If I train you well enough, you could cook all the dinners. I could breeze in after school and have a hot meal waiting for me."

Holden laughed. "Only if you wanted spaghetti and meat sauce five days a week. Seriously, though, this wasn't hard at all. I wish I would've learned to cook before now."

"You never watched your mom cook?" she asked.

"No," he said, knowing it was time to go beyond surface conversation with Finley. "She was usually at work."

"Oh, what did she do?"

"A little of everything. She cobbled together a bunch of part-time jobs. Juggled three, four, five at a time. She cleaned houses on her own and office buildings with a janitorial service. Waited tables. Worked retail and at a movie theater. I didn't see her much."

Sympathy shone in Finley's eyes. "What about your dad?"

"He went out of his way not to work— and I went out of my way to avoid him as much as possible. He was a drunk, Finley. A mean drunk. I learned from an early age to stay out of his way. We weren't that happy, middle-class family who ate dinner together every night. I lived on canned soup and peanut butter sandwiches. A box of Kraft Mac and Cheese was a real splurge in our household."

She took his hand. "I'm sorry, Holden. I didn't know. You seem so urbane and sophisticated. You're so put together. You have this casual elegance about you. You told me you grew up poor, but everyone has a different definition of that. I thought you meant your family didn't take elaborate vacations or you drove used cars. I had no idea things were so difficult. The fact that you earned two college degrees and have become a successful novelist is incredible."

"I won an academic scholarship to college. Had a perfects score on my SAT. That's the only way I was able to get a degree. I paid attention to the way kids in class dressed. How they spoke. Acted. I told you I'm a quick study, so I picked things up easily. What you see today is who I became after a long time of living in poverty."

He shook his head, memories he hadn't thought about in years crowding into his mind.

"My dad berated me for majoring in English lit, telling

me it was a worthless major. That I'd never amount to anything. His words haunted me, so I made sure I earned my teaching certificate on the side to have that to fall back on. Teaching paid the bills those two years before I was accepted into the writing workshop."

He sighed. "I'd had a romantic vision of teaching by day and writing by night. As an English teacher, though, all I did was come home and grade essays for hours. That was pretty soul sucking. Winning a place in the Iowa workshop was a dream come true. I knew it was my only shot at becoming a writer. I left there with *Capitol Crimes* finished and an outline for *Hill Country Homicide*. I was fortunate to land an agent early because very few in the program did. Evan shopped *Crimes* to all the major publishing houses, and they got into a bidding war over it."

He sipped the wine, enjoying the taste. "I'm comfortable now, money-wise. Not only has Evan made some good deals for me, but he encouraged me to see a financial planner. A lot of new authors blow their advances on expensive cars or things which don't last. Mine has taught me about investing. Living frugally, especially since I have a job where my income is so unpredictable. Who knows if the next book will even be published, much less sell well? So, I'm prepared."

Finley grew thoughtful. "Do you ever see your mom? Or your dad?"

"No," he said flatly. "He drank himself to death. Died two days before I started classes at SMU. I didn't bother going to his funeral. Hell, I don't even know if they had a funeral for him. As for Mom? She actually met a guy while cleaning his office. He's quite a bit older than she is, but they just hit it off. He'd lost his wife several years before and was ready to retire. Wanted to move abroad."

Again, painful memories resurfaced, ones he probably should deal with at some point with a therapist.

"She told me they were getting married and moving to Copenhagen. At least, that was the first stop. He had a lot of places he'd visited for business over the years and wanted to take her to several cities. Live there a while. Move on to another one."

Holden swallowed. "She didn't tell him about me. Said she was sorry, but this was her chance to finally have a life for herself. That she wanted to travel and have nice things and never look back. I was a reminder of all the bad things she went through. At least she was nice enough to tell me and not simply disappear."

Her eyes widened in surprise. "You never talk to her? Never see her?"

"No. I'm on my own."

Finley stood and came to him, sitting in his lap, wrapping her arms about his neck.

"No, you aren't. Not anymore. You have me."

9

$\mathcal{F}$inley's heart ached at what Holden had revealed. Something told her that he might not have told his one serious girlfriend everything he had just shared with her.

She gazed into his eyes. "I wish I could change the past for you. Make it different. Easier. Better. But I know what you went through made you who you are today. You're a good man, Holden. You're thoughtful. Caring. Smart. Funny. I don't know if I would have the great attitude you do, coming from nothing. I'm lucky that I still have both my parents in my life. We talk frequently. I wasn't as close to my brother growing up. He's a dozen years older than I am. When I started kindergarten, he was leaving for college. But as adults, we've started talking. We're friends now."

She framed his handsome face with her hands. "I can't begin to understand how rough you had it, with an abusive dad and an absentee mom. One who's still absent from your life."

Hesitating a moment, Finley decided she would simply speak from her heart. "We haven't known one another for long, but the connection between us is greater than anything I've ever felt. I meant when I said you aren't alone. You aren't. You have me. I still have a lot to figure out about myself. Where I'm going. How I'm going to get there. But you are the one who's encouraged me to trust my gut and take the risks I've been too afraid to even think about."

She swallowed. "I need you in my life, Holden. As a friend. And more. I need you to be my sounding board. The person who will always be straight with me, even when I don't want to hear the bad stuff. I'm going out a limb here, but I also want to be your lover. I haven't trusted a man in a long, long time— but my heart tells me you're the man who can change everything for me. Help me be a better person. Push me to reach my full potential. And enjoy life along the way while I'm heading to my destination. I've always been a person who plays it safe. I don't rock the boat. I sometimes go along to get along and keep my feelings and opinions to myself. I'm methodical. A bit of a neat freak. I love structure. But you're pushing me out of my comfort zone. And I like that."

She paused. "I like you."

Finley had never spoken so openly— or boldly. Then again, she'd never met Holden before. This man made her feel things unfamiliar. Express herself as never before.

He stared at her. The longer he did, the more worried she became.

"You've got to say something," she insisted. "Or it's going to be very awkward climbing off you and going back to eating my spaghetti."

A slow smile appeared. "I was just drinking you in. You are the most beautiful, most honest, most talented person I've ever met. I keep thinking why would a woman like you be interested in a man like me?" He paused. "I guess, deep down, I'm still that little, neglected boy, not thinking he's good enough or smart enough to be somebody. My dad didn't just beat me down physically. He constantly belittled me, shaving away any confidence I ever had."

Holden took a deep breath and slowly let it out. "I think I've pushed myself to be successful just to prove him wrong."

"Don't measure your worth by a bitter alcoholic," she cautioned. "Or what anyone else says about you. *You* are the sole judge of your value. Your worth. And let me tell you, I believe in you, Holden. I think you can pretty much do anything you set your mind to. How many people even write a book, much less get it published? And yet you've done that twice. That's amazing. Not only that, both novels have been so outstanding, they've become movies. Or one has and one will be soon. You've even challenged yourself by going out on an artistic limb and agreeing to write the screenplay for one. With absolutely no training, just your instinct guiding you. And you know what? It's going to be incredible. *You* are incredible."

His hands had gone to her waist. Now, they moved to

her face. "My own personal cheerleader. You're the incredible one, Finley. You have such heart. You're creative. Loyal. Compassionate. Nurturing. What did I do to deserve someone like you?"

"You opened yourself to the universe, Holden. It led you to Lost Creek. We were meant to find one another."

Their lips met, the kiss a solemn oath which promised the other that good things lay ahead.

Holden was the one to break it. "I do want to make love to you. Not now. I think we need to give each other a little more time. But soon."

He kissed her again, murmuring, "Very soon," against her mouth.

This time, she was the one to break the kiss. "I'm going to hold you to that, Mr. Scott. In the meantime, I want to try your spaghetti."

He laughed. "It's probably cold by now."

"That's all right. I think it'll be perfect."

Finley pushed up, returning to her seat. Surprisingly, they were able to return to mundane, normal topics after such honesty between them about a hurtful topic to Holden. She saw a resiliency in him, something that had to have seen him survive such a terrible childhood.

She told him about her day at school and how her class was studying about inquiry and research, learning to put that research into their own words and organize it in order to write about it.

"My focus is on language arts and social studies. My partner on the team covers the math and science objectives. That's a good thing because while I liked science, especially geology, I was awful at math."

"Tell me about your students," he urged. "The good ones— and those bad ones."

Finley found herself talking through the rest of dinner, Holden asking insightful questions, even making a suggestion on how to handle one of her problem students.

"I was pretty badly behaved in fourth and fifth grades," he shared. "I read way above grade level. Most of the bad behavior was because I was so bored. And then it became habit. At first, the other kids were in awe of me because I would talk back to my teachers. Dare them to knock the chip off my shoulder. Then the novelty wore off, and I went back to being the sullen, quiet kid who didn't have any friends."

"What changed?" she asked.

"I didn't always have a lunch to eat. My mom was too proud to fill out the papers for me to get on the free or reduced lunch program. I guess she thought I could exist on pride alone. I started spending lunchtime hanging in the boys' bathroom, hiding in a stall, reading. Then our janitor found me in there one day. Mr. Hamilton."

She watched his face soften with the memory.

"He took me to his office, which was pretty much a broom closet with a desk and shelves of cleaning supplies. Shared his lunch with me, even pouring soup from his thermos. Homemade soup from his wife. Mr. Hamilton was the first adult who really talked to me. I mean that he asked me questions— about me —and actually listed to my answers. For the first time, I felt seen. Heard."

"He fed you more than food. He fed you attention," she observed.

"Exactly. Soon, I was taking his advice. Doing my homework and turning it in on time. Not smarting off to my teachers. I'd never really cared about getting good grades, and neither of my parents ever emphasized that. But Mr. Hamilton wanted to see my papers and my report card. He noted my progress and urged me to do better.

"That man changed my life."

Finley smiled. "I'm glad he came into your life and helped you turn things around."

"We ate lunch together every day. Talked about all kinds of things. Mr. Hamilton was a news junkie. He followed presidential elections. World events. Sports. The weather. Soon, I was reading newspapers and magazines, talking about every topic under the sun to him. He even put in for a transfer to the middle school I was supposed to go to, and we continued our lunches during the three years I was there. By then, I was on the A Honor Roll and reading voraciously. Mr. Hamilton was the first person I told that I wanted to be a writer. He didn't laugh. Didn't judge. Merely told me that he thought I'd be good at it."

"That's wonderful. I wish every kid had a Mr. Hamilton in his life. Do you still stay in touch?"

"He had a heart attack the last week of my senior year in high school. Pushing a heavy-duty floor scrubber one minute— and dropped dead the next. He left me a letter, telling me how proud he was that I'd won a scholarship to college. How I'd been the best friend he'd ever had. Even left me a little over two thousand dollars, which I never mentioned to my parents. That was my mad money in college. I had the scholarship but also worked to pay for room and board. If there was a movie I wanted to see, I'd dip into that fund. A book I'd checked out and wanted to own? I bought it with the money Mr. Hamilton left me. I used the last of it to put down the deposit on the apartment I rented when I started teaching."

"What an inspirational man," she said. "He changed your life, Holden. Mr. Hamilton was a father to you in every sense of the word."

He wiped his eyes with his napkin. "I never really thought of it that way, but you're right. He helped me become interested in the world. He saw potential in me when no one else did."

"I think you need to write his story," Finley encouraged. "Or the story of him mentoring you. I know that would be really different from the political thriller you wrote and the murder mystery. It's a story that needs to be told, though, whether you do it as fiction or non-fiction."

Holden nodded to himself. "You're right. I'll have to think about it, though. I've got several ideas on the back burner. Right now, I'm concentrating on the script for Wolf. It's my first priority. Then I've got a solid first draft of my third novel. I always complete it. Let it sit for a bit. Then come back and read it straight through with fresh eyes. Once I finish those two things and send the novel off to Evan, I'll definitely run with your idea."

"It would be a great way to honor Mr. Hamilton," she said.

By now, they had finished their meal. Finley poured them both a second glass of wine.

"Take this into the den. I'll clean up and join you."

"Nope. I'm not going to leave you with a mess. Put away the leftovers for Emerson. We'll clean together." He smiled at her. "It always goes faster when you have a helping hand."

Within minutes, the kitchen was sparkling. They took their wine to the den and were sitting on the couch when Emerson arrived home, carrying a white bakery box.

"Dessert for tomorrow," she said. "I think this will be a real hit."

"How did your cake tasting go?" Finley asked.

Emerson set the box in the kitchen and returned to them. "The groom doesn't like chocolate. The bride wanted nothing *but* chocolate. They argued for a good half-hour before I stepped in and read them the riot act. In the end, the wedding cake stayed traditional. The groom's cake is now the bride's cake. Chocolate on chocolate on chocolate. Both are happy."

"Holden made spaghetti and meat sauce," Finley said. "There's some in the fridge for you."

"You cook?" Emerson asked, eyeing him up and down. "If I would've have known that, I might have vied for your attention and knocked Fin out of the way."

"I don't even know how to toast a piece of bread," he admitted. "In New York, every meal was takeout. Finley is the one who said she's going to teach me how to cook. Tonight was pasta with meat sauce."

Emerson chuckled. "Not my dream man after all.

Sorry, Holden. I'll continue to hold out for someone who knows how to grill a steak. Make divine mashed potatoes. Fry chicken or bake bread. But I do thank you for the leftovers."

Finley heard Emerson heating up the spaghetti in the microwave. Her roommate took her bowl and waved at them on the way to her bedroom, saying, "Papers to grade. See you tomorrow at dinner, Holden."

"Goodnight," he called. Then his gaze turned to her. "Will Emerson stay in her room?"

"At least for an hour. Maybe longer."

"Do you have papers to grade, Miss Farrow? Or can I convince you to spend the next hour kissing me?"

"I think I can work you into my schedule, Mr. Scott."

Suddenly, his mouth was on hers, filling Finley with warmth.

And the hope they might have a future together.

10

$\mathscr{H}$olden rose at six thirty, sending off a quick text to Finley, wishing her good morning. She had told him she was usually in her classroom by that time each morning so that she could prepare the learning centers and lessons of the day and still have time to check her email and tutor students who came in before school started at seven thirty.

She replied right away, telling him that she looked forward to seeing him tonight at dinner. He asked if he could pick up Emerson and her, and she told him to come by their house at a quarter till six.

He made a cup of coffee and put on his jacket, going to sit on the porch of the cottage, mulling over what he would be writing today. He decided to go for a walk once he finished his coffee, which always seemed to spark creativity within him. As he hiked along a nearby trail, though, he couldn't get Mr. Hamilton out of his mind.

Pulling out his phone, Holden began dictating memories of his mentor and friend.

He talked of the day they met and how Mr. Hamilton was curious about everything. A few months into their friendship, Holden had asked why Mr. Hamilton was a janitor because he seemed so smart and should be doing something else that paid a lot more money. He never forgot what the custodian told him, which had shocked him.

Mr. Hamilton had earned two history degrees and was an ABD— a doctoral student who'd finished all requirements except for his dissertation. The custodian had put his academic career on hold and entered the military, going to fight in Vietnam during the last eighteen months of that war, seeing tremendous horrors there, ones which he refused to share with Holden. At the time, Holden thought it was because he was so young. As an adult, he realized even if he had been an old man, Mr. Hamilton would have kept those terrible memories to himself.

Mr. Hamilton had come home a changed man, not wanting to work in some dusty museum. Instead, he told Holden that he'd decided he needed to make a difference in the lives of others. Even if he only helped one individual, Mr. Hamilton said it would be worth it. He liked caring for the school he worked at. For the staff and students.

It was only after his friend's death that Holden learned that Mr. Hamilton had donated everything he had to charity since his wife had passed away two years before him. He'd lived frugally during his years of working for the Austin school district. Not only did he leave Holden with a few thousand dollars, but Mr. Hamilton had contributed sums to organizations such as the Boys and Girls Clubs, the YMCA, the Salvation Army, and the SPCA.

All Holden knew was that Mr. Hamilton had changed his life for the better. He only wished his friend could see the man he'd become.

And the man he was becoming, now that he had returned to his roots in Texas.

Making his way back to his rented cottage, Holden knew that he would be writing Mr. Hamilton's story, be it in a fictional setting or a non-fiction one. The world needed more Mr. Hamiltons. Though he'd told Finley he would put this project on a back burner, it excited him too much. Immediately, he typed up what he'd dictated into his phone and then began outlining a few other ideas that came to mind. Holden decided he could work simultaneously on the screenplay and Mr. Hamilton's story.

He read over and then fired off the pages he had written the last couple of days to Wolf and then showered and shaved, dressing in slacks and a sweater. Knowing Wolf most likely wasn't awake yet, he called Ana.

She answered on the first ring. "How is the script coming along, Holden?

"Really well, In fact, I just emailed Wolf more pages."

"Would you believe my husband is already up and in his office— and it's only ten o'clock! He told me last night that he was eager to meet with you again. Why don't you drive down and have lunch with us? By then, Wolf should have finished reading what you sent to him and have some feedback for you."

"I'll see you in a hour then," Holden told her.

When he arrived at the ranch, Wolf greeted him at the door. "You've hit it. Your rhythm. Your stride. I knew it would click for you. All the pieces are falling into place, my friend."

"So, you think I'm on the right track?" he asked.

"The pages you sent today? I wouldn't change a thing about them. You seem on fire now. I think you'll wrap this up in another month— even less —at the rate you're writing."

As they entered the den, Holden said, "I do feel like I've established a rhythm. I want to get this first draft down because I know when you start putting out feelers for casting, it will help immensely if you have a version of the completed script."

"You're right about that. Ana and I are going full steam ahead on all other aspects of the project now. I'll be using a lot of the same crew I have in previous films. Even though Ana has never produced before, she's been with me every step of the way on the ones I have directed. I think we're going to have an excellent partnership." He smiled at Holden. "I'm just glad you were willing to come on board."

"I have another idea. I'm not sure of the form it'll take, but I'd like you to look at it when I'm done."

"I'm intrigued," his friend said.

Ana entered the den. "Lunch is ready. Come on into the kitchen."

Over sandwiches and chicken tortilla soup, Holden told the couple about Mr. Hamilton and the lifeline the custodian had thrown to a very lost, angry boy.

"I wouldn't be here with you today if Mr. Hamilton hadn't taken such an interest in me."

He talked about their lunches together. How Mr. Hamilton would give Holden newspapers and then quiz him over various articles. How he had taught Holden how to play chess.

"I've never really talked about this with you, but my home life was pretty abysmal. My dad stayed drunk, and my mom was gone all the time, working jobs to keep a roof over our heads. I pretty much raised myself. Mr. Hamilton was not only my friend, he was a true father figure to me."

"I think it's a very moving story, Holden," Ana said. "You could fictionalize it, of course, adding in your own experiences with Mr. Hamilton. Or perhaps it could be a memoir of your time with him. You might have to stab at it a few different ways before you settle on how you want to share Mr. Hamilton's story with the world." She paused. "After all, you would also be sharing your own story, too. A big part of you will go into the writing of this."

"Ana's right," Wolf said. "You'd be baring your soul. For the record, whatever form this story takes, I think it would have film potential, Holden. Not everyone is into super-hero or big action films. Ana and I have started WEBA Productions because we know there's a market for audiences who sometimes want a quieter, more reflective film about the human experience. This Mr. Hamilton story is exactly the kind of projects we want to bring to the screen." He paused. "Just think about it. I know you haven't even started writing yet, but once your story starts taking form, keep WEBA in mind."

He thought of all the kids out there like him, and how not all of them had had a Mr. Hamilton to help steer them in the right direction. Bringing this story alive on both the page and the screen might be exactly what needed to be done.

"I'll definitely consider it."

They finished eating and he and Wolf retreated to the director's office, where they viewed the storyboards Wolf had drawn up based on the novel since the script wasn't completed yet.

Holden snapped pictures of the storyboards as Wolf said, "These are the scenes from the book which I feel are the most critical. The beats that I need you to hit. How you get there is up to you. Right now, you've exceeded my expectations, Holden. It's not many writers who can make a transition from writing a novel to writing a screenplay. A script has to be so tight. So terse. Yet it has to have all the emotional wallop and excitement of a novel. I'm proud to be collaborating on this project with you."

He basked in the director's praise. "I think the more I write, the better the script will get. Once I finish the first draft, I'll go back and tweak it."

"Are you going to try to work on this Mr. Hamilton story at the same time?"

"Let me assure you that I will not neglect *Homicide*, Wolf. It's my top priority. I told Finley about Mr. Hamilton, and she's the one who suggested I turn it into a story. While I would have to put off the actual writing of it until I finished up with the screenplay, I plan to at least work on character sketches and plot points for Mr. Hamilton. I can juggle laying the groundwork for the new story while I'm working on the script. I know how many pages I want to put in on the screenplay each day. Any time left over is to rejuvenate my creative juices, and that includes working on the Mr. Hamilton story."

Wolf said, "Speaking of Finley, how are things going between the two of you?"

"Really well. Almost scary well," he admitted. "When I left New York, I severed all ties with Madison. My focus was to come back to Texas and put one hundred and ten percent into this script. The thought of getting involved with another woman so soon after splitting with Madison never entered my mind."

He paused. "Meeting Finley came out of nowhere. I didn't want to like her— but how could I not?"

"She is delightful," the director said. "Ana has really taken to her. Finley sent the photos she took of the children to us. It's remarkable what she was able to capture from them. I can see such joy. Not only on their faces but in their body language. It's as if these photographs have given Ana and me a slice of Eva and Bear which time will never capture again."

"You know how talented Finley is. You saw the landscapes of the Hill Country she took. Hell, you offered her a job based on that series."

"Finley has a good heart. Also, she refused to accept

any payment for the pictures of the children. She said being given the opportunity to work with WEBA Productions would be payment enough."

"That sounds like her. I haven't known her long, but Finley is generous to a fault. I'm having dinner with her and a few of her friends this evening. You remember Dax and Ivy from Java Junction?"

"Yes, they are a very interesting couple. We had a good conversation about their Harmony & Hues series and the possibility of turning it into a documentary. We tabled it for now, but I plan to take it up with them again once it draws closer to summer. I still want to see some of Ivy's paintings, though. Who else will be at this dinner?" Wolf asked.

"Finley's roommate. A fellow teacher named Emerson. She has a second job working as a cake baker for Weddings with Hart. It's a business Ivy's sister runs at Lone Star Winery. Ivy manages the tasting room there, and Finley wants me to come for a tasting sometime since I know next to nothing about wine."

"Perhaps Ana and I could join you and Finley for this tasting," Wolf suggested. "We are a bit isolated here at the ranch. Ana is busy with the children, of course, and now juggling a dozen balls with WEBA Productions, but she needs female friends in her life. She really likes Finley and also liked Ivy quite a bit."

"I'll bring it up tonight at dinner. See when we might be able to work out a time for the tasting. Finley stays pretty booked on weekends, photographing events held at the winery, and also doing portrait sittings."

Wolf's face softened. "Those photographs she took of that newborn and the parents moved me, Holden. I like to play the tough, macho man, but inside? I am squishy soft. Ana can tell you this."

"That's what makes you an outstanding filmmaker, Wolf. You have access to your heart and soft side and everything in between."

"Go home, Holden. Write some more this afternoon and then enjoy your dinner with your new friends tonight. Send me whatever you finish."

"Not right away," he said, reminding Wolf that he liked to let things sit a day or so on the screenplay before he fiddled with the pages and then forwarded them to his friend.

"I will eagerly await whatever I get, whenever I get it."

Wolf walked him to the door, and Holden said, "I'm going to need to return your truck to you. I can't drive it forever. I told you that I'll be staying in Texas. There's no reason for me to return to write in New York. Evan has told me that himself. That's the beauty of being a writer. I could do it on a raft in the middle of the ocean or sitting on a lounge chair by a pool."

"Keep the truck until you find something of your own. Maybe Finley might help you find a new vehicle."

Holden drove the short distance to Lost Creek, thinking about if this would be the town he might settle in.

With Finley.

He was crazy having such wild thoughts after having only known her such a short time, but he had never been more certain of anything. Wolf and Ana liked her. And if Mr. Hamilton had been here, Holden would have been proud to introduce the custodian to her.

He downloaded the photos he'd taken of the storyboards to his laptop and studied them several minutes, referring back to his novel and then his outline. Then the creative spark hit, and Holden began typing madly, trying to get everything down while it was fresh in his head.

Two hours later, he set aside his laptop, raking his fingers through his hair. He didn't often have such a marathon of writing. Usually, things came to him in bits and spurts, but he'd clearly seen what he'd just captured on the page, as if the movie ran in his head as he wrote.

Glancing at his watch, he saw he had half an hour before he needed to pick up Finley and Emerson. He decided since Finley had been so delighted with the flowers he'd brought her, he should bring Harper Clark a bouquet.

He stopped on the square at the same florist, getting all roses this time, and then drove to Finley's house.

Knocking on the front door, Emerson answered again.

"I'm curious as to what is in that bakery box," he told her as she retrieved it from the kitchen counter.

Finley entered the room. "I've kept out of it though I'm dying to see what's inside. I will admit that I leaned down and took a big whiff. The chocolate smell was heavy and sweet."

Holden offered to carry the box to the truck for Emerson.

"Flowers?" Emerson asked as she slid into the back

seat, picking up the bouquet and setting it beside her as she reclaimed the box from him.

"I asked if I could bring something tonight. I was told no. You can't wrong with flowers, though."

"If you get tired of being Finley's boyfriend— and you learn to cook —I'd be open to a relationship with you, Holden," Emerson teased.

He glanced to Finley in the passenger seat next to him, seeing her blush.

Was he her boyfriend?

He was thirty-one. The terms boyfriend and girlfriend seemed so antiquated. Yet he would happily wear the label if Finley wanted him to.

Emerson gave him directions, and they reached the Clarks' home about seven minutes later. As they got out of his truck, Dax and Ivy pulled up behind them. They both got out, each holding two bottles of wine in their hands.

"We're always in charge of the wines," Ivy said cheerfully. "I check with Braden or Finley, whoever's cooking, so I know what's appropriate to bring."

"What are we eating tonight?" Dax asked his wife as the five of them approached the front door.

"Fajitas," Ivy said.

"What?" Finley asked. "Emerson should have made her sangria since we're eating Mexican food." She looked to Holden. "Emerson is famous for her sangria. It's a little hard to transport, though. You can repeat Mexican for us next week and make a batch of sangria then so Holden can taste it."

"Don't think you have to invite me every week," he said. "I don't want to horn in on anything."

Dax rang the doorbell, and a tall blond man answered. "Welcome to Casa Clark, everybody."

As the others crossed the threshold, Finley slipped her arm through his. "I don't want you to feel obligated to come each week, but these are my friends, Holden. They're important to me. Just as you are."

Holden hadn't felt needed—or wanted—in a long time.

He decided it felt damn good.

he others moved passed their host, and Holden and Finley stepped toward him.

"I'm Braden Clark," he said, offering his hand. "Happy to have a friend of Dax's join us for dinner." He paused, noting Finley's hand tucked through Holden's arm. "Or should I say a friend of Finley's?" he asked, interest lighting his eyes.

"Thanks for inviting me this evening," Holden said.

"Happy to have you," Braden replied, closing the door.

The group left the foyer and entered a large den, what Madison had always called a great room when they had visited her parents. A woman who resembled Ivy, thought she had auburn hair and was a bit taller, came toward them.

"You must be Holden Scott," she said, smiling warmly at him. "I'm Harper Clark. Welcome to our new home."

He handed the flowers wrapped in tissue paper to her. "These are for you. Happy housewarming."

Accepting them, she inhaled the roses. "How thoughtful. Let me put them in some water and place them on the table. Then we need to give everyone a tour of the house."

Harper disappeared into the kitchen as Braden looked to Holden. "We just moved in on Sunday. We'd been renting a house a few doors down from Emerson and Finley, but we got married last fall and had been looking for a place ever since then. When this one went on the market, we knew it was the one for us."

Harper rejoined them. "Finley is familiar with the house since she helped us furnish it. Let's go ahead and show everyone around, though."

They toured the house, which Holden estimated to be about twenty-five hundred square feet. It was roomy and even though the Clarks had only recently moved in, it already had a homey feel about it. The tour ended outside, where Braden showed off the covered outdoor kitchen.

"This may have been what sold me on the place," Braden shared. "I do all the cooking, and it's nice to have some outdoor living space. There's also a fire pit to gather around after dinner if we'd like."

"Since we've added Holden to our group, I think we should hold all our weekly dinners here," Harper suggested. "That is, if Finley doesn't mind cooking here. There's just so many of us now. We've got a large dining room, which will be more comfortable than eating on the couch, balancing plates in our laps, and on the floor."

"I'm happy to do that," Finley said. "I'm already in love

with your kitchen, especially those double ovens and that large island."

"Things are pretty much ready for us to eat," Braden told them. "Give me two minutes to get all the garnishes for the fajitas out, and then you can assemble them to your liking."

The group followed him into the kitchen. Braden apologized, saying, "I didn't have time to make anything more elaborate this week. Not after the big move and settling in. I thought a fajita bar would be easy."

"I hope you used that fabulous marinade on the beef strips," Ivy said.

"I did," Braden assured her. Looking to Dax, he asked, "Want to open the wines for us?"

"I also have iced tea if anyone wants that," Harper said.

By the time the drinks were poured, it was time to form a line. They headed clockwise around the large island, taking warmed tortillas and filling them with beef fajita meat and the toppings they wanted. Holden chose cheese, grilled onions and peppers, and sour cream for his, adding some refried beans and rice to his plate, as well.

"Queso and chips are over on that countertop," Braden told them. "Don't miss them."

They took their plates into the dining room, and the conversation was quick and witty. He hadn't realized how starved he was for good conversation— and friends. He had lived a quiet, solitary life these past few years in New York, but he could see how fun it might be, being around a large group such as this.

"What are you working on now?" Harper asked him. "I

devoured your first book, but I haven't gotten to the second one yet. I've recently started my own business, and it doesn't leave much free time."

"I'm juggling several projects. Something I've never really done before," he explained. "Usually, I write something and then take a break before starting a new piece."

"I totally get that," Ivy chimed in. "I have to finish an entire painting before I can start something new. I deliberately avoid even thinking about anything new until I've completed what I started."

"I'm not like that at all with songs," Dax revealed. "While I have been inspired at times and written an entire song, I usually have three or four melodies going in my head at a time. I'll work on one. Skip to another. That's just my process."

"Just before I came to Texas, I finished the first draft of my third novel," Holden shared. "I always put aside a novel for a few weeks before I go back and do a hard edit on it. If I don't, I find I'm simply too close to the material and the characters, in particular. Once I have some distance and perspective, though, it's a little easier to edit."

"What's it about?" asked Emerson. "Your first two books are very different from one another."

"It's more of a psychological thriller," he explained. "I have a detective whose marriage is on the rocks. He follows his wife one night, trying to figure out if she's having an affair or into something she shouldn't be doing. He has trouble putting the pieces together, watching from afar as she meets certain people. The next day, he and his partner are called to a homicide scene, a place he'd been the night before. The victim is someone who spoke with his wife. A woman who resembles her quite a bit. He begins to wonder if the victim was the intended target— or if the killer meant for his wife to be the victim. It becomes a game of cat and mouse after that."

"That sounds exciting," Dax said. "And it has movie written all over it."

"I haven't even let my agent read it yet, but I have told him the premise. He would agree with you. I'll work on polishing it once I finish the project I've been hired to do now. It's a screenplay for *Hill Country Homicide*."

"I think I remember reading in your bio that you were from Texas," Harper said.

"I grew up in Austin," Holden confirmed. "I thought it would be a good place to set a murder." He grinned. "I didn't have to do nearly the research that I did for *Capitol Crimes*."

"What is like, writing a screenplay?" Braden asked. "It's got to be different from writing a novel."

Holden chuckled. "It's *way* different."

He told them a little about his friendship with Wolf and how the director had started his own production company.

"Wolf asked me to take a stab at writing the script for *Homicide*. I'm not trained in screenwriting, so I did a crash course on my own, trying to figure it out. I also re-read *Capitol Crimes* and the screenplay for it, trying to see the difference between the two. I believe I've found my rhythm now, and things are starting to move faster. Wolf is reading scenes as I write, making suggestions. He'll help me polish the script so that it's a tight, filmable piece."

He glanced around the table. "Enough about me. I'd like to hear something about all of you."

Harper took the lead, and Holden saw she was comfortable in doing so.

"I worked for an event planning company in Austin for several years before I decided to return to Lost Creek and open my own event center at our family's winery. More and more brides are not going with traditional church weddings, and I wanted to capitalize on that. The winery makes for a wonderful location for a wedding, whether it's held indoors or outdoors."

"A friend of Harper's designed the center," Braded added. "One wall is entirely glass, looking out over the vineyards. It makes for a truly special setting for a wedding. She also has space designated for an outdoor wedding, as well. A covered area and benches for guests. Again, the grapevines are in the background, and they make for some spectacular memories."

Braden smiled at his wife, a tender look in his eyes.

Ivy spoke up. "Harper and Braden were the first couple married at the event center. She had a huge opening party to kick off the opening. People who showed up had no idea they were attending a wedding— and that included our parents."

"I didn't mind making our wedding the guinea pig to see how things might run," Harper continued. "I figured as long as we had all those family and friends present, we might as well truly celebrate with our marriage."

Braden said, "I'm from California. My family had a winery in Napa. Things didn't end well there. My dad embezzled a bunch of money and went to prison. I found myself with no job or home and a very particular set of skills which didn't transfer to many other jobs. I was radioactive in the wine community. No one in the industry wanted to touch me and have my name associated with their business. Bill Hart gave me a chance to be his viticulturist." He paused. "That's the person who specializes in the cultivation of grapes. Nowadays, I've since moved up and am the chief winemaker for Lost Creek Vineyards."

"I haven't been much of a wine drinker before now," Holden confessed, "but I've enjoyed Lost Creek wines at my friend Wolf's house and also here in Lost Creek itself. Finley has suggested that I do a wine tasting with Ivy to learn more about wines and discover what I'm drawn to. Wolf and Ana would also like to come."

"I'd love to walk you through a tasting, Holden," Ivy said. "The tasting room is open seven days a week. If you'd like, I can give you and your friends a private tasting. We close at five-thirty this time of year, so if you want to come after that, I'd be happy to let you sample both reds and whites. Would tomorrow or Friday be good for you? I'm working both days."

"I'd like to be there if I could," Finley said. "I need to go to the varsity basketball game at the high school Friday night, though. One of my former students who's a sophomore is getting his first start at center, and he asked me to come watch him play. If tomorrow works for Wolf and Ana, that would be terrific."

Holden pulled out his cell. "I'll text Ana. She's the keeper of the schedules. I know enough to always run something by her."

He finished the text and set down his phone as Ivy said, "If tomorrow isn't good, we can pick a day next week."

His phone buzzed, and Holden read the message, saying, "Tomorrow works for them. Ana says they could be at the winery by six."

"Perfect," Ivy said, smiling at him. "I'll have everything ready."

Talk turned to other things then. He learned a little about the town of Lost Creek as they shared with him what it had to offer. Dax suggested a few restaurants for him to try. Braden told him to stop by the winery for a tour of the vines, saying he'd be happy to walk Holden through the process of how the wines were made. Ivy encouraged Holden to drive around the area and soak up the beauty of the landscape.

"Wolf would really like to see your art, Ivy," he mentioned.

"After tomorrow's tasting, you're welcome to stop by my studio and see what I have going. I'm preparing for a showing in New York. It's my first exhibit."

"That would be great," Holden said. "I'd also like to see your art. What type of paints to you use?"

"Almost exclusively oils, but I'm experimenting some

with watercolors recently. I'm not certain if any of those will be in my show, though."

Emerson looked around. "I think we're all ready for dessert. Be right back."

She rose and Harper joined her, saying she'd get the dessert plates. When they returned, Ivy had removed the cake she'd made from its box, and every eye was drawn to it.

"Oh, my gosh. That looks fantastic," Finley said. "What is it?"

Emerson cleared her throat. "Tonight, I've baked for you a coffee-chocolate layer cake with mocha-mascarpone frosting. I used an instant espresso powder in both the batter and the frosting. I doubt you'll have eaten anything like this."

Everyone groaned, and Dax said, "I'm full from the fajitas, so I'll limit myself to one slice."

His remarks caused the group to laugh.

Emerson sliced cake for everyone, Finley passing the plates around the table. Holden placed the first bite into his mouth, and an explosion of chocolate erupted.

"Mmm," he said, not able to describe the richness in the cake and its frosting.

Emerson smiled. "I'll take that as a compliment, Holden."

He swallowed. "You do this every week?"

She nodded. "I try out all kinds of desserts. Puddings. Pies. Cakes. Cookies. I experiment with different flavors. Sometimes, I strike gold. Tonight seems to be one of those nights."

Braden and Dax gave her a thumbs up.

"Sometimes, it's good— but not great. Then again, that's what baking is all about. What I learn, I use in new cakes. Brides don't simply want a vanilla cake and vanilla icing these days for their wedding cakes. They want new, interesting flavors and decorations no one has seen before. Everyone wants their guests wowed."

"You can't imagine what Emerson can do with icing," Finley bragged. "Just her piping of delicate rosettes alone is a work of art. Oh, remember that vanilla almond rainbow petal cake you did a few weeks ago? The rainbow was all buttercream petals. Absolutely beautiful— and delicious."

Holden tasted another bite of the cake, savoring its richness. "I hate to ask this, but why are you still teaching when you can make creations such as this?"

"I like teaching," she told him. "School was always important to me. I grew up without much. School was my haven. My safe place. I loved learning and wanted to be a teacher my entire life."

"When did you start baking?" he asked.

"I worked in a bakery my last two years in college. That's when I really began learning. I'll be honest. If I hadn't already finished two years of college— and had my scholarship and grants paying for the remaining two years —I might have thought about going to culinary school and specializing in baking."

"Emerson worked at The Bake Shop here in town on weekends," Finley said. "Until Harper talked her into coming to work for Weddings with Hart."

Emerson nodded. "I was able to work on a lot of wedding cakes at the bakery. I would've been happy staying there, but Ethel, the owner, encouraged me to accept Harper's offer. She said I needed the creative challenge. I make good money on the side, baking wedding and groom's cakes, but it's not as much as my teaching salary brings in."

"What about opening your own bakery?" Holden asked, placing the last forkful of cake into his mouth.

"I would never want to compete with Ethel," Emerson said. "She's such a sweet lady. Besides, I'm good at teaching."

"The kids love her," Finley said.

"Maybe I could write a book about a baker," he mused. "He could put poison in a cake."

"I'd read that," Dax said. "Or how about winemaker? You've got a lot of resources at this table, Holden. We could keep you busy for years, helping you research and kill people."

The group all laughed, but Holden didn't think it was a bad idea. He would definitely take Braden Clark up regarding a tour around Lost Creek Vineyards. You never knew when a plot would hatch and what sparked it.

"Time for teachers to go home," Finley announced. "I know it's early for a New Yorker, but Emerson and I go to bed early because we're at school so early each morning."

"Not a problem," he said. "With so many here, cleanup will be a breeze."

"No, we'll handle that," Harper said. "It was just nice to see everyone. Is next Wednesday good for everybody?

We've been letting the day bounce around. Maybe we should pick one and stick to it."

They all agreed Wednesdays worked. Holden was pleased he was included.

"Let me slice cake for everyone to take home," Emerson said, taking what was left of the dessert into the kitchen and divvying the cake up as everyone took their plates and wineglasses from the dining room to the kitchen.

Harper pulled him aside. "I'm glad you came tonight, Holden. I've known Finley over twenty years. She was a year behind me in school. At UT, I was her big sis in our sorority." She paused. "I can tell you're good for each other."

"Glad I got the Harper Clark stamp of approval," he said lightly. "Thank you again for having me tonight. I really enjoyed myself."

He accompanied Finley and Emerson to the truck and drove them to their house. Emerson leaned up, touching his shoulder.

"I'll let you two say your goodnights," she told him, getting out and going into the house.

"How was tonight for you?" Finley asked.

"Tonight was good. Very good," he told her. "You have a great group of friends. They made things comfortable for me."

"They all liked you." She brushed the back of her fingers against her cheek. "I like you," she said softly, leaning in and kissing him.

Holden tasted the chocolate cake and the wine and something else that was simply innately Finley.

He could have kissed her all night, but he broke the kiss. "I'll see you tomorrow at the tasting room. Can I pick you up?"

"I'll meet you there. I've got a faculty meeting after school and some projects coming in tomorrow that I'll need to grade."

He cupped her cheek. "Okay. Six at the tasting room then." Once more he kissed her and then pulled away, knowing he better let her go now.

As he watched Finley walk up the sidewalk, a peace settled over Holden. He was living in Texas again, making headway on the screenplay. He'd been introduced to a wonderful group of people close to his age, ones he hoped would become friends over the coming weeks and months. Contentment filled him, something he'd never experienced before.

And as Finley turned and waved goodbye to him, Holden realized that he had fallen in love for the very first time.

12

Finley left the teacher's lounge early, returning to her classroom while her students were still at lunch. She rearranged the furniture some so that it would be easier to place them in groups as they returned from eating for the project she had in mind. She sat at her desk when finished, her thoughts turning to last night.

The private tasting with Ivy had been enjoyable. Finley had done a couple of these with Ivy before, and each time, she learned more about wines. Ivy was so knowledgeable and natural when she dispensed information, making those sampling wines feel at ease as she imparted interesting tidbits, helping them discover the wines they enjoyed.

Ana had been partial to whites and rosés, while Wolf went for the darkest of reds. Finley had watched Holden's reactions to the different wines as he found he liked those in the range from Pinot Noirs to Merlots best.

After the tasting ended, Ivy took them to her studio, a place Finley had never visited before. It was on the square, located above Mayor Bennett's hardware store, and usually was rented out as an apartment. The last tenant had left a broken-down sofa. The rest of the space was filled with Ivy's canvases and art supplies.

Her friend had taken them through the paintings which she had completed, and Finley thought how breathtaking the landscapes were. The only time she had seen Ivy's work was the single painting of Lost Creek Lake that hung in Java Junction. Ivy had painted the lake again from a different perspective, but she had also painted much of the surrounding area. Finley recognized different places they had driven to, Ivy sketching them, as well as taking photographs on her phone, while Finley used her various cameras to capture the geographic features of the land.

She had hugged Ivy, complimenting her on her work. Ivy had even suggested that someday they might try something unique and do an exhibition together, with photographs Finley had taken of places Ivy had painted. Ana had seconded the idea.

Wolf had wanted to buy several of the paintings to hang at Meadow Creek Ranch, but Ivy told him everything in the room would be viewed by Clive Crutchfield, the Soho gallery owner who would put together the show for her. Ivy had told the director that she would give Crutchfield Wolf's contact information, saying the two might come to an agreement to have at least one painting already sold when the show began, still displaying it, while giving Wolf a chance to bid on other ones.

Afterward, Holden had come back to her house. It was a little after eight o'clock, and they both were starving. Finley had made omelets for them, walking Holden through the steps and telling him the next time, he'd be in charge of making the omelets. She also had toasted slices of sourdough bread, her favorite, and they had sat at the kitchen table, eating and talking for two hours. It amazed her how long they talked and the gambit those topics ran. Holden was well-informed about so many different things in the world and kept up with the news both here and abroad.

He had kissed her at the door as he told her goodnight, telling her it was a school night and she needed to get some sleep.

Tonight would be different. Finley planned to spend the entire night with Holden.

The bell rang, and she pushed aside thoughts of the handsome writer, going to the door to greet her students as they returned to the classroom, assigning them to different pods. Once they were all seated, she gave them their instructions, and they began to work, happily chattering about the news stories they would write about the Old West. Circulating through the room, she answered their questions, glad they were all on task. This was the best group that had come through in her six years of teaching, and she would miss them when they left for middle school.

"Miss Farrow?"

She startled, looking at the student standing in front of her.

Josh said, "It's almost time for the bell. Can we get our backpacks?"

Pulling herself from her reverie, having slipped into more thoughts about Holden, she inwardly chastised herself. Glancing at the clock, she saw less than two minutes remained before school would end for the day. Fortunately, her students were well-trained, and Finley saw they had already cleaned up and were moving the furniture back into place.

"Thank you for getting so much done this afternoon and cleaning up without being asked," she said brightly. "Collect your backpacks and line up."

Students rushed to their cubbies, claiming their backpacks, and she went to the door, watching as they lined up in an orderly fashion. The bell rang, and she dismissed them, telling them to have a great weekend.

Lisa stopped at the door. "Are you coming to the basketball game tonight, Miss Farrow? My cousin Barry is playing on varsity."

"I'll see you there, Lisa. I'm glad Barry is making his first start tonight."

She went to the parent loop, her afternoon duty this week, and supervised traffic for the next quarter-hour. Once it thinned, she headed back into the building, stopping by her room to pick up her coat, purse, and tablet for her meeting. She couldn't help but be a but resentful that Sheena, her team leader, had called a meeting of their team on a Friday afternoon. Finley had been team leader and asked her principal if she could pass along that responsibility this year to someone else so another teacher could gain that experience. It freed her up from a ton of paperwork and additional meetings, which helped since she was devoting more and more time to her photography business.

Sheena had taken her place, and it seemed the small bit of authority had gone to her head. Where Finley was organized and efficient and aware of others' time, Sheena was downright anal about everything and thought nothing of calling meetings at inconvenient times, including the afternoon they had let out early for the winter holidays. The new team leader was also pregnant and experiencing mood swings. Sheena was six weeks out from her due date. If the baby came at spring break, as he was supposed to, Sheena wouldn't return for the remainder of the year. Finley had already agreed to be the acting team leader in Sheena's absence.

She had also arranged with Mary Martin's secretary to meet with the principal next Monday afternoon. Mary had been gone, attending an educator's conference, and Finley was ready to break the news to her boss that she wouldn't be returning next school year.

Entering Sheena's room, she saw the team leader bustling about.

"Anything I can help you with?" she asked.

"No," Sheena said sharply, picking up her tablet and coming to sit at the table where Finley had already taken a seat.

The other two members of the team strolled in and joined them. Neither looked happy. They were both regulars at the happy hour many teachers went to at Hill Country Hangout each Friday afternoon.

"This won't take long," Sheena said primly, proceeding to talk non-stop for the next forty-five minutes.

It was nothing that couldn't have been covered during their regular conference period during the day. Finley decided she would mention the way Sheena threw her authority around when she met with Mary on Monday. While she knew Sheena was a good teacher and thoroughly covered all state required topics during instruction, Finley didn't think Sheena had the right characteristics to continue in the role as team leader. Hopefully, the principal could give Sheena some delicate, sage advice as to when was the best time to call a meeting outside normal school hours. Maybe she could even suggest that Sheena might want to relinquish her duties as team leader next year in order to spend more time with her newborn.

Much of the notes Finley took were related to what would need to happen once Sheena went on maternity leave and how she wanted things done. While Finley understood that Sheena wanted her team to be ready in case she went into labor early, this discussion could have been between the two of them and didn't need to include their other teammates. As it was, Finley would be in charge of seeing how the rest of the year played out. She decided everything would get done her way. She had experience Sheena didn't, especially in closing out a school year and submitting budget information to central administration.

Since she'd brought her things with her, Finley went directly to her car and headed home once Sheena wrapped things up. It was almost five o'clock when she arrived home, and she changed from her school clothes into a red cashmere sweater and a pair of black pants, the high school's colors. Holden was taking her to an early dinner at Lone Star Chophouse before they went to the basketball game.

She spritzed on some perfume and left her bedroom. Since she didn't see Emerson, she figured her roommate was at the event center, putting final touches on the cakes for tomorrow night's wedding. The couple marrying each had children from their previous marriages, and in addition to a wedding and groom's cakes, the three children also would have small cakes of their own. Finley would be photographing the wedding and reception and had already shot the bridal portraits a month ago when the bride's dress came in.

The doorbell sounded, and she went to answer it, thinking it thoughtful Holden always came to the door to collect her. The last few men she'd dated merely texted from the car, telling her she should come out.

Opening the door, she caught her breath, seeing how handsome her date truly was. His black hair shone and his moss green eyes drew her in. She'd never dated a man who wore glasses before, but they suited him, making him look sexy and smart.

"Hi. Come on in. Let me grab my purse and coat."

She went to the breakfast bar. Suddenly, Holden's strong arms encircled her from behind. He nuzzled her neck, his lips moving to her ear, where he tugged gently on the lobe with his teeth, sending a frisson of desire running through her.

Turning her in his arms, he said, "You look beautiful tonight, Finley."

"You clean up nicely yourself, Mr. Scott."

He wore a navy blazer over an open-neck, button-down shirt and dark slacks. Up close, he smelled divine, his cologne subtle, reminding her of the woods in autumn.

"I didn't know the dress code of the restaurant. I hope I can get away without wearing a tie." He dipped his hand into his pocket and pulled, revealing a pin-striped tie. "But I brought one just in case."

"This isn't New York. It's rare you'll see a tie in any restaurant in Lost Creek," she told him, pulling him down for a kiss.

Finley broke it, telling him, "More kissing later. Right now, we need to make our five-thirty reservation. The basketball game starts at seven-thirty, and I want to make sure we get a good seat."

He threaded his fingers through hers and led her to his truck, opening the door for her and seeing she was settled before closing it.

The restaurant was only half a mile outside the city limits. They parked and went inside, Holden giving the hostess his name. She led them to a booth for two, and their server brought two waters. They both ordered iced tea, skipping wine, Finley telling him they could open a bottle after the game tonight at her place and savor it.

They both ordered steaks, medium for her and

medium rare for him. They decided to share sides and ordered roasted garlic mashed potatoes, mushrooms bordelaise, creamed spinach with parmesan, and toasted garlic bread. Each of them ordered a wedge salad, as well.

"I need to go car shopping," he told her. "I've been driving a truck which belongs to Wolf." His gaze met and held hers. "Since I plan on staying in Texas. I need wheels of my own. Maybe you can go shopping with me."

She hoped that she might be the reason he had decided to remain and boldly asked, "If you're buying a truck, where are you going to put down roots?"

Without hesitation, he said, "Lost Creek. It's quickly become home."

The server appeared, setting down their salads and bread, and they dug into them.

They talked about events in the news recently as they ate. A politician being impeached. Another school shooting, this time in East Texas. An earthquake in Japan. Finley had never been a person who followed the news much, but Holden's curiosity had piqued her own, and she found she enjoyed talking about things outside of Lost Creek. He also knew a lot about the world of entertainment, reading several trade papers online, sharing about books to be published and new movies coming out.

They finished their meal and she excused herself, going to the ladies' room while Holden paid their check. She freshened her lipstick and returned to the table, giving him directions to the high school gymnasium's parking lot. As she had known, it was almost full, and they had to hunt for a space to park. Only a handful of district games remained, and Lost Creek was good about turning out for sporting events held at the high school.

She flashed her teacher ID, which gave her entrance into all school events from games to plays to concerts, while Holden purchased a ticket for himself. They entered the gym, weaving their way up the stairs and to a section just to the right of center. Though they had to go up several rows, they found enough room on the end and would have a good view of the entire court.

Several people stopped by to say hello, and Finley proudly introduced Holden as her boyfriend. A few recognized him from his author picture from a book jacket, while two more mentioned they'd read an article about him in *People* magazine.

"I didn't know you were so famous," she teased as the teams took to the court.

"Hey, you're the famous one," he countered. "Probably half the people at the game tonight had to stop by and say hi to you. Former students. Parents." He smiled, taking her hand. "You've really touched a lot of lives, Finley."

Holden continued to hold her hand, giving her a warm glow. She hoped he was ready to take the next step in their relationship tonight because she certainly was.

At halftime, the Lost Creek Lobos led by two baskets. Holden asked if she wanted anything from the concession stand.

"Popcorn. It's better here than at the movies. And a Dr. Pepper," she told him.

He grinned. "Two state drinks and a large popcorn. Be right back."

Finley watched him head down the stairs, admiring his lean, strong frame, ready to see him out of his clothes.

Suddenly, her view was blocked, and she looked up.

"Hey, babe. How's it going? You're looking good."

Randy Foster sat next to her. She'd dated the football coach for a short while. He was still built like the former college linebacker he'd been. Good-looking and knew it. She'd grown tired quickly of his cocky attitude.

And the cheating.

"This seat's taken, Randy."

He grinned. "I know. I'm sitting in it."

13

*H*olden ran into Bill and Bud at the concession stand. The retired brothers had been in real estate development together in Houston. Bud had never married. Bill was a widower whose only son lived with his family in Lost Creek and convinced his dad to move here to be closer to his grandkids. Bud had followed Bill here. He saw them almost every time he went to write at Java Junction and had taken to speaking with them briefly, either before he got started writing or once he'd completed a scene. They were in their late seventies. Funny. Kind. And huge fans of his.

"Hey, guys!" he greeted, stepping up behind them.

"Have you seen Tommy tonight?" Bill asked. "My grandson is dominating the boards."

"The blond power forward? He's your grandson?"

"Yup," Bill confirmed. "His daddy also played basketball."

"But nothing like Tommy," Bud added. "Coach says that Tommy has a real shot at a scholarship when he graduates next year."

"Why are you here, Holden?" Bill asked. "I didn't know you liked basketball."

"I don't really follow it much." He grinned. "But I'm with someone tonight who came to see her former student start at center."

Both men's eyes lit with interest, and Bud said, "Barry's kept his head tonight. It was good move by Coach to bring him up from JV because of the injury. Nice he's getting some varsity experience." He paused. "Who's the teacher?"

"Finley Farrow."

Bill nodded. "Miss Farrow has a wonderful reputation around Lost Creek. Her brother runs the water sports place at the lake. All my grandkids went to her parents' Montessori school."

"Is it serious?" Bud asked.

"It is," he confirmed. "At least on my end."

Bud waved a hand in the air. "You're a nice-looking fellow, Holden. Smart. Good personality. I'll bet she's crazy about you."

They had reached the front of the line, and Bill placed his order and one for Bud. Looking to Holden, he asked, "What'll it be?"

"Two DP's. A big popcorn."

Bill added it and though Holden tried to pay him for it, he said, "Nope. I got this one. But maybe you can introduce us to your girl sometime."

"I'll do that," he promised, accepting the bucket of buttered popcorn and two soft drinks.

He returned to the gym, glancing at the scoreboard, seeing seven more minutes before the second half started. Already, players were returning to the court, shooting from the arc. He spotted Tommy and watched him hit four three-pointers in a row. He'd have to tell Finley about Bud and Bill and their connection to the forward.

As he began up the aisle, he noticed someone had joined Finley. From the sour look on her face, she wasn't happy with the company.

He studied the guy as he eased up the aisle. All his life, Holden had observed others. He was good at nailing personalities merely by sizing up someone's physical appearance and facial expressions. The man seated next to Finley looked like he had played ball, most likely football. He was nice-looking but had an arrogant air about him. Holden had a pretty good idea that this was the coach she had dated, the one she said was a real player.

Reaching his row, he looked down. "I'll need my seat back," he said, his voice neutral, smiling at the guy.

Glancing up, the man said, "It's mine now, buddy. Move along."

"Randy, I told you my boyfriend was sitting there," Finley insisted, her voice low. "Get up and go. Please."

Holden wished she hadn't added the *please*. It was a word that made a guy like this Randy creep dig in.

"Babe, I just—"

"You were stupid enough to screw up your relationship with a class act like Finley," he said calmly. "She's done with you. Vacate the seat, *buddy*." He emphasized the last word because it's what this guy had said to him.

Randy glared at him as he stood. If he were a cartoon character, Holden would have seen steam coming out of his ears.

Finley, too, came to her feet, so the three of them were close together. Her eyes pleaded with him, and Holden knew she didn't want any trouble.

He passed the drinks to her and set the bucket of popcorn where the coach had been sitting so that he wasn't juggling the items and off-balance. Holden didn't think the guy would take a swing at him, but he wanted to be prepared.

"Listen, window face," Randy growled.

"No," he said firmly, keeping his voice level. "You listen. Finley has told me you dated, and she called you a player. That's a guy who toys with the emotions of a woman he's going out with. Players don't care if the other person gets hurt because it's all a game to them. A player doesn't want to get to know someone. He's just looking for a good time. Yes, I'm sure you showered Finley with compliments, but you didn't bother to ask her questions and get to know her. For men like you, it's all about the chase. You can't commit because all you're interested in is something physical."

Randy's jaw dropped, but Holden pushed further.

"You're an employee in this district. By now, people are looking at us. At you. Thanks to the ever-churning gossip mill, most of the fans in this gym know you used to go out. And that you don't anymore. Finley's a lady and wouldn't have put it out there that you're a player. But the speculation has to be there. If you slam a fist into my face, not only will you lose your job— but I'll press charges for assault. You'll be ruined. I won't have had to lift a finger.

"So, smile at us, Randy," Holden said, smiling broadly at the coach. "Let's not give anyone anything to talk about."

He leaned in, his mouth close to the other man's ear. "And stay the hell away from Finley. Or you and I will be trading more than words."

Holden leaned back and laughed, slapping Randy on the back. The coach played his part, smiling widely. Only if someone were up close would they have been able to see the rage seething in Randy's eyes.

"Nice meeting you," he said amiably, stepping back to allow Randy to exit the row.

The coach trotted down the steps, pushing a hand in the air, waving without turning around.

Finley sat again on the bleacher, Holden picking up the bucket of popcorn and placing it in his lap as he, too, sat. He brought an arm about her waist and leaned in. She turned toward him.

And he kissed her.

Not for long. Just enough to let the people inside this gym watching— and he knew they had garnered their fair of attention as the buzzer sounded for play to start —to know he'd staked his claim.

She handed him his Dr. Pepper, and he took a long

draw on the sugary drink before setting it on the concrete floor beside him. Then he picked up a piece of popcorn and fed it to her. She chewed thoughtfully, her gaze never leaving his. Holden them scooped a handful for himself and downed it.

Leaning close, she said quietly, "If you were a dog, I'd say you just marked your territory. Since you're not, I'll say you planted your flag."

He fed her another bite of popcorn. "I may have asserted my rights. It never hurts to establish your position. And I take my position of being your boyfriend very seriously, Miss Farrow."

Laughter bubbled up from her. Holden relaxed, knowing all was well between them. He turned his attention back to the game—and left his arm around her waist. Just in case Randy Player still had them in his sights.

By the time the game ended, the Lobos winning by seven points, several people had stopped by their seats to chat during timeouts. No one brought up Randy, and neither did Finley or Holden. The home crowd stood while the school song played, and then it began vacating the gym.

"Do you think Randy will be waiting outside?" Finley asked.

"Not a chance. He can't afford to. He would lose his job if he assaulted me. Even if he got off by some odd chance, this district would find a way to let him go by the end of the year. The old 'we're going in another direction' speech. And he would be poison which any other district would be afraid to hire."

As they walked to the car, he put his arm around her shoulders. "The people in the row in front and behind us might've heard a little of what I said. If they did, so be it. I can't stop the tide of gossip. I have a feeling, though, that the jerk won't bother you again. That he'll put out feelers and land another position far from Lost Creek by next year."

They reached the truck and got in. Holden started the motor, letting it warm up a bit, not trying to pull out since the parking lot was a madhouse.

"He was everything you said," Finley said. "He gushed over me, but he never really took the time to get to know me. He wanted to be physical right from the start. I heard a rumor he was also seeing the friend of an acquaintance. I had my friend put the two of us in touch. Yes, Randy was also seeing her. She lived in Burnet and thought they were serious. Who knows if he had another other women he was stringing along?"

Holden leaned over, his hand capturing her nape, pulling her close for a long kiss.

"I hope you know I'm faithful. That you're the only woman I'm seeing." He kissed her lightly. "The only one I want to see. I know your free time is almost non-existent, and I don't want to smother you. But I'll take whatever time you're willing to give me, Finley."

Those aquamarine eyes sparkled at him. A smile tugged at her lips as she said, "I've got all night free, Holden. And it's all yours. *I'm* all yours. If you want me."

He removed his hand from her nape and quickly put the truck into drive.

"Let's go sip some wine at my place," he told her. "And if we get tired of that, I can think of a few other things to while away the night."

"You writers. You're always full of clever ideas," she purred.

Holden roared with laughter.

14

―――――――――

As they approached the turn to The Inn on Lost Creek, where Holden was renting a cottage, Finley's heart sped up, beating wildly in her chest. She knew she was making the right decision. She already felt emotionally committed to Holden. A physical commitment was merely the next step.

"You need to text Emerson," he told her, glancing over at her and then back at the road. "Girl code."

He was right about that. Women always let their friends— and especially their roommates —know where they were going to be and who they would be with.

"Good idea," she said, removing her cell from her purse and tapping a message to Emerson.

> Do not wait up for me. Will be with Holden tonight.

Emerson replied immediately. All that appeared on the

screen was a heart emoji. Though she and her roommate had not talked much about Holden, Finley knew that Emerson liked the writer and would approve of them being together. Emerson had thought Randy was a tool and had told Finley that up front. She wished now she had listened to her longtime friend. That was in the past, though.

Holden was her present— and possibly her future.

She didn't want to get ahead of herself, though, weaving fantasies about this man. They hadn't known one another long, but already, she believed she knew him better than any other man she had dated. That included her years with Jeb. Her college sweetheart had turned out to be as self-centered as Randy Foster, and Finley was glad things hadn't worked out between them.

Because it had given her this chance now to be with Holden Scott.

He pulled past the B&B itself, the truck going down a narrow road to where the cottages for rent stood. Cutting the engine, he turned to her.

"I don't know what tonight will be like between us, Finley. It's something I've wanted. *You're* someone I've wanted. I just want to make sure before we walk through that door that this is the path you want to follow. I don't want you to feel rushed. Hurried into something you're not ready for yet."

She gazed at him, once again grateful he was such a gentleman. "This is something I want, Holden. To get to know you better. To show you what I'm feeling for you. I know some people might believe we're pulling the trigger too soon, but of all the decisions I've made regarding a man, this is the one I'm feeling best about."

His serious expression faded, a smile turning up the corners of his beautiful mouth.

"I'm ready for this adventure with you."

He got out of the truck. Finley waited, allowing him to come to open her door for her. He slipped his hand around hers, leading her to the door of the cottage and unlocking it.

Once inside, she placed her purse on a table by the door and shrugged out of her coat, draping it atop the purse. He removed the blazer he wore, and his hands cradled her face, giving her a tender kiss.

"Do you want a glass of wine?" he asked. "Relax a little?"

She gazed at him steadily. "Maybe later. All I need now is you."

The air between them crackled with electricity, and Holden yanked her to him, his mouth crashing down on hers. She had always enjoyed kissing, but all the men she had previously dated only used it as a quick stepping stone to other things. Not Holden. He was a man who excelled at kissing. They had already spent hours doing so, and he wouldn't rush things now.

He scooped her into his arms, walking to a chair and sitting. Finley wound her arms around his neck, matching him kiss for kiss. She lost track of time as they took turn sharing control, dominating and then yielding, deepening each kiss until her body was afire, trembling with need.

Wordlessly, he came to his feet, carrying her into the

bedroom. Leaning over, he switched on a lamp sitting on the nightstand and then gently placed her on her feet.

"I hope you don't mind a little light," he said. "I don't want to miss a thing about you."

He anchored his hands on her waist and kissed her again. Desire poured through her. Desire for him and what they were about to do. She unbuttoned his shirt to his waist, slipping her hands inside it, flattening her palms and moving them over the hard plains of his chest. She heard a noise in the back of his throat, a low growl which sent shivers dancing along her spine.

His hands left her waist. He tugged the shirt from where it was tucked into his pants, unbuttoned the last few buttons himself and discarded it.

Her eyes roamed over his chest, watching the muscles bunch as her palms glided over the ridges of his abs.

Holden took the hem of her sweater and lifted it from her, tossing it to the ground. His fingers lightly stroked her neck and then her shoulders, moving to her back and unfastening the clasp of her bra. He pulled the straps from her shoulders, and the bra joined her sweater on the floor.

"You are incredibly beautiful," he said huskily, his hands cupping her breasts.

As he caressed her breasts, his lips found her throat, licking and nipping. She could feel the slight stubble as it grazed her neck, the touch stoking the fire within her. His lips traveled down the slope of her shoulder, nibbling as he went.

Suddenly, he twirled her in his arms, facing her away from him. One arm pinned her to him as his free hand kneaded her breast. Holden continued kissing her neck and shoulder as his fingers circled her nipple, teasing it until it pebbled in need. Slowly, he rubbed the pad of his thumb back and forth across it, causing a deep ache within her. One only this man could fill. Then he tweaked it playfully, making her gasp aloud.

His hand left her breast and traveled south, finding the button of her trousers. He slid the button through the buttonhole and slowly pulled down the zipper.

His teeth grazed her earlobe as he said, "I don't want to let you go, but I need to. Just for a moment."

Trembling, Finley leaned against him as his hands pushed the pants over her hips. They pooled at her feet, and he held her waist, allowing her to step from them. She kicked them aside. His arm went around her waist again, and her fingers gripped his muscled forearm. She gazed down at it, having never really thought how sexy a man's forearm could be. It made her think of the Regency romances she'd devoured in high school. How women's hearts had fluttered if a man rolled up his sleeves, exposing his forearm.

She got it now.

Holden held her firmly in place as his palm caressed her belly, moving lower, slipping into her panties. He began stroking her, causing desire to flare within her. She was already on fire from the heat of his own body pressed against hers. As he pushed a finger into her, Finley mewled like a kitten.

"You like that?" he asked, he voice low and dangerous, his mouth near her ear.

"Yes," she managed to get out, his movements causing all rational thought to flee.

He stroked her deeply, his fingers knowing exactly where to touch her. She began moving against him, writhing as he increased the pressure. His kisses blazed hot against her throat as the fingers sped up, and Finley became a bundle of quivering limbs. A feeling built steadily within her, and she knew where this journey would end.

Then the orgasm erupted with a ferocity she had never experienced. Her body quaked. She had no control over it as she moved against his hand, whimpering. Finally, the wave of pleasure subsided, and she went limp in his arms. Holden seemed to know she wasn't capable of standing on her own. He lifted her into his arms, placing her on the bed. Going to the other side of it, he pulled down the comforter and sheet before returning to her.

"I can stand," she said, not certain she actually could as she pushed off the bed.

Thankfully, his strong arm went about her waist, steadying her as his other hand pulled the bedding down. He eased her back to the mattress and quickly shed the rest of what he wore, his glasses the last thing he removed. As he set them on the nightstand, it made her realize she still had on her black stilettos.

Finley leaned down to unbuckle the strap, but his hand covered hers.

"No. Wait. Let me."

She lay back against the pillow, admiring his wonderful physique, eager to touch him.

Holden perched on the bed and undid the shoe's strap, easing it from her foot, doing the same with the other shoe, setting the pair on the floor. He looked up at her, his moss green eyes darker than usual. It was a bit different seeing him without his glasses, but he was handsome with or without them.

Finley touched his face with her fingers, again feeling the slight stubble. He took her fingers, kissing them gently, then slipped them into his mouth, sucking on them. A jolt of desire rippled through her.

"Love me," she said.

"I plan to," he told her, his gaze unwavering. "But I'm going to take my time."

Holden proceeded to do just that. Finley felt on fire as he touched every part of her. With fingers. Mouth. Tongue. She also enjoyed exploring his body, so hard and firm. His masculine scent was unlike any other man's, drawing her in, making her heart race.

He worshiped her. There was no other word for it. He made her feel like a goddess. No man had ever taken such time with her, seeing to her needs above his own.

For a moment, he pulled away. She reached out, wanting him back, then realized he'd opened the drawer to the nightstand. He removed a foil packet and ripped it open, placing the condom on his cock and rolling it down. Then his mouth returned to hers, demanding more of her as his hands stroked her to new heights.

When he hovered over her, pausing a minute, their eyes met. She saw his had gone dark with desire.

"I've never needed a woman like I do you, Finley."

Then he moved from her, lying beside her, confusing her. She'd thought he was about to enter her. Already, her core throbbed with need, wanting him inside her.

Before she could ask why he hadn't thrust into her, Holden turned on his side, his hands seizing her waist. He lifted her, rolling to his back. Now, she was hovering over him, his strong arms keeping her in the air.

"You're the one in control," he rasped. "I want you to be in charge of this first time we come together."

Shock filled her. No man had ever ceded control to her.

Confidence rushed through her. "Lower me onto you," she told him.

Slowly, he brought her down. She grasped the base of his erect penis, holding it in place as her body took him in. Finley was seated on him, filled with him. Her gaze met his. She smiled.

And began to move.

She rode him, taking them both on a wild, magical ride. Never had she felt so free. So fearless. So powerful. It was incredibly liberating, to feel such feminine power, to see how she moved him.

When her orgasm hit, it was the most powerful rush ever. He also climaxed, his fingers digging into her hips as she rode him, the wave of pleasure like a surfer dominating a hundred-foot wave. Finley collapsed on his chest, breathing heavily, totally spent.

His arm cradled her to him as his hand stroked her hair. No words were necessary and they wouldn't have been adequate. She rested her head against his shoulder, feeling the beating of his heart as it eventual slowed.

"Your knees must need a stretch," he finally said.

Reluctantly, Finley pushed her knuckles against the mattress, rising so she was in a sitting position again. She eased off him and out of the bed, feeling the blood race through her.

Holden took a tissue and removed his condom, wrapping it and setting it on the nightstand.

"Come back," he said, his voice low and rough, holding a hand out to her.

She eagerly returned to the bed, his body wrapping around hers, blanketing her in warmth. They kissed several minutes until she grew sleepy.

"I know. I'm exhausted, too," he said. "But in the best way possible."

He leaned down and brought the covers over them. Finley snuggled against him, her cheek resting on his bare chest, her arm around his waist.

As she drifted into sleep, she was aware of one thing.

She loved Holden Scott.

15

$\mathcal{W}$hen Finley awoke early the next morning, she could tell Holden was already awake. He kissed her deeply, morning breath and all.

That's when she was certain she was meant to be with this man.

They made love again in a rush of heat this time. Where last night had been slow and incredibly steamy, a dance of passion and exploration, this morning was all about the driving need to consume one another. A frenzy of limbs and tongues. While Holden still took an extraordinary amount of time on foreplay, each scorching touch built until they exploded in one another's arms.

In the aftermath, she lay sprawled half atop him, one leg thrown over him, her arm possessively around his waist, needing to touch him.

And they talked. For an hour. Finley had never been around a man who she enjoyed talking with more than

Holden. Her other sexual partners had either fallen asleep soon after they coupled or, in a morning situation, they were up and out of the bed, in the shower, then gone for the day. She liked that Holden didn't rush from the bed. That he held her tenderly, his hand absently stroking her back, talking about mundane things. Maybe it was the writer in him, that he was so comfortable conversing with someone because he wrote characters who conversed. Or possibly because he was so comfortable with who he was.

This was what she wanted.

She doubted they were on the same page, however. This was a man who had uprooted the life he'd lived for several years and left behind a woman. While Holden had assured Finley that she wasn't a rebound, she knew she couldn't begin creating a new narrative for them. Not until Holden had time to heal emotionally from his previous relationship. She didn't know if she should back away now and give him more space or continue to allow them to grow closer, both physically and emotionally.

Whatever she decided, she would not—under any circumstances— tell him that she loved him. That would be the kiss of death.

She did fear being hurt again, despite his reassurances, but she didn't believe Holden was leading her on. No man could fake what had occurred between them last night or this morning.

Deciding to test the waters a bit, she asked, "Would you consider coming to Sunday lunch at my parents tomorrow? We do it once a month."

Without hesitation, he said, "I would be honored to

meet them and tell them what an incredible daughter they've raised."

His words filled her with warmth. "It wouldn't just be Mom and Dad," she warned. "My brother and his family would be there, too."

He took her chin in hand, raising it until their gazes met. "You trusted me enough to introduce me to your friend family. It would mean a lot to me to meet your blood family. What time is lunch?"

"Twelve thirty," she told him.

"Do I bring anything?"

Finley smiled. "Flowers worked with Harper. I think Mom would appreciate them, as well."

Holden ran his fingers through her hair, the touch light and sensual, causing her to want him again. "Maybe I shouldn't learn how to cook after all. It's way easier picking up a bouquet of flowers than making a dish. Speaking of, I'm starved. Would you like to go into town and grab some pancakes at Lone Star Diner?"

She arched her eyebrows. "You want me to turn up, in public, wearing the same bright red sweater I wore to the game last night? Talk about a walk of shame."

He laughed. "I forgot Lost Creek is a small town. Growing up in Austin was a little different. Would you like to go home and change clothes and meet me there?"

She had something else in mind for this morning. "No, I've got some things to do. *You've* got writing that needs to get done, young man."

Finley untangled herself from him and started to rise from the bed. He caught her wrist.

"When can I see you again?" he asked, hunger in his eyes.

"I'm working a wedding later today. I'll take pre-wedding pictures between three and five thirty. The wedding is at six, with the reception afterward. I probably won't be free until ten or so tonight."

He grew thoughtful a moment and then asked, "Could I come with you? Watch you in action? I'd like to see what you actually do."

"That would be fine with me. Honestly, I think you'll be bored, but I know Harper wouldn't mind. I dress to blend in. Evening weddings I wear a black pantsuit or a black or dark dress."

"I've got a dark suit I can wear. Since I can't come sit in your class and watch you teach, I'm glad you'll let me tag along this evening and see what your photographer world is like."

She leaned down and kissed him. "Get a lot of work done today. Maybe even take a nap—because I plan to keep you up late tonight, Mr. Scott."

"You'll come home with me after the wedding. And stay?"

"It's all I want to do," she admitted.

Finley quickly dressed and drove home. She wanted to talk to her mom about lunch tomorrow, but she didn't want to call her from the car. Even though Mom was always up early, she would wonder why Finley was calling before seven from her car. Once she pulled up in front of the house, she cut the engine and dialed her mom's cell number.

Dianne Farrow answered on the second ring. "Good morning, Honey. I see you're up early as always."

"I could say the same thing, Mom. I get my early bird-ness from you. Are you going to be around this morning? I thought I might stop by for a cup of coffee."

"I have the house to myself. Your dad has gone golfing with the mayor. In fact, he just left. Do you want to come for breakfast? If you leave now, I'll at least have the coffee made when you get here."

Knowing there was no way she could show up smelling like sex, Finley said, "Actually, I just out of bed. I'll need to hop in the shower. Could I come in an hour?"

"I'll have French toast and coffee ready."

"Sounds good, Mom. See you soon."

Finley unlocked the door and entered the house, hearing Emerson bustling about in the kitchen. She went to greet her roommate and before she could say a word, Emerson threw herself into Finley's arms, hugging her tightly.

"What is this about?" she asked.

Emerson released her and grinned. "I don't have to ask how last night went. You are glowing. I've known you ten years now, and I want it on the record— Holden Scott is the perfect guy for you."

She felt her cheeks heat. "So, you really like him?"

"We're all wild about Holden," Emerson assured her. "Yes, we've been texting furiously behind your back. Harper, Ivy, and me. We've never seen you look happier."

Sighing, she confessed, "I've never been this happy in my life, Emerson. I think I've kissed a lot of frogs in my time, but Holden is a prince of a guy." She hesitated and then revealed, "He's coming off a long-term relationship, though. That's the only thing that worries me."

"I'm not worried at all. You know I'm a terrific judge of people. If he were meant to be with this other girl, she would've have come to Texas with him."

"He did tell me he would be staying in Texas. Not going back to New York."

Emerson hooted in triumph. "See? I'm right. Holden is staying for *you*, Finley. And you two are such a great fit. He stepped into our friend group at dinner so easily. Sometimes, that can be *so* awkward, but Holden fit right in. I'm telling you now, the two of you can't break up. It would mess with the dynamics of our friend family."

She laughed. "I need to shower. I'm going over to see Mom and tell her about him. He agreed to come to Sunday lunch with me tomorrow."

Her friend nodded approvingly. "Big step. But a necessary one. He needs to pass the Farrow test."

Finley showered, putting on her makeup and blow-drying her hair. She dressed casually now in jeans and a Dallas Cowboys sweatshirt before driving the short distance to her parents' house. She had always been extremely close with her mom, thinking of Dianne Farrow as one of her best friends. She thought herself lucky to live and work in the town she'd grown up in and able to see her family as frequently as she did.

Using her key, she let herself in, calling out, "I'm here!"

"In the kitchen," her mom replied.

When Finley entered, she saw her mom pouring tall

glasses of milk to go with the French toast on the table. The only time she ever drank milk was when she ate pancakes or French toast and loved that her mom always remembered that. She sat at the breakfast table.

Her mom held up a coffee pod. "French vanilla okay?"

"Sounds good."

Mom replaced the used pod with the new one, removing her own cup of coffee and bringing it to the table as Finley's brewed. She went to the fridge and retrieved a carton of creamer, doctoring her own coffee with it. By the time she did so, Finley's coffee was ready, and her mom brought it to her.

Finley put a splash of creamer in it, along with a packet of stevia, stirring and inhaling deeply before she took a sip.

"Perfect," she declared before taking her first bite of French toast. "Yum. Thank you for teaching me to cook," she told her mother.

"I was glad you were interested in it. Ches never was. Of course, I made him learn how to cook a few of the basics. Still, I know Sally does all the cooking now. At least your brother splits household duties with her."

"And he's a great dad," she said. "He was never one to shy away from changing diapers, and he's always read to and played with the kids."

They talked a little about what was going on at the Montessori school, and Finley shared the units her fifth graders currently worked on. Being teachers, they both loved talking shop. She wondered how her parents were going to feel about her leaving her career in education for photography. She would address that later, once she had both of them together.

Finally, school talk wound down. She picked up her coffee, finishing it before setting down the mug.

"I'm glad you had some time this morning to talk because I want to tell you about someone I've been seeing."

Dianne Farrow chuckled. "I don't know how much you have to tell me that I don't already know, Sweetheart. His name is Holden Scott. He's written two novels, both of which I've read, by the way. And your dad loved the movie of the first one. He's handsome as sin, and you went to the basketball game together last night, where he put Randy Foster in his place."

"You're on the mark about everything. The only thing I'm going to add is how much I like him, Mom. I really, really like him."

Her mother studied her a long moment. "You walked in today, looking like the Finley of old. The confident woman who knows her place in the world. You have a glow about you, Honey. One that's been missing for a long time now."

"I can be myself with him, Mom. I know relationships take work. I don't shy away from that, but right now? Things are so easy between us. We can talk for hours and never run out of things to say." She paused. "We can also kiss for hours and never get tired of doing so."

Mom's smile widened. "You found a man who likes to kiss for that long?"

"I absolutely have," she said, not hiding her own smile.

"I've never met a man who wanted to kiss that long. Hey, *I've* never wanted to kiss anyone that long before, but it's different with Holden." She sighed. "Everything is different with Holden."

Mom squeezed her hand. "You're in love with him."

She nodded. "I am. I'm usually so cautious, but he's so open. Such a wonderful man. It's been easy to give him my heart."

"And your love," her mom added.

Tears stung her eyes. "Yes. I do love him. I haven't said that to him, though. He hasn't said it either." She swallowed. "I want to bring him to Sunday lunch tomorrow if that's okay with you."

"Of course, we want to meet him," Mom encouraged. "Tell me a little about him. Other than how hot he is."

"Mom!"

"Sweetie, I Googled him the minute I got the first call, so I know exactly what he looks like. And he *is* hot."

Finley couldn't help but laugh. "He is."

"And he must be a great kisser if you can do that with him for hours," Mom said, mischief twinkling in her eyes.

"That, too," she agreed. "He grew up in Austin. His family life was non-existent. Alcoholic father. Mother who worked all the time and was never around. Holden pretty much raised himself."

She told her mom about Mr. Hamilton, the janitor, and his influence on Holden.

"I'm glad he had such a fine man come into his life," Mom said. "Holden is fortunate he had an adult looking out for him."

"He taught a couple of years before he entered that famous Iowa writing workshop. Sold the book he wrote while earning his master's degree there. He's been writing ever since."

"If he's been living in New York all this time, why is he in Texas now? Better question, will he be returning to New York anytime soon and taking my daughter with him?"

"He's writing a screenplay based upon his second novel. I don't want to tell you everything. You can ask him about it tomorrow. As for New York, he's left it behind. He's from Texas and says he's back to stay."

They talked about what her mother would serve at lunch tomorrow, and Finley assured her that Holden would eat everything on the table.

"I've got to go," she said. "I've got a thousand things to do and a wedding to shoot later today."

Her mom walked her to the door, embracing her. "I'm so glad you came over and we talked. I'm looking forward to meeting Holden. Can I tell your dad about this?"

"Yes, tell Dad. I'll see you tomorrow."

As she drove home, a text popped up from her brother.

> I have to hear you are dating a new guy from Sally, who heard it from someone in her book club?

She called Ches "Hey. New guy and I will be at Sunday lunch tomorrow."

"I hear he's famous."

"A little bit. He's written a couple of books."

Ches laughed. "You know I don't read. Unless it's something about football."

"His first book was turned into a movie. *Capitol Crimes*."

"We saw that! It was great," her brother said. "Okay, just wanted to touch base with you. Since I'm meeting new guy tomorrow, I won't pump you about him now. Sally's better at that anyway. She can get anyone to tell her anything. See you tomorrow, Fin."

As she hung up, Finley had high hopes that lunch with her family would help add another stamp of approval to Holden. He already had stamps for being hot, smart, friendly, and fun to be with, not to mention her friends' ringing endorsement. Last night had let her know their chemistry wouldn't fizzle. If anything, that would only grow in her estimation.

All she needed was to know if he loved her— and that wouldn't be coming anytime soon.

as it too soon to tell Finley he loved her?
Yes. Definitely yes.

Or maybe not.

He went back to his laptop, trying to delve into the scene he was currently writing. He couldn't. Every time he attempted to get his characters to talk to one another, all he could think about was Finley.

He loved her. Without a doubt, he loved her. But he couldn't tell her. No way. It was too soon to let his head go there. Finley was bright. Sweet. Talented. And cautious. She'd been burned badly before. If he declared his feelings now, she would think he was insincere.

No, he would keep his mouth closed and do what he had been doing. Let her be in control.

Restless, he thought about going for a walk, but even that didn't appeal to him. He decided to go into town.

Stop at Java Junction for coffee and a Danish. Walk around the square. Turn up Main Street. See if that could get him back on track.

Holden drove into town, thinking again that he needed to return Wolf's truck soon. Maybe after coffee, he could drive into San Antonio and stop at a couple of dealerships.

He parked on the square, seeing it had a nice-sized crowd for ten o'clock on a Saturday morning. Once inside the coffeehouse, he ordered a drink. As he waited for it, he glanced around, seeing the place was mostly full.

Then Dax stood, waving him over. Holden saw he sat with Braden. He liked both men. Hoped they would both become friends. He already felt a friendship forming with Dax.

Holding up a finger in acknowledgement, he saw Dax take a seat again. The teenaged barista called Holden's name, and he claimed his coffee, taking it across the room and joining the two men.

"Good to see you," Braden said, offering Holden his hand.

Dax did the same, and Holden sat, placing his coffee on the table in front of him.

"How is the writing going?" Dax asked cheerfully.

"It's not," he said flatly.

"Why?" Braden asked. "It's your source material. I'd think you would know these people and the plot inside and out. I understand it's the first time you're trying to write something in a different format, but doesn't every writer get stuck at some point anyway?"

"It's more than being blocked. It's not as if I'm stymied. I simply can't concentrate."

"Because of Finley," Dax said, a knowing look in his eyes. He looked to Braden. "We've been there. We get it."

"I've always been able to block out everything when I'm writing. Escape into the world I've created. But every time I've tried to do that this morning, all I can think about is Finley."

"You're in love with her," Braden stated.

Holden nodded. "I am. How can I be so miserable and elated at the same time?"

"You've never been in love before, have you?" Braden asked.

"No." He was silent a moment. "I lived with someone a long time. I thought I was in love with her. Now that I'm with Finley, though, I realize just how wrong that relationship was. It had nothing to do with love and everything to do with convenience."

"So, you're not still hung up on this woman?" Dax asked.

He shook his head firmly. "No. Not only were the feelings not there, we parted on a pretty bad note. In fact, I didn't think I would be giving any woman the time of day — much less falling in love with one." He smiled wryly. "What do I do now?"

"You tell Finley that you love her," Braden said simply. "I know that sounds easy. It won't solve every problem. Being in love with a woman means working on your relationship. I do know from experience, though, that once you do tell her? Not only will you be on top of the world, but you'll be better for it. Sharper. More focused. About your work and life, in general."

"You sound as if you know what you're talking about."

"I was engaged. Before meeting Harper," Braden told him. "I thought we had a lot in common. I thought we loved one another and would be able to weather any storm. The scandal which slammed my family, though, hit us like a ton of bricks. She couldn't take it. She left. And I was alone. I blinked and had no job. No family. No friends or fiancée. Looking back, I'm surprised I wasn't suicidal. My brother was."

Holden couldn't imagine things becoming so terrible that he'd want to check out on life.

Braden took a deep breath and blew it out slowly. "Bill Hart gave me a chance when no one else in the wine industry would. I packed up and came to Texas, ready to do my job and never look at another woman again. Yet meeting Harper was the best thing that ever happened to me. She changed my life. I can't imagine *not* having her in my life."

"I was married before I moved to Lost Creek," Dax revealed, shocking Holden since he couldn't see Dax with anyone but Ivy. "The marriage had lost its luster a long time before we split. I wanted to fix something that was so irretrievably broken, it was impossible. I found out my wife was cheating on me with my best friend. Talk about a double blow."

He let out a low whistle, sympathy filling him.

"It shook my world to the core," Dax said. "I knew I had to get as far away as possible and start a new life. I went from being an accountant with a rigid schedule and reinvented myself as a coffeehouse owner and singer-songwriter. Along the way, I meet Ivy— and that changed everything for me."

Dax paused, taking a swig from his mug and continued. "Like Braden, I'd pretty much sworn off women. Ivy, though, is the sweetest soul on the planet. She's so loving and giving. I found myself being drawn to her, swept away by feelings I'd never experienced." He shrugged. "I was smart enough to simply surrender to them. It was a battle I didn't care to fight, trying to keep her out of my life."

His gaze met Holden's. "You need to do the same. It's obvious to all of us that you're meant to be with Finley. When it's right, it's right. Give over to it, and I promise you that you'll never regret it."

Their words bolstered him, and Holden knew it was the right thing to do. To tell Finley that he loved her. The only decision that made sense.

"I'll tell her tonight. She's working a wedding and coming home with me after it."

Having made the decision, a peace descending over him. Holden spent the next half-hour relaxed and engaged with Dax and Braden. By the time he got back to the cottage, he was on fire to write.

Two hours later, he'd finished a scene, his gut telling him it was one of the best he had ever written. He went back and red through today's pages, changing very little. He felt so confident that he immediately emailed them to Wolf, eager for the director's input.

He closed his laptop and set it on the coffee table in

front of him, leaning back, pillowing his head in his hands. He didn't think he would scare Finley off by his declaration of love. If she were feeling the same as he did, she would tell him. If she didn't seem as far along as he was, she would let him know that, too. One thing they did do well was communicate. He felt like there wasn't a topic under the sun they couldn't tackle and looked forward to having her in his bed again tonight. He believed making love to her would be even more special once he'd told her how much he loved her.

Glancing at his watch, he saw he had an hour before he needed to meet her at the winery. He went to the bedroom and dressed in a suit and tie, thinking he would spend the time before he left scrolling through some of his favorite sites. Instead, his cell rang, and he saw it was Evan McGill wanting to FaceTime with him. He had traded a few emails with the agent, but it would be good to talk with Evan now.

Holden answered and said, "How have you been, Evan?"

"Nothing ever changes with me," his agent said happily. "And that's a good thing because I like to make money. Just thought I'd check in with you, Holden. How is the writing going for you? How far along are you on the script?"

"As I told you, it was slow going when I first started. I'm really getting a feel for it now, though. It's an entirely new way of writing, but I'm really enjoying the challenge."

Evan scratched his chin. "Hmm. If you really do have a talent for it, it could open up a new world of opportunities for you. Maybe you could alternate, writing a novel and then a screenplay."

"Wolf has been complimentary of the pages I've sent to him so far. We had thought I would have a first draft by the end of February. That's still my goal, but it might happen a bit sooner."

"Why don't you send me the draft of the novel you finished before heading down to Texas?" Evan suggested.

"No," Holden protested. "It's not ready for you to see yet. I've got to polish it. You know how I am about that. I like to let it lie a while before going back and cleaning it up."

"I know it's not set in stone," his agent assured him. "If I read it now, though, it'll give me an idea what I'll be pitching. I can form a plan of attack."

He laughed. "I know you too well, Evan. Even though I know it still needs work, you'd start putting out feelers to my publishing house and other ones. You're simply going to have to be patient. Let me finish this first draft of the screenplay. Then I promise I'll turn my eyes back to the novel. Actually, I don't believe it's going to need a lot done to it. I felt really good when I finished it." He grinned. "I think I'm getting the hang of this writing thing."

Evan laughed heartily. "Okay. Keep me posted about when you finish the screenplay. I know you'll do some back and forth on it with Wolf, but do you think you'll stick around for the filming?"

"I'm staying in Texas permanently, Evan. It's home. I didn't realize how much I'd missed it until I was back."

"Will you get a place in Austin since you're from there?"

He shook his head. "I'm going to stay right where I'm living now. It's a small town in the Hill Country called Lost Creek. I'm making friends. Learning how to cook. I've even fallen in love."

Evan's eyes widened in surprise. "What? You haven't been there that long, Holden. I don't care how beautiful she is, she's sidled up to you because you've got fame and money. Don't let some stranger jump on your gravy train."

Holden burst out laughing. "You've got it all wrong, my friend," he told the agent. "Finley is amazing in her own right. She's a talented photographer. She doesn't need to sponge off me."

Evan still looked dubious. "Nose to the grindstone. Get the script finished for Wolf, and don't let this woman keep you so off-balance that you can't work."

With a sudden clarity, Holden said, "That woman is going to be my wife."

He ended the call with Evan, owning what he had just told his agent.

He wanted a life with Finley. Forever.

Holden had never thought in those terms in his entire life. Everything had always been in chunks. He always wanted to move to the next goal. First, it had been to get out of middle school. Then graduate from high school and escape his house. Earn a scholarship to college so new opportunities would open up. Graduate. The loftiest goal had been to be admitted to the Iowa workshop, and he had bided his time teaching until he gained admission to the program. Then it had been to sell a book. Write another and sell it. Rinse and repeat.

Things changed when Wolf threw a new goal into the mix, a challenge that came at the perfect time for Holden to accept. It was funny how he now realized Madison had never been a goal, much less a part of any of the goals he set for himself. He'd done a disservice to both of them, taking her for granted and not working on their relationship more. If he had, he would have quickly become aware of the fact they weren't a true fit and ended things long before he had.

Then again, relationships were a two-way street. Madison could also have tried harder from her end, as well. She hadn't. Instead of sharing things with him, Madison had vanished for hours at a time each day. He wondered now if she had actually been writing— or if she had been seeing someone else. Maybe her indignant anger directed at him when he wanted to end their relationship might have been a reaction to the guilt she felt.

He would never know. He never planned to speak to Madison again.

His new goal was a life goal, one to work on over years. Nothing related to his career. He wanted to love Finley. Marry her. Build a life with her. He'd never pictured himself as husband material, much less being a father. Not after the father he'd had and the childhood he'd escaped. Still, he wanted a chance at being a dad. He could think of no better partner to parent with than Finley. She would have to teach him what true family life was like. Once he met her family, he would understand more how to do so.

Holden pictured a life for them in Lost Creek. Buying a house. Getting a dog. Raising kids. Pursuing their art. It brought a deep satisfaction to him. Yes, he was meant to spend the rest of his life with Finley Farrow.

And he would let her know that tonight.

17

*I*f Finley didn't get her act together, she was going to ruin the Anderson/Peters wedding.

She had actually left the house without her two cameras. One, her go-to, was a top-of-the-line Canon which provided pristine images and was ridiculously easy to use. It had cost her almost four thousand dollars — and had been worth every penny. Thank goodness, it had been a tax write-off. The other, a Nikon, which had great resolution and a rapid shooting speed, was her back-up.

What photographer would head to a wedding without their cameras?

Her head was in the clouds today. Because of Holden. It made her angry when she should be celebrating her feelings for him. Sex with Holden had been off the charts. She'd found a man who could be tender and yet full of passion and wild abandon. One who was definitely the most thoughtful lover she'd ever had. He was the dream package.

She wondered if she should have admitted to her mother that she was in love. Mom would definitely tell Dad. Finley had even said it was okay to do so. She only hoped the two of them would keep things to themselves. She didn't want that particular cat released from the bag until she had told Holden of her feelings toward him. Finley could only imagine her brother's teasing if he found out.

Back in the car, cameras in tow, she called her Mom and got voicemail. She waited for the beep and said, "If you only told Dad I'm dating Holden, that's great. If you told him I'm in love, *please* promise me you'll keep this between the two of you. Don't tell Ches and Sally. Don't tell anyone else. Please. Holden needs to hear it first from me. When I'm ready to tell him. Thanks. And delete this message!"

She reached the winery and turned down the road, passing the tasting room, which had a nice little crowd, based upon the cars in front of it. Looking ahead, she saw Holden's truck and pulled in beside it. He climbed out and literally took her breath away. While she all about the casual look, there was absolutely nothing as fine as a hot guy in a white dress shirt and dark suit.

He opened her door and held out his hand, helping her from the vehicle before he brushed his lips against her cheek.

"You look amazing," he told her.

"I was thinking the same about you."

"I was surprised no cars are here yet."

"They will be. I like to get to the venue before everyone arrives. I've got a shot list in my head, and some of those need to be snapped when no one else is around."

Finley claimed her two cameras, handing him the Nikon. "If you'll keep up with this one for me, I'd appreciate it. I only use it occasionally. I'm wedded to this baby," she said, holding up the Canon.

"What's so special about it?" he asked.

"Crystal-clear images. The best AF around."

"AF?"

"Auto focus. And not only is it incredibly easy to move between photography and videography, the video is just as flawless as the photos themselves. Even better, I can pull stills from the videos I shoot."

Holden accompanied her to the event center.

"I already have stills of the outside that I use for every bride. I shoot a few each season in order to get the landscaping at different times of the year. Inside, though, is always different. Harper is a genius in helping brides select the layout they want and how to maximize their dollars when it comes to the flowers and candles used to decorate the venue."

They entered the building, and Finley took several shots of the area where the wedding would occur. The florist Harper used usually delivered the flowers and finished decorating just before Finley arrived. She also left the various bouquets and boutonnieres in the dressing rooms for the bridal party.

"You mentioned a shot list. Is that the photos you want to take each time?" Holden asked.

"Yes," she said, snapping pictures of the decorated tables. "I break it down into different parts of the day. Getting ready photos for both bride and groom and their attendants. First look photos, which are all about capturing the emotion of various firsts. The groom waiting for his bride. The first married kiss. Then there are ceremony shots. Group pictures after the ceremony when the guests are consuming appetizers and drinks. The hardest to capture are reception photos. I do the traditional ones. Speeches. Cake cutting. Father-daughter dance. But I circulate constantly during the reception, looking for those little gems."

"This is fascinating. Maybe I need to write a wedding photographer."

She laughed. "Knowing you, he or she would be murdered during the reception. Or *be* a murderer and kill someone at the wedding. Or be a CIA agent pretending to be a wedding photographer and causing all kind of havoc."

"Hey, you're giving me all kinds of plot ideas," he teased. "Okay. I'll be quiet. Stay out of your way but stay close in case you need this camera." He indicated the Nikon he held. "Is there a videographer?"

"Not a professional one. Harper hired a teacher at the high school who teaches photography to be the center's videographer. Obviously, I can't do both. I do shoot some videos as I go along, but this guy simply films the ceremony in its entirety, from the groom waiting for his bride until they come down the aisle together as Mr. and Mrs."

The bride arrived, giggling and teary-eyed at the same time. Magically, Harper appeared, along with her assistants who had already set up the center for the wedding. Her friend had weddings down to a science, being able to comfort the weeping, laugh with the jolly, and make certain everything ran like clockwork. Harper's efficiency made Finley's job a smooth one.

She moved about surreptitiously, snapping shots of the invitation, program, and welcome bags. Moving about, she caught small moments between the bride and her mother and grandmother, as well as the bridesmaids. She took a photo of the wedding dress suspended from a hangar. A close-up of the bride's shoes and the bottle of perfume she used. She would the same with the groom's cufflinks and his pocket square, as well as the bouquets and boutonnieres.

Finley got the bride in a chair, having her hair and makeup done, along with her attendants. They were drinking champagne as they did so, everyone having a wonderful time. She smiled as she took a sweet snap of the flower girls and their baskets as they sat on each side of their grandmother, holding her hands and talking animatedly.

When she had all she needed, she slipped from the room. Holden waited outside.

"You can come in and watch as I photograph the guys," she told him.

Repeating some of the photos from before, she got the groom's tuxedo hanging and his shoes. Took shots of the groom and best man, who held the box with the wedding ring in it. She would also make certain to get close-ups of the bride and groom's hands with their new rings displayed.

The guys were drinking beers and watching a basketball game as Finley moved about them, taking candids, other times asking them to group together for a more formal, posed picture.

She signaled Holden, and they left the dressing room.

"That was a terrific one of the mom pinning her son's boutonniere on," he remarked.

"Those are the money shots for parents. Those small, hidden moments. I like to capture them so they can pull out the photos and relive them for years to come. Okay. Off to the ceremony. This is really where the magic begins. It's the culmination of the couple's love story, so I try to take a ton of pictures during it."

She caught different guests arriving and being seated before the ceremony began and then followed up with photos of the couple's parents being seated. The rest went like clockwork. Flower girls and wedding attendants moving down the aisle. The groom's reaction to seeing his bride. Her being handed over to him by her father.

The ceremony itself was a short one. The exchanging of vows and rings passed quickly. Finley was poised for the kiss and recessional and even snapped a few shots of audience member's reactions to various moments.

Once the cocktail hour started, she was all business, knowing guests didn't like to be kept waiting long. The teacher in her really came out at these times, and she found she was good at managing the group shots, from bride with her parents and the groom with his to adding in both sets of parents with the couple and then immediate family. In-between she took candids of the couple as they held hands, gazing at each in wonder. She made certain she got some great photos of the couple with their children from previous marriages. She wanted them to have some great portraits to display, showing the night they had all come together for a first time as a family.

After the obligatory wedding party photos were finished, she had the couple stand alone at the glass, looking out over the grapevines before she took the pair outside for some wonderful shots.

All the while, she was aware of Holden watching. Assessing. Admiring.

Dismissing the couple, she then asked everyone to wait two minutes before they entered the reception. Harper organized everyone so parents would come in first, followed by attendants, and then finally the couple themselves. In that brief time, Finley raced to set up at the reception so she wouldn't miss a single thing.

She took candids of all the tables and their guests, as well as close-ups of the food during dinner. Harper always left Finley a small plate of appetizers with the DJ or near the band, easy things she could pop in her mouth. She did so now, fueling herself the rest of the night, giving Dax a wave. His band, the Lone Star Rebels, often played receptions at the winery. When they didn't, Dax frequently served as the night's DJ.

The rest went in a blur. Toasts. Cutting the cakes. Various dances. She got shots of the couple dancing on the floor, alone and with others, even dancing in a large group, their faces flushed with excitement.

Finally, it was time to bid the newlyweds goodbye, and these would be some of her best photos. It was a blessing to capture the joy of the happy couple and everyone who attended their wedding.

Once the newlyweds had driven off in their limousine, other guests began departing. As usual, she felt exhausted, going inside and collapsing in a nearby chair. The cleanup crew was already in motion. Emerson was boxing up what was left of each cake, giving them to the bride's parents and her maid of honor, who was her sister.

Holden came and sat beside her. "I'm tired— and all I did was watch you work. You must be ready to drop. You were in motion all night long."

Harper came and took a seat. "How do you think it went from your end?"

"Terrific," she said honestly. "They'll be pleased at what I got."

"The bride was already raving about everything. The food. The wines. The music." Harper sighed. "Another one in the books."

"You love it," Finley said. "You're so good at this."

Holden spoke up. "I was really impressed, Harper. Everything ran flawlessly. If anything went wrong, no one would have guessed."

"Tonight was on point," Harper said. "I need to check on a few things. You two go enjoy what's left of the night."

After Harper retreated, Holden asked, "Do you even have the energy to come home with me? I mean, if you want to go home and fall into bed, I'd definitely understand."

"No," she told him. "I'm looking forward to going home with you." She gave him a sexy smile. "Sleep is the last thing on my mind."

He leaped to his feet. "Energy levels amazingly restored, Miss Farrow. May I walk you to your car?"

Laughing, she took the hand he offered and went to the parking lot with him. He opened her car door, and she slid behind the wheel, placing her camera on the passenger seat and then accepting the second camera from him.

"I'll see you at home," he said, leaning down for a kiss.

He started to pull away, and Finley stopped him, pulling him back and extending the kiss. Finally she released him.

"I think we've got a long night ahead of us," he told her. "And I'm saying that in a good way." Holden smiled. "A very good way."

She watched him start up his truck and followed him from the winery back through town, her heart racing out of control by the time they pulled into The Inn on Lost Creek.

"Breathe, Finley," she told herself, parking beside Holden.

As she got out of the car, he met her, his arms going around her, their mouths fusing together in heat and desire. She wrapped hers around him, holding tight, wanting moments like this now and in the future.

Holden broke the kiss. "I love you," he blurted out.

FInley blinked. "What?"

"I love you," he repeated, his eyes searching her face. "I know it's way too soon and I'm an ass for even saying it because you might—"

She cut him off, yanking him back to her, pouring heart and soul into the kiss.

Holden loved her...

Joy filled her. Pure, utter joy. She broke the kiss, beaming up at him.

"I love you. I was so afraid to tell you. I—"

This time, his mouth came crashing down on hers. Every nerve in her body was now firing, her breasts tingling, her core tightening. She clung to him, drinking him in.

Finally, he pulled away. Just barely.

"You love me," he said softly. "I love you."

"Yes," she agreed, her breathing shallow, her head spinning.

His green eyes twinkled at her. "Then I say we go in and celebrate our love."

Sweeping her into his arms, he headed toward the door. Finley was laughing while crying at the same time, tears of joy streaming down her cheeks. She loved Holden Scott—and he loved her back.

Nothing would ever be the same again.

18

Holden unlocked the door and rushed inside the cottage before Finley could even mention the weekender she had brought along for tonight. Immediately, he backed her against the door, his strong body pinning hers to it as he ravished her mouth. It was hot. It was wild.

It was love.

He threw off his suit jacket and tossed his glasses aside, as well, his mouth finding hers like a heat-seeking missile reaching its target. As they kissed, she unknotted his tie and manage to unbutton a few buttons of his white dress shirt, her hands slipping inside to glide along the sleek muscles of his chest.

Breaking the kiss, he buried his lips against her throat, his hands moving under her black cocktail dress, the heat in his fingers singeing her thighs. He pushed the dress up to her waist, his fingers going to the thin scrap of black lace, tearing it away. He began stroking her, stoking the inferno raging within her. His fingers pushed inside her, caressing her deeply, and she felt the orgasm erupt. It didn't even have time to build.

Finley clung to him, her body shuddering, wave after wave of pleasure dancing through her.

Dazed, she heard him murmur, "I can't wait. Need you. Now."

She heard his zipper and reached down, clasping the velvet rod. It throbbed in her hand.

"Condom," he got out, his mouth devouring hers again as she squeezed him.

Holden picked her up. Instinctively, she wrapped her legs around his waist as he carried her the few steps to the bedroom, tossing her onto the bed. Opening the night-stand's drawer, he found a foil packet and tore it open, sheathing himself before coming down atop her, thrusting into her hard.

It felt so good. *He* felt so good.

"More," she demanded greedily.

He thrust again.

"Harder," Finley commanded.

He pumped into her, his breath coming in spurts, hers doing the same. They climaxed together, and she shattered in his arms.

He collapsed atop her, breathing harshly, lying there a moment. The he raised himself slightly on his elbows, giving her a lopsided grin.

"So, this is love," he teased.

Finley died laughing. "This *is* love," she declared.

He continued to kiss her for some minutes, still inside her. All she could think of was how they could always have this.

Forever…

Holden eased off her and sat on the bed, saying, "I should apologize for being such an animal, but you drive me wild, Finley Farrow."

She pushed up, enveloping him, draping herself over his back and slipping her arms around him. "You can be an animal with me any day, Holden Scott."

As he looked over his shoulder, she kissed him, long and deep.

"I hope I didn't ruin your dress," he said apologetically.

"You didn't. I do need to go get my bag from the car, though."

His fingers brushed against her cheek. "I'll do that. Why don't you meet me in the shower?"

His words sent a thrill up her spine. She dropped a kiss upon his nape. "Will do."

Finley slipped off her dress and bra and went to the small bathroom, lamenting the size of the cottage's tiny shower, wondering how this was going to work. Her fears were pushed aside because her very clever writer made it work. She had never made love in a shower, and it was an exciting experience.

He toweled himself off and then did the same for her. He wound a second one around her damp hair, chuckling. "Miss Jean is going to wonder why I'm using so many towels."

"Let her talk," she said flippantly, as if she were Marie Antoinette telling others to eat cake.

They climbed into bed together, Holden wrapping his arms around her as they spooned. A deep contentment filled her, unlike anything she had ever known.

"I hope you know I want this to be forever, Finley," he told her. "If you need a long engagement, I'm fine with that. Just know I plan to be in your bed the next sixty or seventy years."

"Maybe we'll set a Guinness World Record for the number of times octogenarians have sex in a day," she teased sleepily.

His lips brushed against her hair. "I love you, Finley. I'll marry you wherever and whenever you say."

"Good. Let's talk about it… tomorrow."

Her last conscious thought was how much she loved this man.

HOLDEN AWOKE TO WARM LIPS GLIDING ALONG HIS CHEST.

"You are insatiable," he said, pulling Finley to him and kissing her mouth.

They made slow, leisurely love. He would categorize it as weekend love, when a couple had time to thoroughly enjoy one another.

"Can I get you some breakfast? I could cook you an omelet. I think I'm confident enough to have a go at it."

She took his knuckles, rubbing them against her cheek. "That's okay, Chef Scott. Mom will have a feast prepared. I just need a little something to tide me over until lunch."

"Stay here. Toast and coffee coming up."

He left Finley in his bed, looking rumpled and sexy. It took all his willpower to walk out of the bedroom and go to the small kitchenette to turn on the coffeemaker. He couldn't believe his good fortune. Doing something he loved for a living— and now he had someone by his side. Someone he loved and could share each day with. Coming back to Texas had been the best decision he had ever made.

He returned with a cup of coffee and toast on a small plate. She pushed up, placing a pillow behind her back as she sat up. The covers were draped to her waist. Thankfully, those beautiful breasts were still on display.

"Sorry I don't have a tray," he said, handing both over. "I don't think Miss Jean thought about me serving a guest breakfast in bed. Be right back."

He went and claimed his own breakfast, placing it on the nightstand before climbing back into bed with her. As they ate, she told him a little about her family which he would meet in a few hours.

"Be prepared," she warned. "They're going to grill you unmercifully. I don't bring around dates often, so they will know you're special to me."

Her cheeks pinkened slightly, and he asked, "What's going on?"

"I had breakfast with Mom yesterday. I told her about you." She swallowed. "I told her that I loved you." She winced. "I know. I shouldn't have done that. You should've been the first one to hear it from me."

He dropped a sweet kiss on her brow. "I think it's great that you have such a terrific relationship with your mom. That you could share that with her. I guess I should be glad I didn't hear it through the Lost Creek grapevine."

"Oh, I told Mom not to tell anyone. Except Dad. They could never keep a secret from one another, especially one so happy. But she knows not to say another word, not even to Ches and Sally."

"Are you comfortable with us telling them today that we're going to get married?"

Finley gave him a wicked smile. "I'm ready to put it on the City of Lost Creek's website."

He laughed, kissing her again, knowing married life was going to be rich and full with this woman.

"Lunch is at twelve thirty. I always try to get there about noon to visit a bit and help Mom in the kitchen. I need to go home and get ready there. Do you want to pick me up about ten till noon?"

He kissed her soundly. "It's a date. What do I wear to Sunday lunch?"

"Not a suit a tie," she said, laughing. "Jeans are fine. Ches seems to live in shorts year-round. It's always casual."

She dressed in a shirt and leggings she had brought, and Holden threw on his robe, walking her to her car. It was hard to let Finley go, even if he knew he would see her soon.

Going back into the cottage, he showered and shaved,

pulling out his notes for the next scene and then tucking them away again. He didn't want to get lost in another world as he wrote and lose track of time. Instead, he read the Sunday *New York Times* and browsed a few other sites on his laptop before leaving to pick up Finley.

They arrived at her parents' house, a one-story, brick ranch with a beautiful yard. Sam and Dianne Farrow couldn't have been more wonderful, welcoming him as if he were a Lost Creek native they'd known their entire lives. Ches Farrow was quite a bit older than his sister, probably ten- or twelve-years Finley's senior. He was the teasing, older brother, while Sally Farrow was warm and friendly. Ricky, their eight-year-old, and Tiffany, who was ten, were both adorable, Ricky favoring his father and Tiffany looking like Sally 2.0.

They asked him the typical questions about his writing, and Holden talked a little about his relationship with Wolf Ramirez and the new production company Wolf had started.

"Writing a screenplay must be difficult," Dianne Farrow said.

"It has been. At least at first. I'm not trained in screenwriting. It's been a little trial and error for me, but I'm getting the hang of it. So far, Wolf has been pleased with the pages I've turned in to him."

"You said you'd been living in New York for several years," Sam said. "Do you plan to return there once you finish the screenplay?"

"No. The beauty of being a writer is that I have a job that I can do anywhere. As long as I have my laptop and a good Internet connection for research and emailing, I'm golden."

Holden reached for Finley's hand. "I've decided to stay in Lost Creek permanently. Because I want to spend my life with your daughter."

Finley's mom and sister-in-law gasped in surprise. Ches gave his sister a knowing smile. Sam Farrow nodded approvingly.

"You're getting married," Dianne managed to say. She leaned over and kissed Finley's cheek.

"Will you get married at the winery?" Sally asked eagerly, looking from Finley to Holden.

"This is pretty new," Finley replied. "We haven't set a date. We haven't talked details." She looked up at him. "But I'm ready to be Finley Scott."

"Weddings take time to plan," Dianne reminded.

"Actually, all we need is a license, Mom," Finley said. "But I do think the winery would be the perfect setting. Harper would pull out all the stops for us."

"You should wait until school is out," Sam said. "Then you won't have lesson plans and grading to worry about."

Finley frowned. "The winery will be pretty booked then. I'm not sure any summer dates would be available."

"Maybe on weekends," Holden said. "But no one said we have to get married on a weekend. We could do it at six in the evening on a weekday if Harper agreed."

"Oh, that would be a good possibility," Sally said. "Most of the people you would invite would be right here in Lost Creek anyway." She looked at Holden. "Where is your family?"

He stilled. "I don't have any family left. I was an only child. Even the man who was like a second father to me passed away a number of years ago."

Finley squeezed his hand. Only she knew that his mom had cut all ties with him and that Holden had no idea where in Europe she now was. Or even if she was still in Copenhagen.

"I've never imagined a large wedding for myself," Finley said. "Something small and intimate would suit us better, I think." She paused. "Let me text Harper and see what she's up to now."

She did so, everyone at the table looking on eagerly.

"I told Harper that Holden and I wanted to stop by this afternoon. She said we could in an hour."

"Then that's plenty of time to have dessert," Ches interjected. "I saw that apple pie in the kitchen."

"And ice cream?" Ricky asked eagerly.

"I've got your favorite, Ricky. Blue Bell," Dianne said. "Let's get these dishes cleared away, and then we can have dessert."

They talked about the wedding over pie and ice cream. Finley said they would have to postpone any kind of honeymoon because she was booked solidly through the summer, photographing weddings and then taking senior pictures, along with being on Wolf's movie set some.

"I'll also be working on the movie this summer," Holden told them. "Wolf wants me on set in case any writing adjustments need to be made. Since it takes place in the Hill Country, he'll be shooting it here. So, we'll both be tied up."

"Honeymoons can be overrated," Ches said. "Sally and I flew to Greece. We were exhausted by the time we got there." He grinned at his wife. "And then we didn't see much of it after we got our second wind."

"I've told Ches we need to go back someday and take the kids," Sally said. "So we could see the sights."

"Yeah, nothing like taking kids on a trip so you can get all that sightseeing in," Ches agreed smugly, his wife punching him in the shoulder.

Dianne insisted they leave the dishes and head over to see Harper. Everyone hugged them goodbye, and he was touched when Dianne said, "We always wanted more children. I hope you don't mind if we claim you as a second son, Holden."

He swallowed, his throat thick with emotion. Holden felt he was being given the family he'd never had.

They drove to the Clarks, where they shared their good news with the couple. More hugs were exchanged, and then Harper said, "You've got to let me do the wedding for you. Everything will be comped. That can be our gift to you." She paused. "But we'll have to find someone who can photograph it!"

"When are you getting married?" Braden asked.

"That's why we're here," Finley explained. "To look at Harper's calendar and see what might be available."

She explained the idea of a small, weekday wedding, and Harper nodded enthusiastically.

"Those are actually starting to become more popular, especially for couples who don't want to wait a year or two and wait for a date to open up at their dream venue."

"I'd thought about once school is out." Finley consulted her phone. We get out the Friday before Memorial Day this year. We just want something small."

Harper flipped a page. "If you want to wait for school to end, we could do that Tuesday, Wednesday, or Thursday after Memorial Day. Anytime you'd like. Indoors or outdoors. The choice is yours."

Finley looked to him. "Do you have a preference?"

"I think outside would be nice," he said.

"Sunset is around eight-thirty that time of year," Harper said crisply, all business now. "I'd hold the ceremony no earlier than six-thirty. Beginning at seven would be ideal. The heat of the day would be dying down. Then you could move inside the center for your reception. I'm assuming Blackwood BBQ could do the catering."

"Yes," he and Finley replied in unison.

"It's up to you," Harper told them. "I'd pick the date now, so it'll be on the calendar. Even with a small wedding, you have a lot to consider. The meal. The wines and beers. Cakes. Music."

Holden took Finley's hand. "How about that Tuesday? That way, school obligations would be out of the way. I'm assuming you're already booked to photograph weddings that weekend. That would give us a couple of days together. Maybe a mini-honeymoon in San Antonio for a couple of days."

"I like that idea," she said, her aquamarine eyes sparkling at him.

"Got it," Harper said, inputting the info into her tablet. "I'll work on finding a photographer. You can talk with

Emerson about cakes. I can set up an appointment for you with Shy Blackwood if you'd like. With a smaller crowd, how about Dax as the DJ?"

"Perfect," he said.

Holden couldn't believe how quickly things were coming together. He knew it would be smooth sailing from here on out.

19

$\mathcal{H}$olden felt Finley's lips brush against his brow. He reached out and cupped her nape, giving her a kiss as she bent over him while he lay in bed.

"Have a good day," he told her.

After she left for school, he decided to get up and go home. Although they weren't living together, they spent every night with one another, whether at his cottage or her house. It was impractical for them to move to either place. The cottage's rental agreement would end soon, and he would have to give it up. At her house, he had Emerson to consider, though she had assured Holden he was welcome at any point.

The house was cramped, however, with the third bedroom serving as an office to both women and their side businesses. Emerson had cookbooks and sketchbooks for cake ideas stacked everywhere, while Finley had photography equipment and various samples of her work stored. Though he didn't have much, no closet space was available. The house only had the one bathroom, and he didn't think it fair to move in, no matter what Emerson said.

Because of that, they were looking for a house they could move to, hopefully before the wedding. A local realtor, Cyndi Johnson, had shown them two houses so far. One had potential, but the other had far too many renovations to do to bring it up to being livable. They didn't have time to take on such a huge project.

Whatever they chose, it needed to be large enough so they both had a home office to work from and still have bedrooms for them and the family they wanted to raise. That had been one of the first things they had discussed after they became engaged. Coming from a loving family, Finley definitely wanted children. She told him she didn't want to assume he felt the same, though. Holden assured her that he did want kids. They had talked of having at least two, possibly more, and they would start trying after a year or so of marriage. They both agreed they needed time to grow as a couple before adding children to the mix.

Holden rose, dressing and driving to Java Junction. He grabbed a morning coffee and pastry before returning to The Inn on Lost Creek. Once at his cottage, he ate his breakfast while flipping through various news sites on his phone. He checked his email and then went for a long walk, thinking about the outline for his Mr. Hamilton story which he had sent to Evan McGill.

His agent had called it schmaltzy as hell, but he had

loved it, all the same. Evan said it had the perfect mix of nostalgia and realism and was the kind of uplifting tale that would do well in the market. Evan had told Holden he thought it had book club potential written all over it. That was what an author hoped for, writing a book which not only would a lot of people buy and read, but that they would gather and discuss it.

He took a long, hot shower after he returned and readied himself for the day. He had a meeting with Wolf and Ana this afternoon at two. By now, he had completed his first pass on the script and used Wolf's notes to tinker with a second draft, deleting two scenes and adding three more, along with tweaking the dialogue throughout it. Wolf had passed the script along to Ana to read, and the three of them would talk today about what changes— if any —needed to be made before the script was considered complete.

His cell rang, and he answered.

"It's Cyndi, Holden. I know Finley is at school now, but I have a pocket listing that I want you to see ASAP."

He knew a pocket listing was a property which had not yet officially gone on the market and asked, "Will I be the first to see it?"

"You will. It's a little larger than what I think you're looking for, but it checks off pretty much every box the two of you gave me."

"Can I see it now?"

"I was hoping you'd say that," Cyndi said.

He asked for the address and told the agent he would meet her there.

When Holden pulled up to the house, he was pleased that it sat on a cul-de-sac, one of four houses. The house had terrific curb appeal, with a manicured lawn and flower beds in bloom. He could imagine their kids riding bikes in the circle and shooting baskets at a portable hoop.

He saw Cyndi's car turn onto the cul-de-sac and got out of his vehicle, greeting the realtor as she did the same.

"The bones are good," she told him. "Although it's almost forty years old, you couldn't tell by looking at the outside. New roof. New paint. New landscaping, with the yard resodded in the front and back. It recently was renovated inside, as well. The owner passed away, and the interior hadn't been touched since he moved in decades ago. His son inherited it, but he lives in Austin and doesn't want to uproot his family to come to live in Lost Creek, so he had the entire inside updated to get the best price possible. He wants it sold as quickly as possible. It's just over four thousand square feet."

As they moved up the sidewalk, Holden thought it might be too large and then decided it could be something they grew into, especially when kids came along. It would be easier to find and purchase one house now than having to buy something larger ten years down the road.

Cyndi let them in and said, "I'll let you wander about since that's what you like to do." She pulled out her phone and began tapping away. "I'm sending you and Finley some details about it now."

Holden moved throughout the house, excitement filling him. He liked what he saw and thought Finley would, too. The floor plan was fairly open, and he suspected a few walls had come down to make it so. The kitchen was the showplace of the house, with double ovens, six gas burners, and even a pot filler, something he'd known nothing about but which Finley raved about. Since she was such a great cook, he wanted her to have a dream kitchen.

He walked the entire ground floor, opening drawers and checking inside closets, and then ventured upstairs, returning to the kitchen when his tour was completed.

Cyndi put away her phone. "You can check your email about the particulars of the house. I haven't even had a photographer come in yet to take pictures, or I would've sent those, too. Besides what I mentioned previously, the house has a new HVAC system. The wood floors laid throughout are also new." The realtor paused. "What do you think of it?"

"What I think is why didn't we start with this to begin with. It's perfect, Cyndi."

"The owner just contacted me yesterday," she explained. "He drove down from Austin and handed over the keys and listing to me. I thought of you and Finley immediately."

"What's he asking for it?"

Cyndi told him, and Holden nodded. "I need Finley to see it, of course, but I'm going to ask that you not show it to anyone else, Cyndi."

She smiled brightly. "That's what I thought. Something like this rarely comes on the market in Lost Creek. I can easily sit on it for a few days. In fact, let me give you the key so you and Finley can see it today when she gets out of school."

"Thanks, Cyndi." He accepted the key. "I don't think we'll be needing to see any more houses."

He returned to his new SUV, having bought it a couple of weeks ago. While he'd liked driving Wolf's truck, he didn't think it was practical to buy one for himself since he had no need for such a large bed. An SUV was roomy and suited him.

Holden decided to text Finley.

> Think I've found our house. Turnkey and large. On a cul-de-sac. Cyndi emailed you info, & I am inside it now. Hope we can look at it together today once you are out of school.

He drove back to the cottage and by the time he reached it, Finley had replied.

> Have a faculty meeting. Will not be free until 4:30 or later. Can meet you then. Excited!

Holden replied, sending her the address and telling Finley he'd be waiting for her once her meeting let out. He was in limbo now, waiting to hear about his script and not wanting to start on the Mr. Hamilton story just yet. He decided it was time to pull out *Inside Threat* and begin his re-read of it. He could get through a couple of chapters, doing his usually fine tuning and hunting for any typos.

Going inside the cottage, he set an alarm on his phone,

so he wouldn't get caught up in the story and forget his meeting with Wolf and Ana.

The alarm went off, startling him, pulling Holden from the world of Washington, D.C. He had researched the city and government in-depth while working on *Capitol Crimes*, and he'd been able to use some of that research which had been untouched for *Inside Threat*. Already, he liked what he read. The pacing was spot on. His protagonist was smart and likeable. Holden decided he would devote the next few days to polishing his manuscript before he sent it off to Evan. They had talked about it, deciding to give his current publishing house first dibs on reading it and making an offer.

His publisher had liked *Capitol Crimes* so much that they'd signed him to a two-book deal, which included *Capitol Crimes* and what had eventually become *Hill Country Homicide*. They had wanted to lock him up for a three-book deal, but Evan was cagey and had pushed for only two, wanting to give himself wiggle room down the line in future negotiations on Holden's behalf, seeing great potential in his new client. If his current house wasn't interested or his agent didn't think their offer up to snuff, Evan had said he would open up the bidding to other houses.

He drove to Meadow Creek Ranch, Ana greeting him with a hug.

"You know I'm a fan of your writing, Holden, but I had some doubts as to how you would tackle a script. Not only did you capture everything from your novel, you tightened it like a pro. I would've thought this was the tenth screenplay you'd authored and not your first."

Holden glowed at her compliment, knowing Ana did not shower praise lightly. "Thank you. The format is tricky, but I told Wolf I might like to try writing another screenplay again in the future."

As they moved to the den, Ana said, "Wolf has already tasked me to look at other books we could make into films, as well as read screenplays which are starting to come in. Do you think you'd be more comfortable working with your own source material, or do you believe you could take someone else's novel and turn it into a screenplay?"

"I have no idea," he said honestly. "Part of me thinks it would be simpler using my own work since I'm so familiar with it. Then again, it was difficult to take a hatchet to my book and chop out so much. I would be interested to see what I might do with a novel if I were given a fresh start with turning it into a screenplay."

"I know you already know your next project. As much as I've loved what you've written so far, I think your Mr. Hamilton story will become my favorite. But after that? You'll have to see where you wish to go in your career."

They went into the den, where Wolf was watching ESPN. He turned off the TV as Holden took a seat, setting his laptop on the coffee table in front of them. Wolf reached for a legal pad and consulted it.

"First, my friend, let me congratulate you on completing your first screenplay. I liked the additional scenes, especially two of them. It was a good move to cut a couple of others, but I put one deleted one back in. I think it flows better with it included."

The director told him which one and why he'd reinserted it, and Holden agreed it could stand as is.

Glancing at the legal pad, Wolf told Holden about two minor tweaks he wanted. Holden called up the first scene on his laptop and asked for a couple of minutes to revise. He knocked out what Wolf requested within ten minutes and then asked what the second revision was. The adjustment was so small, Holden completed it within two minutes.

He handed over his laptop and allowed Wolf to read what he'd done. Ana came to sit next to her husband so she could also read the changes at the same time.

While he waited for them to finish, Holden scrolled through his phone, seeing where the vote on upping minimum wage had finally passed and there was yet another new push to keep the country on Daylight Saving Time year-round. He had just opened the *Publishers Weekly* site to peruse when Wolf spoke up.

"This is fantastic, Holden," the director praised. "We have ourselves a finished script, and I know exactly who will be receiving it. First, though, we need to protect it before I send it out."

"Do I file for a copyright?" he asked. "Evan and my publisher usually handle that kind of paperwork for me, but I have no idea how things work with a screenplay."

"We could go the copyright route as backup, but it needs to be registered with the Writers Guild of America. A final script always should be registered with WGA.

That'll provide a public record and will state your claim to authorship."

"Both our names should go on this," Holden insisted.

"No," his friend said flatly. "I may have passed along a few ideas to you, but you're the one who put the words on the page. If I would've written a scene and you'd written the next one, that would be different. Yes, I helped you polish it a bit, but it's all your work, Holden. You should receive sole credit."

He raked a hand through his hair. "Okay, how do go about it?"

"Remember how I had you join WGA when you agreed to write the screenplay?"

"Vaguely," he said, thinking how swiftly things had happened as he'd left Brooklyn for Texas.

"The Writers Guild of America has two offices. One on each coast. L.A. and New York. I had you join the California branch. Give me your laptop."

Wolf had called up the site and turned it so Holden could see.

"You can submit your script online, but I'm a little old-fashioned when it comes to things such as this. Ana can handle this for you. They state you should mail one unbound copy of the script with a title page and your name, plus a check. WEBA Productions will cover the cost, which is minimal."

"I'll print it out after I pick up the kids at school," Ana said. "I'll swing by the post office in Bandera tomorrow morning after I drop them off and send it off."

"Thanks. I appreciate it."

The three of them talked over some of the actors Wolf wished to approach. Ana threw out an unusual choice for the murderer, but Holden saw just how good the actor might be in the role.

"Not being a large studio, we can't offer the flashy salaries a couple of these name actors are used to," Ana said. "Still, I think we should shoot for the sky and try for everyone we suggested, then go from there."

"I agree," her husband said. "I've already been dangling hints to Jack Calder. I knew not to go through his agent, who's a greedy little bastard and would never let him sign for what we can offer to pay him. We can always offer Jack points off the back end, just as we have with you, Holden, in case he does decide to do it."

"I want you to be able to make money off this movie, Wolf," he said. "If you give away too many points, where will the profit be?"

The director's eyes gleamed. "Oh, we are going to make money off this, my friend. I guarantee it."

They talked a while about some of the places Ana had scouted. A few of them he was familiar with because they were in or near Lost Creek.

"I do want you on the set as much as possible, Holden," Wolf urged. "Not every day, of course, and not all day. Just enough to get a feel for things throughout the shoot. I know you'll be juggling other projects by the time filming begins."

"Yes," he said. "I've started my read-through of *Inside Threat*, the novel I finished just before I came to Texas. It's fermented enough, and I want to spend the next few days cleaning it up before I send it off to Evan. Then I'll be starting the Mr. Hamilton story."

"If you don't mind, send it to me when you finish tweaking it," Ana suggested. "After all, WEBA Productions is always interested in anything Holden Scott writes."

He agreed to do so and glanced at his watch. "I need to get going. I think I've found the house for Finley and me."

"Oh, that's wonderful," Ana exclaimed. "Is it in Lost Creek?"

"It is. It's got plenty of space for both of us to work from home."

Since Finley had already turned in her resignation, they had shared with Wolf and Ana her plans to go into photography full-time. The couple had been delighted with the decision.

Holden drove directly to the house in Lost Creek and parked in the driveway. Satisfaction filled him as he studied it.

This would be their home.

Since Finley wouldn't be here for another five to ten minutes, he picked up his phone. It opened to the Publishers Weekly site, which he had forgotten to close. He tried to check it once a week, just to see what books had been sold and what they were about, trying to gauge the market.

His eyes fell on a familiar name. A wave of nausea washed over him.

Winston Press has acquired the rights to *Assassination Games*, the first novel from newcomer Madison Parmalee.

Publication has not yet been set. The two-book deal was brokered by Amanda Sommers of SGR, who said the political thriller is '*a thrill ride and glimpse into the shadowy dealings of how Washington is run.*'

Madison Parmalee is a graduate of the University of Iowa's famed Iowa Writers' Workshop. She is now working on a sequel to *Assassination Games,* which will also be published by Winston Press.

Holden had forgotten that he'd given Madison a copy of *Inside Threat* to read.

And she had hijacked his book.

20

A thousand things were swirling through Holden's head. He had to stop this book from publication. Now. Fortunately, Winston Press was one of the largest publishing houses in New York. They had bid on *Capitol Crimes* and come in a close second. Holden had liked Vincent Winston, the head of Winston Press. They had met twice and even had dinner together. Thank goodness he had a personal connection with the publisher—because he knew this was going to be Shit City.

Immediately, he FaceTimed with Evan, wanting to get the ball rolling.

"Hey, Holden. How—"

"Fucking Madison stole *Inside Threat*," he ground out. "My book. *My* book, Evan!"

The agent whistled low. "I saw the sale in PW yesterday. I know Amanda Sommers, the SGR agent listed who brokered the sale. How the hell did this happen, Holden?"

He cursed aloud. "I always let her read my stuff, Evan. Even when she stopped sharing hers, I kept passing pages to her. She would give me notes. Pretty good ones, actually. When we broke up, I never gave it a thought. All I wanted was out of there. I didn't realize she still had a copy of *Inside Threat*, much less that she'd try to pass the work off as hers."

Evan went totally business, and Holden was glad he didn't share any I-told-you-so's.

"My personal attorney has an IP attorney at his firm. Intellectual property. I'm going to call him now and share the situation. Wasn't it Winston Press that bought the book?"

"Yeah," he said, anger churning within him.

"I won't notify them of anything yet. Let me talk with the lawyers, and I'll get back to you. And under no circumstances are you to call Madison. Do you hear me, Holden? Not. One. Word."

"I hear you," he said sullenly, itching to call his ex and scream at her. Which was so out of character for him. Holden rarely raised his voice. He couldn't ever recall ever arguing with Madison, other than that last time they spoke. Bitterness bubbled up within him, thinking of how great this betrayal was.

"Sit tight, buddy," Evan urged. "I'll call you as soon as I know something."

He ended the call, taking deep breaths, trying to get his anger under control. Trying not to imagine dismembering Madison into tiny pieces.

Five minutes later, his phone rang. It was Evan.

"What did you find out?" he barked. "I'm sorry. I'm not mad at you. I'm beating myself up, and I'm furious with Madison for what she's done."

"My lawyer is setting up a meeting with Rutherford Baxter, the firm's IP guy. I'm heading over there now. Hopefully, I'll call you in an hour or so with a plan of attack."

"Thanks, Evan. For being my advocate and friend."

Holden hung up and saw Finley's car pulling in next to his. He couldn't ruin this for her. They were about to look at the house he hoped they would share for a very long time. He didn't want Madison's treachery to infringe now on this moment. Besides, he wouldn't know anything until Evan called back.

Putting a smile on his face, he got out of his SUV and met her, giving her a kiss. For a moment, he clung to her, wishing all the bad things to come in this fight over *Inside Threat* wouldn't touch their relationship and yet knowing they would.

Breaking the kiss, he asked, "What do you think?"

Her sunny smile washed over him, calming him, melting the tension.

"Already, I like it. I've always had a thing for Colonials. And look at how long the porch runs. The flowers are beautiful, and the grass is immaculate."

"Did you have time to see what Cyndi sent about it?"

She giggled. "I read everything during my faculty meeting. Held my cell in my lap under the table. Felt like a kid trying to get away with something. I love the floor plan. But it's huge, Holden. I didn't think we were looking for something so big."

He shrugged, slipping an arm about her waist as he guided her to the front door.

"I thought the same thing at first when I toured it. Then again, we don't have to use every room right away. We could close some off. Furnish it as we need to. Right now, it's definitely got office space for both of us, and that's the most important thing since we'll both be working from home."

Pulling the key from his pocket, he added, "We can kept bedroom doors shut, only opening them once another kid arrives."

She leaned into him. "I like the sound of that."

Holden unlocked the door, pushing aside all other thoughts. He wanted to be here, in this moment, for Finley. He followed her around the house as they talked about each room, even discussing some of the furniture to place in it.

When they reached the kitchen, her jaw dropped. "This is fabulous!" she cried.

"I thought you'd like it."

He watched her open cabinets. Test burners. Open the oven. All the while, her smile grew larger.

"Let's look at the back yard. Not much has been done there," he told her.

Outside, Finley immediately said the patio was too small. "I would add to it. And cover it. Actually, I'm jealous of Braden's outdoor kitchen. Maybe someday we can put one of those in."

"We can do it now," he assured her. "We've got the money."

She frowned. "I don't want you paying for everything, Holden."

He cupped her face. "Let's face it. The State of Texas doesn't pay its teachers nearly what they're worth. And you've put a lot of your savings into your business, which I think needs a name. What's mine is yours, Finley. I've done really well with my books and selling the film and foreign rights to the first one. We can afford this place—and an outdoor kitchen —if that's what you want."

She slipped her arms around him, resting her cheek against his chest. "How about a pool?"

Holden laughed. "We can put in a pool."

"Yes!" she exclaimed. "I always wanted one growing up, but Dad said we could never afford one. This is so exciting! Come on, let's go back inside and see the rest of it."

He caught her enthusiasm, and they continued their tour.

"The primary suite is really large," Finley commented. I like the fact we'd each have our own closet."

"Cyndi said the entire place has been renovated. The seller inherited it. Updated it. And now wants to sell as quickly as possible."

Her eyes widened. "We might actually be able to move in before the wedding."

"I was thinking that," he said. "So, are you ready for us to put in an offer?"

"Yes!" she squealed, throwing her arms about him.

Holden wanted nothing more than to put her on the

kitchen island and make love to her, but he didn't want the call he expected interrupting them.

"Then let's call Cyndi and get the ball rolling."

They called the realtor, putting her on speakerphone, and she was thrilled that she had a sale. After discussing it, they decided what they wanted to offer. Cyndi said she would contact the owner immediately and let them know if he accepted.

"I can also handle booking an inspector for you," Cyndi said. "But I won't get ahead of myself just yet. Hope I can get a hold of him now. Talk to you soon!"

He hung up. "I have a feeling we just bought a house."

"We need to celebrate. Maybe we could stop for dinner on our way home."

Hesitating, he said, "I need to talk to you about something. Something serious."

Her brows knit together. "What's wrong, Holden?"

"A whole hell of a lot," he said flatly. "I screwed up— and now I'm being taken advantage of." He paused. "Let's go sit in the car and talk."

They went to his SUV. She reached for his hand. "Whatever it is, you know you have me. Team Scott is invincible."

"I think things are going to get pretty ugly. I may need to go to New York."

"Then I'm going with you," she said stubbornly.

"Babe, you don't even know what it is yet," he protested. "And you've got school."

"I've got so many sick days built up, I could take off the entire rest of the year and not use them up. I wouldn't do that to my students, but you get what I'm saying. I'm here, Holden. Tell me what's going on. You said you've screwed up. I know between us, we can fix whatever is wrong."

"It's Madison."

He saw the wind go out of her sails. "What about her?" she asked warily.

"Madison is a writer, same as me. You know we met at the Iowa workshop. She's smart. Has a great eye for details. I would let her read my work, and she would give me hers to critique. After the movie of *Capitol Crimes* came out and was such a success, Madison stopped letting me read her stuff. I got it. She was probably a little bit jealous. A little down on herself. Writers are hard on themselves, and I'm sure she doubled down after my initial achievements."

He took a moment, gathering his thoughts before continuing.

"She always had some good suggestions, so I continued to let her read my work. Including *Inside Threat*. I finished it just before I spoke with Wolf and agreed to come to Texas to work on the screenplay for *Homicide*. Madison and I both said some pretty ugly things when I left. I never even thought to ask her to return whatever copy she had of my latest novel. That's been out of sight, out of mind, while I've been working on the script."

Finley squeezed his hand encouragingly. "Go on."

"Out of habit, I check every week to see who's sold what manuscript. And today? I saw where Madison had sold a political thriller called *Assassination Games* to a major New York publishing house."

She went still. "It's your book, isn't it?"

"I think it very well might be. The description was too brief, but between it and the title, my gut tells me she took my novel and claimed it as her own. She didn't even have an agent when I left New York, and now she's represented by one at SGR, one of the biggest literary agencies in the business."

"Have you called your agent? He needs to know," she insisted.

"I did. He should be calling me back soon. He's meeting with his lawyer and another one who specializes in intellectual property. That's what novels fall under."

His phone buzzed in the cup holder where he'd placed it. He saw Evan's face appear on the screen.

"It's them."

"Can I be here with you, or would you prefer privacy?" she asked.

"Here with me. I need you," he said.

Determination filled her face. "Then answer it."

Holden did. "I'm here with Finley. What have you learned, Evan?"

"I'm going to pass you over to Rutherford Baxter, Holden," his agent said. "I'll be in the room, listening."

"Okay."

Evan turned the tablet before him, and a man in his late fifties with salt and pepper hair appeared on the screen. He looked rich. Confident. Almost arrogant.

Holden would take all three in the attorney who would lead them into battle.

"Holden Scott," he said, introducing himself. "My fiancée, Finley Farrow, is also here with me."

"Rutherford Baxter. I am an intellectual property attorney, Holden. I'm going to be asking you some questions and then giving you some advice. First, let me say, IP can include just about any kind of original creation. Intellectual property can be the logo for a company. A song—both its lyrics and music. And most certainly, a novel."

"That's good to know."

"You own the copyright to each and every sentence you write, whether it's on a physical, paper page or a document on a computer. As soon as it's recorded, it is copyrighted from that moment, going forth. Your manuscript is protected by U. S. law even though it is not published or has yet to be formally copyrighted. What it is important is that you need proof that you wrote it."

"What kind of proof?" he asked.

"Usually, proof is to submit it to the U.S. Copyright Office and obtain a copyright of it. Another option— one which is very old school —is to mail yourself a copy of the manuscript and refrain from opening it when you receive it. The date of the postmark can often prove in a case such as this that the work was yours. I understand, however, that you were not quite done with writing the book."

"No. My process is to finish a work and then let it vegetate a while. It's too hard to edit something when you're so close to the characters. I give it some time and distance, and then I go back in when I'm already in the midst of writing something else. I find I'm not as attached to everything and can be more objective as I fine tune the manuscript."

Baxter nodded. "It is my understanding that you gave permission for Madison Parmalee to read your work-in-progress."

"Yes, that's correct." His belly roiled with guilt for having placed himself in this situation.

"What I will need you to do is gather evidence—written evidence —of anything that you used to write this novel. Character sketches. An outline. Research notes. Even early drafts of the work."

"I have everything except previous drafts," Holden shared. "Tons of research notes. A fairly detailed outline of the plot. Definitely the character sketches. I keep everything on my laptop in a folder with the name of the book." He sighed. "The only thing I come up short with is different drafts. With a computer, I simply open up the doc and begin working. I go back and make adjustments directly and then save. So the file only has the most recent time and date I worked on it."

"That will be helpful. More than you think," Baxter assured him.

He thought a moment. "Wait. I'm also paranoid about losing what I've written. Besides saving in the cloud, I also save to my computer. And I email myself every night with the latest draft of the manuscript. I delete the previous emails, but I should have the January email where I sent myself the book, my summary, and cast of characters."

Baxter smiled, reminding Holden of a shark encircling his prey.

"That's excellent, Holden. Did you send any of this to a friend, beyond Miss Parmalee? Or discuss the plot with someone? Evan said you didn't speak to him about anything, other than sharing the title."

"That's right. I'm pretty private when I work, Rutherford. I don't throw a lot into the universe. I guess I'm paranoid of this very thing happening. Will it hurt, not having anyone else I talked to about the book?"

"It would if we went to trial, but that's not going to happen," the attorney assured him. "In the future, I recommend emailing a copy once a week to Evan, at the minimum. Or discuss it with your fiancée or a close friend or two, people whom you can trust. For now, I believe we have ample proof to prove ownership to both Winston Press and SGR."

"Thank you so much," he said, squeezing Finley's hand tightly.

"I would like you— and your proof —to come to New York, however," Baxter continued. "First, I need you to email me copies of everything associated with *Inside Threat* that you've mentioned. All Word docs. I'd also like you to forward the earliest emails you sent yourself."

"I can do that," he said, making a note of the email address that Baxter now provided to him.

"I will set up a meeting with all interested parties. I'd like you here a day or two before that, so I can look over everything and prep you on how to phrase certain things. You won't be testifying in court, so it's nothing illegal. It's just best if I prepare you for what's ahead and how to appropriately respond. And whatever you do, you are not to contact Miss Parmalee."

"I won't," he promised. "When do you need me there?"

"Today is Tuesday," mused Baxter. "I'll set up the meeting for Friday. Can you get to New York by tomorrow afternoon? That way we could talk and then meet again Thursday if anything needs to be continued."

"Yes. I'll book a flight now."

"I look forward to meeting with you, Holden," Baxter said. "Let me turn you back over to your agent."

The screen shifted, and Evan came into view. "I'm glad you're coming, Holden. Text me your details. I'll have a car meet you and bring you to my office first."

"Will do. Thanks again for acting so promptly, Evan."

"If Amanda Sommers is repping this book and Winston Press jumped on this quickly, I know we have a winner on our hands. And your final version will be better than Madison's." Evan snorted. "Knowing her, she only changed the author's name on the title page and ran with the rest as her own."

"I'll text you in the next few minutes once I have flight info," he promised.

Finley pulled her hand from his and furiously tapped at her phone. "We can get an American Airlines flight out of San Antonio, but it's early. Six in the morning. Lands a little after noon Eastern time. The next one won't get us there until six tomorrow evening."

She did a new search. "Austin has a flight at eight tomorrow morning. Arrives around two in the afternoon. But Austin is a bit of a drive from here."

"I say we book the San Antonio one. We can pack and drive down tonight. Stay close to the airport," he suggested.

She asked if he had a frequent flyer number. He did but didn't remember it.

"I'll use mine," she said.

He watched her work, ever the teacher, efficient and practical.

"There. Done," she told him. "I know the hotel we should stay at. I'll book a room for us. Go home and pack and head to my place. I'll need to call for a sub for the next three days. Hopefully, we'll be done by Friday."

He kissed her. "If we are, let's stay and enjoy Saturday. Fly home Sunday. I'd like to show you a bit of New York since you said you've never been."

"I'd like that," she said, her face growing serious. "I know you're upset about this Holden. But we're in this together. We'll get your book back."

He smoothed her hair. "I'm glad you're in my corner, Finley Farrow."

His phone rang, causing his gut to tighten. "It's Cyndi," he said, relaxing slightly. "Hello?" he said, putting the call on speaker.

"Holden, your bid was accepted," Cyndi told them. "The buyer wants a fast closing. I'll do everything I can to expedite things on my end, including getting that inspection done right away. I'll need you to put down the earnest money, and we'll be official. I'll need a check for that."

"Finley and I have to go out of town unexpectedly,

Cyndi. I'll have someone drop the check and key off to you."

"Oh, keep the key. It's going to be your house soon anyway."

"Thanks, Cyndi."

"Anytime."

Finley said, "Emerson would be happy to drop off the check for us."

He grinned. "You think she wants you out of the house that badly? And by you, that includes the extension of me."

"Emerson adores you. But I do think she isn't going to worry about finding another roommate for a while."

He kissed her soundly. "We may just have ourselves a house, Mrs. Scott-To-Be. Go home and pack. I'll try to swing by for you in an hour."

Holden watched Finley get in her car and allowed her to pull out of the driveway before following her part of the way, turning toward The Inn on the Creek.

As he packed, Holden was glad he was marching into battle with Finley by his side.

21

---

*H*olden had known all along that he would return to New York someday. Just not under these circumstances. As the Manhattan skyline came into sight, he wondered what the outcome would be and if he— or Madison —would walk away with the rights to his novel.

He was glad he had Finley by his side for what lay ahead. She looked out the window now, and he pointed out a few sights to her, trying to remember what he felt the first time he flew into the Big Apple. This was her first trip here, and he hoped they could clear up this situation with Madison so he could enjoy free time here with her.

"It's… enormous," she said, wonder in her voice. "And just beautiful. I love the Hill Country. It's a part of my soul, but this urban beauty also speaks to me. I wish I'd brought my camera with me. At least I can take pictures with my phone."

She turned to him, squeezing his hand. "I'm sorry. I sound like an over-eager tourist when we're here for a very serious matter."

"I understand. I know how excited and overwhelmed I was to see Manhattan for the first time. I don't want to take any of that experience away from you."

"Did you get a lot of work done?"

They had only had a few hours of sleep when they reached their airport hotel in San Antonio. While they waited at the gate and for most of this flight, Holden had continued reading through and tweaking *Inside Threat*. He was almost three-quarters of the way through the manuscript now, and he'd be damned if Madison Parmalee got credit for his hard work.

"I did."

They landed and disembarked, collecting their bags. Once they had those in hand, they searched and found a man holding up a sign with Holden's name, and he confirmed his identity to the driver, who took their luggage. The only thing Holden kept was his laptop bag.

The driver escorted them to a large town car and stored their luggage, telling them that he would swing by Mr. McGill's office and pick him up before heading to the law offices.

As they drove along the FDR, Holden pointed out various places to Finley.

"You know this city well," she said. "Maybe next fall we can take a belated honeymoon trip here. After the filming ends and I've shot all my senior portraits."

He brought their joined hands to his lips and kissed her fingers. "Wherever you want to go."

Holden needed to keep things in perspective. Yes, there was this mess with Madison, but he had an excellent team in place to help him in the fight to reclaim his work. In the meantime, he had a wonderful life waiting for him in Lost Creek. Marriage to Finley. New friends and family who had taken him in as their own. A house to buy and a thriving career. Whatever the outcome regarding *Inside Threat*, he couldn't let any bitterness tinge the happiness he now felt and the life he would lead in the future.

When they got close, the driver texted Evan McGill, and his agent and assistant were waiting for them when they pulled up in front of the building. The pair got into the town car, and Holden introduced Finley to Evan and Delphine.

"I can see why Holden wants to stay in Texas now," the agent said, not bothering to hide his smile.

"Thank you for jumping on this so quickly," he told his friend. "I still can't believe that Madison would do something like this and think she could get away with it."

Evan shook his head. "And I can't believe you're having trouble with that fact. I told you from the beginning that she was bad news and a user from the first time you introduced us. Don't worry. By the time Rutherford Baxter is finished with her, Madison Parmalee will be done in the publishing industry."

Normally, he wasn't a vindictive type, but Holden wanted Madison punished as fully as possible for stealing his work and trying to pass it off as her own.

"Once we're dropped off, Delphine will check you into The Plaza, so don't worry about your luggage."

"Thank you, Evan," Finley said. "You've been very thoughtful."

"Holden isn't just one of my top clients," Evan said. "He's a friend. I'll go to the mat for him."

They arrived at the law offices, and the agent escorted them to the fifty-seventh floor, where they were immediately greeted and taken to a large conference room. Bottles of water awaited them, and the assistant asked if they would also like coffee or tea brought in. Everyone passed and moments later, three people entered the room.

Rutherford Baxter introduced himself and another IP attorney, Leo Turner, as well as his assistant, who would take notes and manage any administrative duties.

"I hadn't read either of your published novels, Holden, but I read several chapters of each last night, simply to get the flavor of your writing," Baxter told him. "Then I read the first thirty pages of the manuscript for *Inside Threat*. Clearly, you have a certain style. The first and third books, both being political thrillers, are very similar in tone, while your murder mystery still has echoes of your style and use of language."

He turned to Leo Turner, who said, "I input the manuscripts into a few AI programs, and they concluded the same thing, noting your phrasing and tone and other similarities. That establishes a baseline for us as to the kind of writer you are and the type of work you produce."

Holden had stayed away from AI, not even using Grammarly, an AI program which looked over a person's documents and social media posts to make certain they read clearly and effectively and were mistake-free. He preferred finding his own spelling and grammatical errors and those he didn't, he left to his agent, editor, and proofreader.

"We've contacted several professors in Iowa, ones who you and Miss Parmalee both took courses from," Leo continued. "Since the culmination of the workshop program requires submission of a creative thesis before awarding a Master of Fine Arts degree, the school had a record of both your novel and Miss Parmalee's. We were able to obtain a copy of hers. Dr. Ingram will also fly in tomorrow to meet with us and make himself available on Friday if we need him at our conference."

"I remember the novel Madison wrote and submitted," he said. "It was a women's fiction piece."

Baxter gave a barracuda smile. "Yes, it was. We also analyzed her writing via AI. Obviously, her style was nothing remotely similar to yours."

"I just wonder how much she changed *Inside Threat* before submitting it to Winston," he wondered aloud. "I wish we could get a copy of that."

"It's going to read like your work, Holden," Leo assured him. "Even if Madison did change a few things, your fingerprints will be all over it. One of our investigators has discovered that Madison's agent submitted *Assassination Games* to Winston Press three days after you left the brownstone."

"She wouldn't have had time to change much then," he

remarked, feeling hopeful. "Does Madison know what's coming?"

"She's going to have an idea," the lead attorney said. "Both Vincent Winston and Amanda Sommers are meeting with us on Friday morning, and we've requested that Miss Parmalee also be in attendance. They know what I do. I would think by now, Miss Parmalee and her submission is under great scrutiny by both SGR and Winston Press."

"She'll be defensive," Holden predicted. "And prepared. Madison has always been meticulous. She'll do everything in her power to make it appear that it was her work that I stole and not the other way around."

"Can you elaborate on anything you read of hers?" Leo asked. "Beyond what we read? Anything about the content or style?"

"Madison started three different novels during our time together. Evan wouldn't take her on as a client, so she went through a few agents. I can give their names to you."

He did so, and Baxter quickly called the investigator, providing the names to him.

"Tell us about what you read," Leo urged.

"She never finished any of these three novels that I know of. One was about a women's book club. Another was about a women divorcing her high school sweetheart after twenty years of marriage and trying to find herself. The last one was centered around a mother and daughter spending a summer together at their beach house on

Nantucket. Madison jumped around a lot. She has ADHD and takes meds in order to help her focus."

Baxter made a note on the legal pad in front of him.

"After a while," he continued, "Madison no longer shared any of her writing with me. I knew she was experiencing a lot of self-doubt. Her doubt was reinforced by the success I was going through. After the movie version of *Capitol Crimes* came out, she never let me read anything else of hers."

"When was that?" Leo asked.

Holden shared the date and then said, "Madison told me she was writing every day. I worked from the brownstone we lived in, and she would leave, being gone for hours at a time. She took her laptop with her, and I would ask her every time she came home how the writing had gone. She was pretty tight-lipped."

"Let's go back to your pattern regarding writing," Baxter said. "Walk me through that again. I want to make certain we're perfectly clear about your process."

"I keep everything in a folder with the name of the book. Title is always the first thing I come up with. I add a variety of blurbs to that folder. What I call the full-blown blurb for the book's jacket, along with a metadata blur of a hundred words or less. Then I have the elevator pitch blurb, which runs between twenty and twenty-five words. Along with those, I create character sketches and then an outline, which are also placed into that folder. Then there's the actual manuscript itself. I don't keep all the drafts of the story, though. I work from the original, adding scenes and chapters as I go along each time. I save that doc daily."

He paused. "I would send Madison the word doc of the manuscript about every five chapters or so, getting her input She's the only person who had eyes on the work."

Baxter prompted, "You told us yesterday that you always email yourself a copy of that day's progress."

"Yes, that's right. Once I email the current version to myself, I delete the one from the previous day."

"Could you leave your laptop with us overnight, Holden?" Leo asked. "Our tech expert can pull all your emails and any files off it we need. I assure you we'll take excellent care of it."

"I'm happy to do so. Whatever will help."

He slid the laptop across the conference room table, and Leo excused himself, taking the laptop with him.

"I think we have everything we need from you, "Rutherford Baxter assured him.

"Will you need us tomorrow?" Holden asked.

"I don't believe so," the attorney said. "Between interviewing Dr. Ingram and getting all the massive documentation printed out and those ducks in a row, we have a strong case to present to Vincent Winston. If we need anything else from you, I'll give you a call. For now, consider yourself free all day tomorrow. I would like you in the offices by eight-thirty on Friday morning, however. That way, we can go over anything additional that we need to."

Everyone rose, and Holden shook the lawyer's hand. "Thank you for what you're doing for me, Rutherford."

Baxter chuckled. "You'll get my bill, Holden. You'll be appalled at how much it is, but I'm the best IP and copyright attorney in this city. Probably the entire country. And after you sell *Inside Threat*—both the book and movie rights—my fee will seem like a pittance."

At the elevator, Evan texted the driver to meet them downstairs and then said, "Baxter's right about the bill. It'll be sky-high, but I'll split it with you, Holden. I have my own investment in *Inside Threat*."

"No," he said firmly. "Madison was my partner. I'm the one responsible for giving her a copy of the manuscript. She's the one who took it upon herself to steal it and claim it as her own. It's an expensive lesson. One I'll never repeat again. I'm also going to start putting you on my daily email to myself when I send that day's pages. You just have to promise not to read it."

Evan chuckled. "I can do that."

His fingers found Finley's and took them as they entered the elevator, needing her assurance.

They dropped Evan at his office, and then the driver took them to The Plaza, giving them the key card which Delphine had passed along to him.

As they entered the lavish hotel, Finley's eyes widened. "I've seen this place in so many movies. I can't wait to see what our room looks like."

They went upstairs and found their luggage waiting for them in their suite. Finley went to stand next to the floor to ceiling window and Holden joined her, wrapping his arms around her, resting his chin on her shoulder. They stared out at Central Park.

"I'm starved," he told her. "Do you like Chinese food?"

"I love it," she replied.

"Then let's head to a spot where I ate my first meal in Manhattan."

An hour later, they were dining on steamed shrimp dumplings, Peking duck, crispy string beans with minced pork, and fried rice.

Finley placed the last bite in her mouth. "You may have to give me an hour to recover. I'm so full, I don't know if I can stand." She yawned. "Sorry."

"It's been a long, exhausting day," he told her, paying the bill.

They returned to their room, the curtains still open, the New York skyline lit up before them. A part of the city would always seem like home to him, but already Holden itched for the wide-open spaces of the Hill Country.

He dropped a kiss on Finley's nape. "Let's get some sleep. I want to take you wherever you wish to go tomorrow."

Holden enveloped Finley in his arms, hoping by the time they left New York, everything would once again be on track.

22

inley and Holden went for bagels and coffee the next morning, stopping at a small neighborhood place not far from their hotel.

After chewing one bite, she said, "These are fantastic! The best bagel I've ever eaten. Was this one of your hangouts?"

"No. To be honest, I rarely left Brooklyn. It had everything I needed. I only came into Manhattan to visit Evan."

"Then how did you know to stop here?" she asked.

Holden laughed. "Any place in New York has great bagels. They say it's partly the water, which is really soft."

"You're right about that soft water. I rinsed shampoo forever from my hair this morning," she said drily.

"Somehow, the minerals in the soft water affect the gluten in the dough. It makes for a very chewy, very tasty bagel. You can't go wrong stopping at any bagel place in New York City."

Finley took another bite, savoring it. "If I wasn't so happy living in Lost Creek, I would move here for the bagels alone," she declared.

They finished their breakfast and took the subway downtown. Holden had asked her what three things she most wanted to do in New York. She had told him she would like to visit the 9/11 Museum and Memorial, take the ferry to see the Statue of Liberty, and walk through Central Park. He said he was happy to show her all three.

"Thanks for indulging me today and playing tourist," she told him as they walked hand-in-hand to the museum, being among the first entering it.

"I've only been here once," he admitted. "It was very moving. I'll let you take the lead."

The museum was a unique experience, presenting the story of that day in September with exhibits from the events of the day told through audio and video recordings, first-person testimony, and artifacts and images. It also displayed exhibits which brought that day into context, spotlighting the events leading up to the attacks, as well as the aftermath of the infamous day.

She found tears welled up frequently, especially when she saw the pictures of the almost three thousand people killed as a result of the terrorist attack, both here, in Pennsylvania, and in Washington, D.C.

After two hours, they left the museum and spent some time at the outdoor tribute of remembrance honoring the dead and located on the site of the former World Trade Center complex. Though her heart hurt, she found a peace viewing the reflecting pools.

"I'm ready," she finally said solemnly, and Holden led her from the area back to the nearest subway station.

He took her to the High Line next, a park built along an historic elevated freight line on the west side of Manhattan. Before climbing the stairs to walk the path, they stopped at a hot dog cart, which had a blue and yellow umbrella shading the pushcart, where Holden told her to let him order.

"Sabretts has carts all over the city. Nathan's is also amazing." He stepped up and said, "Two franks. All the trimmings. Two sodas."

"Franks?" she mouthed as the vendor begin readying their order.

He shrugged. "When in Rome."

Holden paid for their lunch, and they mounted a staircase, stopping at a bench as they ate their hot dogs. Finley didn't think she could ever call them franks.

"The ferries running to Ellis and Liberty Islands get crowded as the day goes on," he told her, draping his arm about her shoulder as they basked in the sun. "We'll do that first thing Saturday morning. I want you to get to see everything on your wish list."

She smiled up at him. "I'm seeing all I need to see right now."

He kissed her softly. "Ditto."

They finished their lunch and walked the entire High Line, the Hudson River on their left. It was wonderful seeing the city from this angle. Finley had always wanted to visit New York, and now she was doing it with her fiancé, which made it that much more special.

Once they finished the High Line, Holden took her to Central Park. They saw the Shakespeare Garden and Strawberry Fields. Belvedere Castle and the famous Carousel.

"We need to come here during late October or November," he told her as they strolled along. "Central Park is at her best in autumn. The array of colors is breathtaking."

"Maybe we could combine New York with a New England fall foliage trip," she suggested. "I've never been to that part of the country. I was always busy teaching during those months."

"I like that idea," he said, stopping to kiss her.

Finley had never felt more loved than in that moment. She decided it would be these small snapshots of their love and lives together that would be the ones which would always stay with her.

She only hoped things went well at tomorrow's meeting. She was dreading being in the same room with Holden's former lover and worried how Madison Parmalee would react when she learned who Finley was.

They went back to The Plaza and made glorious love, the curtains wide open, Central Park below them. After, they showered together, and Holden asked her if there might be somewhere special she wanted to have dinner.

"Anywhere is good with me." She grinned. "I would actually want to go back to the bagel place, but I noticed their hours. They're not open now."

He nuzzled her neck. "We'll get you more bagels tomorrow. We can even bring some back to Texas with us.

They won't taste quit as good since they won't be as fresh, though."

"It doesn't matter. That's a terrific idea. And I'd love for Emerson to try at least one. She used to make bagels sometimes when she worked part-time at The Bake Shop for Ethel. I think she'd really be interested in tasting a genuine New York bagel."

Holden said he was in a mood for seafood, and they went to a place in Midtown that he said Evan McGill had taken him to before. She had donned a black cocktail dress she'd brought with her, knowing they might go somewhere fancy. It wasn't one she usually wore to photograph weddings. It was fitted and flared, with a plunging neckline, and made her feel extremely sexy.

"Why don't you order for me?" she said. "You did so well doing that at lunch today."

He laughed. "Happy to do so."

The server brought them two appetizers, and they shared them. One was Oysters Rockefeller, which had been sautéed in butter, garlic, shallots, and spinach before being topped with breadcrumbs and cheese and baked.

"I'm definitely adding this to my repertoire," she told him, happily eating another oyster.

Holden had also ordered Hudson Valley Foie Gras. The duck liver was so rich and buttery, Finley thought heaven must be full of foie gras and Blue Bell Ice Cream.

After the server cleared the empty appetizer plates, Finley said, "I don't know how the rest of the meal can get much better than that."

"It will," he guaranteed.

They skipped having soup or salad, ready to go straight to the main course. He opted for a seared sesame crusted yellow fin tuna, while she ate Dover sole. They shared sides of lobster mac and cheese and truffle whipped potatoes.

"Dessert?" he asked.

"Will you split something with me?"

He smiled. "Only if it's chocolate."

Finley laughed. "That won't be hard." She picked up the dessert menu. "Either the chocolate mousse or the chocolate pots de crème."

"Let's go for the mousse," he suggested. "It'll be lighter." Holden waggled his eyebrows at her. "And allow me to be a little lighter myself. And naughtier."

She smile seductively. "You can be as naughty as you want, Mr. Scott. I look forward to it."

Suddenly, Holden was drenched, white wine dripping down his face as he blinked rapidly. Before Finley could react, her cold glass of wine was splashed in her face. She grabbed her napkin from her lap, blotting her face, pressing the cloth against her eyes so she could see.

When she looked up, a woman with a bright red face stood at their table, her anger obvious.

Her fingers clamped Finley's wrist, jerking it up. She peered at the engagement ring and then glared at Finley, her hatred palpable.

"How long was this going on, Holden?" the woman demanded. "No wonder you dumped me so quickly. You already had a side piece. I was expendable."

Madison Parmalee...

Finley jerked away her wrist, rubbing it, staring at Holden's former partner through narrowed eyes.

The server had rushed over, along with the maître d.'

"Please let me escort you—"

"Don't touch me," Madison barked at the server. "I'm leaving."

She hurried away from their table, and Finley saw a man jump up from a nearby booth and follow Madison outside.

"I am so sorry," the maître d' apologized. "Miss Parmalee will no longer be served here." He sniffed. "I do not care who her father is. Again, my apologies. May I bring you each a towel? Shall I call the police?"

"No to both," Holden said. "Just the check." He dabbed his face with his napkin.

"Please. Your dinner is on the house, *Monsieur.*"

"No," Holden insisted. "You shouldn't have to take a loss caused by someone else."

Finley noticed he couldn't even use Madison's name. She glanced around, seeing patrons at the other tables still staring in their direction. Slowly, they returned their attention to their food.

The server accepted the credit card Holden offered, and they left the restaurant quickly, their evening spoiled.

By a spoiled brat.

Finley slipped her arm through her fiancé's. "I didn't think she'd take us being together well."

"She's been overindulged by her parents her entire life. I'm ashamed I stayed with her as long as I did."

She squeezed his arm. "You're with me now. And I'm

not judging you. I love you, Holden. Madison will get what's coming to her tomorrow. Don't stoop to her level."

"You're right," he said, looking around and hailing a cab.

They returned to The Plaza, washing the sticky wine from their faces. They changed into the plush robes provided, and Holden called for someone to pick up their clothes and have them dry cleaned. She told the bellhop the stain was white wine, hoping if they had that information, their clothes could be saved.

When the bellhop left, Holden pulled her into his arms. "I was really looking forward to removing that dress from you," he said huskily.

She offered him the tie to her robe. "It's knotted. Let's see how much of a magician you can be. After all, your kisses are pretty magical."

He hugged her to him. "You're taking this really well, Finley."

Smiling up at him, she said, "Madison will get what she deserves tomorrow. And I get to ride off into the sunset with you."

His hand slipped inside her robe, kneading her breast.

"Then let the magic begin."

23

$\mathcal{H}$olden got into the car after Finley, his fingers seeking hers. They had gone for bagels this morning, and he had forced half of one down. The coffee he'd drunk now sat sour in his stomach. They rode in silence to Rutherford Baxter's office, where Evan would be meeting them.

When they arrived, the driver opened the door. Holden escorted Finley inside the high rise.

"Maybe I shouldn't be in the conference room today," she said, her voice small. "Especially after what happened last night."

"I'm not going to let Madison Parmalee chase you away," he said firmly. "She's not going to dictate whether or not you're in that room, Finley." He gazed deeply into her eyes. I need you there with me."

She nodded. "I'm always in your corner, Holden." She gave him a sweet smile.

Once again, they were met and taken to a smaller conference room this time, where Leo Turner awaited them. The copyright attorney said their meeting with Dr. Ingram had gone well and only bolstered their claim that Holden had written *Inside Threat* and not Madison.

"Tell him," Finley urged quietly.

"Tell us what?" Baxter asked, entering the room.

"There was a confrontation last night," Holden began. "At the restaurant where we were having dinner. Madison approached us."

The graying attorney frowned. "What did you say to her?"

"Not a word," he replied. "It's what she did."

Holden filled in the pair how Madison had come to their table and tossed drinks in their faces.

"We didn't say anything to her, but it was obvious she had an inkling about what would happen at today's meeting."

"We can help you file assault charges with the police," Leo told them. "I'm sure there are witnesses who would come forward and confirm your version of the events."

"I don't want to do that," Holden said flatly. "I'm hoping after today, I never have to see or think about Madison Parmalee again."

The lawyers asked if they had any questions and left them in the conference room, saying someone would return for them shortly before ten. Leo also returned Holden's laptop to him.

At a quarter till ten, Baxter's assistant appeared and escorted them to the same conference room they had met in on Wednesday. She remained in the room, setting up to take notes. Evan McGill joined them, and the three of them sat on one side of the conference table, with the attorneys at both heads of the table.

"Do not speak to Miss Parmalee," Baxter cautioned. "The less you say, Holden, the better. That's what you're paying me for. To do your talking for you."

Holden said, "I've met Vincent Winston before. If I hadn't signed with my current publisher, he was my next choice."

"In fact, Winston Press was going to be one of the houses I approached with *Inside Threat*," Evan shared. "Holden previously had a two-book deal, so we're open to bidding once we establish that we hold the rights to *Threat*."

Baxter nodded. "Good to know. Although I'm certain you'll be asking far more than what they're paying Miss Parmalee. Stay seated when they arrive," he added. "This isn't a social gathering."

Moments later, the door opened. Vincent Winston entered, wearing a custom suit of navy, looking powerful and confident. Holden fought the urge to rise and greet him.

Winston's eyes went straight to Rutherford Baxter. "I'm not used to being summoned to a meeting," he said crisply. "Knowing your specialty, Rutherford, I have to say I'm grateful you've kept this quiet."

Winston's gaze flicked to him. "Holden. I'm sorry we're meeting again under such circumstances. I had no idea you would be the author involved."

He gave the publisher a tight smile but didn't reply.

Amanda Sommers breezed into the room, followed by another man and Madison.

The man looked to Baxter and nodded curtly and then glanced at Holden. "I'm Morton Felderman. Attorney for Winston Press."

Amanda Sommers, a cool blond, said, "I'm with SGR and represent Madison Parmalee."

He couldn't help but turn his gaze upon Madison. Her eyes glittered with hate. She looked as if she wanted to pounce upon him or at least verbally lash out at him, but Holden assumed she'd been issued the same warning he had.

"Have a seat," invited Leo Turner.

The four took chairs on the opposite side of the table.

Rutherford Baxter took the lead. "I've asked you here today to straighten out the claim that Madison Parmalee wrote the manuscript you announced you had purchased from her. *Assassination Games*." The attorney paused. "When, in fact, Miss Parmalee committed literary theft in claiming the work as her own. *Assassination Games* might be what she's calling it, but the manuscript is the sole work written by my client, Holden Scott."

Holden listened as his lawyer walked through everything which had been shared with him. Baxter explained how Holden had created blurbs, character sketches, and outline for *Inside Threat*. As he spoke, the administrative assistant placed copies of each of these in front of the publisher, his lawyer, and Madison's agent. She did not provide one to Madison herself.

"At the time Mr. Scott wrote *Inside Threat,* he was cohabiting with Miss Parmalee. They met at the Iowa Writers' Workshop they both attended and became friends and then lived together. They were not partners in writing, however," Baxter emphasized. "They merely resided together in Brooklyn for several years, where Mr. Scott regularly shared his writing with Miss Parmalee, seeking her feedback."

Baxter continued speaking, but Holden lost the thread of it. All he could think about was how much time and effort he had put into *Inside Threat* and how desperate he was to get it back. He didn't want to lose his work, much less allow Madison to pretend it was hers.

"Miss Parmalee has copies of each of the drafts and the dates they were saved as she worked," Felderman stated. "It seems Mr. Scott cannot produce anything such as this from what you've shared."

"But does Miss Parmalee have all the legwork that goes into a manuscript?" Leo Turner interjected. "You have before you— dated —everything Mr. Scott prepared before he even began writing his draft of *Inside Threat.* Its plot. Cast of characters, with detailed character sketches. His research notes on Washington."

Felderman remained silent.

Leo went on to explain how they had analyzed previous writings done by Madison and compared them with Holden's work, concluding with, "We even have Dr. Rod Ingram here in our offices today. Mr. Scott and Miss Parmalee were in classes Dr. Ingram taught in Iowa, and he was Miss Parmalee's thesis adviser, so he has a deep knowledge of her talent and writing style. After studying Mr. Scott's manuscript, which Miss Parmalee has tried to pass off as her own work, Dr. Ingram felt it impossible that Miss Parmalee could have written it."

"Dr. Ingram— and no one here at your office —has seen the manuscript which Winston Press has purchased from Miss Parmalee," Felderman said. "How can you say with such certainty that Miss Parmelee did not write *Assassination Games?*"

Baxter stared stonily at the attorney. "Be glad I haven't hit your boss with a cease-and-desist order. I have asked him and the interested parties here today in order to avoid that very public action. It is a courtesy I was willing to extend, Mr. Felderman, because of Mr. Winston's reputation and that of his publishing house. There has been misconduct on Miss Parmalee's part, and I am placing the ball in your court to handle the matter. Unless you want me to go the legal route."

The attorney shook his head. "I don't need to preach to you about copyright protection. Mr. Felderman. Besides, the fact that everything Miss Parmalee has written up to this point could be classified as women's fiction and that none of her work has been published?" Baxter asked. "You merely have to read a chapter of *Capitol Crimes* and read a chapter of what Winston Press bought from Miss Parmalee. It is obvious that she has falsely claimed to have written that manuscript. We can follow up—"

"Enough!" Vincent Winston interjected. "I'm not going to be drawn into a lengthy court battle and endanger the sterling reputation of my family's publishing house. Mr. Baxter is being more than generous in giving me a heads up about this manuscript and the damage it could cause if I continue on the course to publish it."

Vincent glanced down the table, focusing on his newly-signed author. "I checked the date you submitted your manuscript to us. Even if you changed a few lines here and there, you've obviously stolen Holden Scott's work. Have you no integrity, Miss Parmalee?"

The publisher's accusation broke the dam, causing Madison to leap to her feet.

"You don't know what it's like, trying day after day to put words on the page and nothing comes. Or what you do write is paltry prose, nothing that anyone would ever buy. A piece of me died every day I lived with Holden. He constantly rubbed in my face that he was such a huge success. And then when he became too big a name, he decided he didn't need me anymore."

She turned, glaring at him. "I *made* you! I read everything word you wrote and gave you suggestions on how to improve it. And you accepted my input. You needed me. You *still* need me, or you'll fall on your face."

He had been angry with her, but now only pity filled him. He shook his head sadly, refusing to engage with her.

"You hurt me, Holden," Madison continued. "Every day we were together. Then without warning, you walked out on me. Abandoned me. I wanted to hurt you back. I wanted to have a bestseller and receive the accolades. Do the book tour. Go on the talk shows and be charming and funny and win over America."

Holden glanced to Baxter, who seemed to be silently communicating with Vincent Winston.

"No charges will be filed," Baxter announced. "Though you are guilty of literary theft and violating U.S. copyright laws, Miss Parmalee. As a favor to Mr. Winston, the matter will be dropped since he obviously will no longer be publishing something which never belonged to you in the first place."

"Thank you," Winston said humbly. Then to Madison, he added, "You will return every penny of your advance, Miss Parmalee. Immediately." His tone brokered no response.

Amanda Sommers finally spoke up, looking at her client. "SGR is dropping you, Miss Parmalee," she said formally. "I will make certain that no other reputable agent takes you on."

"No other publisher will ever consider a manuscript you present for submission," Winston added. "You are a pariah, Miss Parmalee."

Madison had gone white as a sheet, only two red spots of anger on her cheeks. She snatched her purse and fled the room.

Vincent Winston looked to Holden. "I read *Assassination Games*. I'm sorry. *Inside Threat*. I should have recognized your style and tremendous pacing, Holden. None of us had any idea of your previous connection with Miss Parmalee. We determined her credentials solid, having graduated from the Iowa workshop. I am giving you my deepest apologies, Holden."

He swallowed. "Apology accepted." The words were soft because his throat was thick with emotion.

Immediately, Winston looked to Evan McGill. "Would we have a chance at bidding on *Inside Threat?* I know Holden's deal has expired with his current house."

The agent looked to him. Holden nodded.

"You need to destroy any copies of what is being called *Assassination Games,*" Evan instructed. "Also, you should make a published announcement that you have withdrawn your offer to Madison Parmalee regarding the sale of her manuscript. Holden is polishing the manuscript now. I should begin pitching it in the next week once he's finished. I'll make certain that you receive his version of the manuscript."

"May I extend my apology, as well, Mr. Scott?" Amada asked. "Your novel grabs a reader and sucks him in. I was hoping Madison Parmalee would be that one incredible author that comes along in an agent's lifetime. I'm sorry for any role that I played in this."

"It's not any of your fault," Holden assured them. "Madison was angry at me and looking for the way she could hurt me the most. Taking away the book I had worked so diligently on was the best way to punish me. I hold no ill will to anyone present. I'm merely grateful that Mr. Baxter and Mr. Turner have helped me reclaim my work."

Vincent Winston rose, and his attorney and Amanda did the same. He offered his hand to Baxter.

"Thank you again for not going on the record and filing the cease and desist and making this incident public knowledge. You saved the reputation of Winston Press. My family is in your debt."

"It's a win for all of us," Baxter replied. "My assistant will see you out."

The trio left and once the door was closed, Baxter offered his hand to Holden. The two men shook.

"I have to echo Vincent Winston. Thank you for keeping this out of the press," he said.

"The full story will never get out, but there will be speculation," the attorney told him. "First, Winston Press' withdrawal will be enough to set tongues abuzz. Miss Sommers will also spread the word. Miss Parmalee's reputation as an author will take a hard hit. Gossip will abound, but hopefully, your name will be kept out of it, and no one will ever make a connection between the two manuscripts. Will you really consider selling *Inside Threat* to Winston Press?"

"I liked Vincent Winston," he said. "He seems like a good guy and a knowledgeable publisher." He turned to his agent. "It'll be up to Evan to field the offers for the manuscript, though, and advise me on what to do."

Smiling, Evan said, "I'll get on it the minute I receive your final version."

"I can have it to you by mid-week," he promised.

Holden thanked the two attorneys again, claiming Finley's hand as they moved to the elevator. They stepped inside it. The moment the doors closed, he embraced her, giving her a kiss.

"Thanks for coming to New York with me," he told her. "For standing with me."

"I didn't say anything," she protested.

"But you were here. I had your support. I hope you realize I'll support you and your career in the same way."

The elevator doors opened, and they left the building, walking across the street and entering Central Park. They found a bench to sit on, and Holden draped his arm around Finley's shoulder.

"I've never felt more supported or loved than I have with you," she told him. "I can't wait to be husband and wife."

He laughed. "Part of me is tempted to take you to a courthouse now and make it official, but I want our family and friends to see us speak our vows to one another. That means waiting until school is out and getting married at the winery."

Finley rested her head against his shoulder. "I'm looking forward to becoming Finley Scott."

"What? No Finley Farrow?" he asked.

She gazed up at him. "Nope. Miss Farrow, the teacher, will becoming Mrs. Scott, full-time photographer, married to Mr. Scott, the famous novelist— and screenwriter."

Pushing to her feet, she grabbed his hand and pulled him to his. "Let's go make a few memories, Mr. Scott."

"I can't think of a better person to do that with than you, Miss Farrow."

24

"I'm so nervous," Finley proclaimed as her mother fastened the necklace. "Why am I nervous?"

"Every bride gets a few jitters," Dianne Farrow assured her daughter. "It's a big commitment you're making to one another. It's forever."

"Were you nervous on your wedding day?" she asked.

Her mom laughed. "I fainted at the altar."

"What?" exclaimed all the women present.

Dianne laughed. "It seems silly now. I hadn't eaten. I had this fear of having something stuck in my teeth, and Sam would turn to say his vows and change his mind. I loved him so much. I just was hedging my bets. But I didn't eat or drink anything. I'd been going non-stop for days. And boom, I went down for the count."

Sally asked, "Is that shadow on your forehead in your wedding pictures a bruise?"

"I always told everyone it was bad lighting. But yes, it was a bruise. I'm just grateful I didn't face plant and break my nose." Her mom smoothed Finley's hair. "Your dad said he would have married me anyway, broken nose and all. Honey, Holden adores you. You're doing the right thing in marrying him."

"I know," she said. "I'm just excited and nervous and eager, all rolled into one."

"I wasn't nervous about marrying Braden," Harper said. "I was more worried about pulling off the surprise wedding. Making certain everything ran smoothly and everyone had a great time. Braden did tell me *he* was a bundle of nerves before the party got started. I could never have told looking at him, though."

Harper hugged Finley. "Going out to check on things a final time. Don't worry. Everything will go off without a hitch."

Emerson said, "Everything looks lovely, Finley. The cakes came out perfectly."

"Because you made them," she teased.

Her friend blushed. "Catering is ready to go. Harper has things decorated so well."

Danny Shelton spoke up. "Can I get a few pictures of the bride and her mother?"

Finley posed with her mom, knowing Danny was doing a good job. He was the high school photography and digital graphics teacher who was the event center's videographer. She had seen his work previously and knew he was getting some great shots as she and her brides-maids got ready. Danny would also be on-call in the future as Harper's back-up photographer in case Finley was unavailable. She would be leaving with Holden next week to go on set for the initial days of shooting for *Hill Country Homicide*, taking stills and working on ideas for the movie's poster and ad campaign. The thought of leaving teaching excited her. While she would miss her students and the daily routines, the thought of running her own business and the opportunities it presented was too good to pass up.

Harper rejoined them, giving Finley a thumbs up. She had everyone gather around and poured champagne for them all, Danny snapping away.

"Here's to my lovely friend," Harper said, holding up her champagne glass. "For your future with Holden and all the good times to come."

The women clinked glasses together, and Finley sipped the bubbly liquid, which tickled her nose. Danny excused himself, going to take some photos of the men.

Ana stopped by with Eva and Bear. Eva was serving as the flower girl, while Bear would be their ring bearer. Wolf was Holden's best man.

"The kids look adorable," she told her new friend, watching Eva twirl in her pastel dress.

"Wolf and I are so happy for you and Holden, Finley," Ana said. "And we cannot wait for filming to begin next week."

They had landed Jack Calder, the only big name in their cast. Finley had met Jack a few nights ago, and he was outgoing and friendly. The actor was working for scale because he had always wanted the opportunity to work with Wolf on a picture. He'd already rented a house in Bandera and was bringing his wife and two kids with him for the duration of the shoot. Wolf and Ana had agonized over the shooting schedule, but they thought they could get the entire film completed in ten weeks.

"It's time," Ivy announced. "You look beautiful, Finley."

Ivy was stepping in and acting as the wedding's coordinator during the ceremony since Harper was serving as the maid of honor. Ivy had them leave the bridal dressing area and escorted them outside, having them line up with the children first, followed by Harper.

Her dad joined them. "Ready to start the next chapter in your life?"

"Mom told me she fainted on your wedding day."

He chuckled. "She did. Don't worry. I'll keep a good hold on you, so history doesn't repeat itself." He paused. "We're really happy for you, Finley. Holden is a terrific guy. You know I wouldn't trust just any man with my favorite gal."

Finley had to blink back tears. "He thinks the world of you and Mom. You've both accepted him with open arms."

"I'm not losing a daughter. I'm gaining a son," Dad declared, and she knew he meant it.

The music began, a piano and cello duet recorded by The Piano Guys of Christina Perri's *A Thousand Years*. Dax had suggested all the music to use, and as Finley watched Eva scatter rose petals and Bear follow her with the wedding rings tied to a small, satin pillow, she was glad about the choice.

Harper went next, looking beautiful and at ease. Her

friend's confidence inspired Finley, and she smiled up at her dad.

"I'm ready," she told him as the music changed to Daniel Jang's sweet rendition of the John Legend love ballad *All of Me*. She had liked Dax's idea to use this song instead of the traditional wedding march as she went down the aisle toward her groom.

Her gaze connected with Holden's, his green eyes shining with love as she floated toward him, the soft breeze causing her veil to move slightly. Holden wore a dark suit and crisp, white dress shirt, his tie matching the color of his eyes. When they reached him and her dad handed her off to her groom, Finley calmed. She now held hands with the man she loved, the man she respected. Adored. And loved so deeply.

They listened together as Judge Grady talked of what a marriage should consist of. How love wasn't enough. That they needed respect. Honesty. Passion and compassion. Hearing his words, her heart swelled with even more love. She glanced up at Holden and saw love reflected in his eyes.

"How did we get so lucky?" he whispered as he faced her, ready to recite his vows to her.

Holden repeated the words after Judge Grady and then accepted the ring Wolf held out to him, slipping it on her finger. Finley repeated those same vows, taking the ring Harper offered and placing it on her husband's ring finger. They looked at one another, and both of them smiled.

Judge Grady said a few more words, and then

announced, "I now pronounce you man and wife. Holden, you better kiss your bride."

Her new husband's arms went about her. Finley had never known such happiness as when he kissed her. Really kissed her. The kiss was long and deep and told her while there might be storms ahead in their future, they would always have each other and work together to face whatever came their way.

Those in attendance applauded when Holden broke the kiss, and they faced outward.

"I give you Mr. and Mrs. Holden Scott," the judge proclaimed.

They walked down the aisle to Bridesmaids Quartet's upbeat version of Taylor Swift's *The Best Day*. Finley didn't think her smile could be any larger or her happiness run any deeper.

Holden guided her all the way to the inside of the event center, catching her in his arms and giving her a searing kiss. She couldn't wait for their wedding night to begin, but first, they needed to spend some time with their guests.

"This is the best day of my life," her husband told her. "And every day after that will just get better and better."

"Well, we won't get wedding cake and barbeque every day," she teased, "but we'll always have each other."

He cupped her face in his hands. "Every day with my Mrs. Scott sounds like a perfect day to me."

FINLEY MOVED QUIETLY ON THE SET. THEY WERE SEVEN weeks into shooting, and it was amazing, seeing how Holden's work was coming alive. She had read both the novel and screenplay several times now, trying to get a feel for the characters and how she wanted to shoot them. She'd asked Wolf and Ana if she could do individual photographic sessions with the main cast, as well as take photos while the cameras filmed scenes. She also had taken numerous candid shots.

Wolf had invited her and Holden to watch the rushes several nights, which consisted of the footage filmed from that particular day. Wolf was known for his spare approach, and so there were only a few takes of each scene to view. Instead, after the read-through with the cast, the director had done two weeks of intense rehearsals, giving suggestions to each actor and allowing them to play scenes in the way they envisioned for their characters. By the end of the rehearsal phase, both Wolf and his actors were pleased and knew exactly what they wanted to capture on film.

She watched now as Wolf filmed a scene between the characters played by Jack Colton and Laura Sidney. Jack was strictly a film actor and already popular with the movie-going public. Laura, on the other hand, had only a handful of minor roles film projects to her credit. She was better known in the theater world, doing productions in Austin and Houston. Still, she had taken to Wolf's direction well and also used tips provided to her by Jack. Finley believed that after the release of *Hill Country Homicide*,

Laura would be able to write her own ticket in movies and step into leading lady roles.

The scene being shot now was one of cat and mouse, though at times it was hard to decipher which actor played which role. Jack, as a homicide detective, was supposed to be the hunter. He took naturally to that role, his commanding presence making him a leader and believable in the part. Laura was slowly becoming his prime suspect. She was a timid librarian, but she gradually turned the scene around until she was the one who appeared to be verbally stalking Jack's detective. It was a killer performance, no pun intended, and Finley knew she was watching the making of a star.

After the scene ended, Wolf called, "Cut! That's it for the day."

Finley smiled at Jack as she passed him and approached Laura, saying, "I have an idea. Can I steal the next fifteen minutes from you while you're still in makeup and costume?"

"Of course," Laura said, always friendly and willing to go the extra mile for anyone on set.

Finley asked for the set to remain lit for a few extra minutes, and she photographed Laura from different angles, explaining as she worked how she wanted to meld the images together with others in the cast.

"Whatever you need, Finley," Laura said breezily. "You've already done a fantastic job of photographing the entire cast. I can't wait to see how this turns out."

Because of Wolf's name and the interest in his new production company— and this film in particular —the press was in a feeding frenzy. Wolf had granted a handful of interviews, one for television and two for print. For the print articles, he had insisted Finley be the photographer. Thanks to that limited exposure, offers were starting to come in for her to photograph other articles.

When she finished with Laura, she thanked her, seeing that Holden stood nearby, watching her work. Love poured through her anytime she caught sight of her handsome husband. She went to him now, giving him a kiss.

"I heard what you were telling Laura," he said. "I'm with her. I can't wait to see the finished product."

She thanked the lighting director for keeping the set lit, and he shut down the powerful lights.

Holden slipped an arm about her waist. "Ana asked if we could come for dinner. I told her I'd run it by you."

"That's fine with me. I love her cooking and even if she doesn't cook, I love her and Wolf's company."

They drove the short distance to Meadow Creek Ranch, where Eva showed them her new doll and Bear had Holden toss a baseball back and forth until Ana called them in for dinner.

Finley liked that the kids ate with them. Yes, there was some business talk, which Ana said was good for the children to hear so they knew more of what their parents did. The rest of the conversation centered around everything from sports to politics to what the children were doing this summer. Both were on local swim teams, while Eva was taking ballet and hip-hop lessons and Bear was involved with drum lessons.

After dinner, Ana told Eva and Bear to brush their

teeth and wash their faces and get into their pajamas. They could then watch thirty minutes of TV together before bed. The adults spent that time watching the rushes, and Ana slipped out to read a bedtime story and put the kids to bed while the other three finished watching the rushes.

Once Ana rejoined them, they talked about the scenes which had been filmed that day.

"We're already ahead of schedule," Ana said, smiling.

"She's a real taskmaster," her husband agreed, smiling wickedly at this wife. "But we are a good team. Ana does everything with purpose. She keeps me focused."

"Because we will wrap early, we will need to see if Harper can accommodate the party we've scheduled with her. I know it will involve rescheduling the catering and music," Ana said.

"Harper is even more organized than Ana," Holden said. "She could be head of the Joint Chiefs of Staff and still have time leftover to be President Clark and run the country."

"I'll give her a heads up," Finley said, and she and Ana looked at the calendar, agreeing on the date filming could finish and the wrap party could commence.

"In the meantime, Ana and I have agreed to do two joint interviews once production ends," the director said. "One is for *Sight and Sound*. That will take place in September."

"I'm not familiar with that," Finley said.

"It is one of the oldest film magazines," Wolf told her. "Started almost one hundred years ago. The British Film

Institute created it, and it celebrates both film and television around the world. I like that it includes essays and film analysis, as well as in-depth reviews and interviews. It is a great honor to be selected for its cover, and it will feature both Ana and me." He paused. "We agreed to the interview *only* if you could contribute the pictures, Finley. That would mean coming to London."

"I'd love to," she said, excitement filling her. "I've never been abroad though Holden convinced me to file for a passport right after we were married."

Holden slipped his hand around hers. "Wolf had already shared this with me. I was hoping we could both go and see some of England while we're there." He grinned. "I even took the liberty of giving the dates to Harper. She can get Danny to cover for you if you want to extend the trip beyond the interview."

"You *and* England? I'm all in, Mr. Scott." She looked to Wolf. "Thank you for recommending me."

"Ana and I love what you have done with our family portraits and our film. I would want no one else."

"A second interview is in the works," Ana added. "Again, we said we would do it if we could provide our own photographer. It's for *People*. Not the cover. Wolf isn't that big. Yet. But it's a guaranteed four-page article with slots for pictures, along with a single intro page to the article. A full photograph with some short copy."

"That is a huge deal," Finley exclaimed. "I am honored to shoot the two of you."

"We already submitted a few photos for them to

choose from. Some you took of us and the kids at the ranch. But we'll need other ones, too."

"I can work my schedule around whenever you want to do it," she promised.

"The writer of the article will be on set next week, watching us both work," Wolf told her. "He also sounded interested in you and Holden. Who knows? Maybe the two of you will also get some publicity out of this opportunity."

They talked a few more minutes and then said their goodnights. Finley had learned that movie people went to bed early because of their early morning calls. She and Holden drove home, turning onto their cul-de-sac. The house they'd purchased was partially furnished, thanks to suggestions from Harper, Emerson, and Ivy. They would add on to the other rooms in the future.

As they entered the house, Holden swept her into his arms. Finley looped her arms around his neck and kissed him.

"How is Mr. Hamilton coming along?" she asked as he carried her through the house and to their bedroom.

"Today was a good day. I got twenty pages done."

Holden was writing a fictionalized account of his relationship with Mr. Hamilton, and Wolf had already said he was interested in Holden writing the screen version of the story. That was on hold for now until Holden finished the novel. In the meantime, he was splitting his time on the set, watching the filming, and working from home the other days.

He set her on her feet, slipping his arms about her waist.

"A year ago, I never would have envisioned I'd be leading such a great life with the woman I love," he told her. "You mean everything to me, Finley. You changed everything about my world for the better. I love you so much."

She smiled at the man who would always make her heart quicken when he stepped into a room. "You've given me the confidence to soar to new heights, both professionally and personally. I can't imagine living my life with anyone but you, Holden."

Their lips met— and the magic began.

EPILOGUE

NINETEEN MONTHS LATER— SANTA MONICA, CALIFORNIA

*H*olden watched as Finley applied her lipstick. She paused a moment, smiling at her reflection in the mirror, and then finished. He had a good idea why she had to stop. As she capped the tube, he came and stood behind her, slipping his arms about her, one palm cradling her burgeoning belly.

"There. I felt her move again," he said.

Finley laughed as their gazes met in the mirror. "I swear she's going to be a gymnast, as much as she's been tumbling around today. I had to stop for a moment and wait for her to be still to finish putting on the rest of my lipstick."

"She's going to be amazing," he said, kissing her nape. "Just as her mother is."

"We should probably get going," she told him.

He twirled her so that she faced him. "You look beautiful tonight. This aquamarine top matches your eyes perfectly."

Her fingers brushed his cheek. "And you look like a handsome winner to me, Mr. Scott."

They left their hotel and walked the few blocks to the beach, where a huge tent had been erected in a parking lot. This was where the Film Independent Spirit Awards were held each year on the night before the Oscars. The atmosphere was much more casual than the Academy Awards, and he and Finley were dressed for the occasion. She wore the long, flowing top over black leggings and sandals, while he had on an open-neck button-down shirt and a pair of jeans. Fortunately, this was their second time at the awards, and they had known which hotel to stay at in order to be able to walk over and not be caught up in the immense traffic jam they now skirted.

They hit the red carpet, seeing Wolf and Ana, and Holden waved to the couple.

An entertainment reporter stopped them. "Holden, can I have a word?" Jane Rodgers asked.

"Sure," he said, slipping an arm around Finley.

"You were here last year," Jane said. "Winning Best First Screenplay for *Hill Country Homicide*. You're nominated this year for Best Screenplay this year for *Mr. Hamilton's World*. Usually, you release your books through a large publishing house, as you did with *Inside Threat* last year. What was different about *Mr. Hamilton's World*?"

"It's a quieter novel— and movie —than what I usually write. I decide to go in a different direction and publish it independently. The reader response has been fantastic.

And of course, it was great to work on the screenplay and film version with my good friend, director Wolf Ramirez, and his producer wife, Ana."

"This is the second novel of yours that WEBA Productions has filmed. It's also the second screenplay you've written for them," Jane noted. "Which do you prefer writing? A novel or a script?"

"Actually, I've found I enjoy doing both, Jane," he told her. "A screenplay is radically different from a novel. I exercise different muscles when writing each. A script needs to be lean and mean, but it has to convey all the heart and soul of the meat of a novel."

"You based this on a true story. You knew the actual Mr. Hamilton, didn't you?"

"I did. He was the custodian at my school. I thought it was important to tell his story. Too many people judge others by what they do for a living. Most people would have written off Mr. Hamilton, simply because he was a janitor. He was the smartest man I've ever known— and the best man. I hope he's looking down on me now, proud of all I've accomplished, thanks to his guidance. Not just being a successful novelist and screenwriter but proud of the man that I've become."

Jane smiled indulgently at him. "You're going to be a first-time father in a few months."

He turned to gaze at his wife, smiling at the woman who made every day a special one.

"Yes. Finley and I are having a girl this coming June. She'll be named Rebecca, after Finley's maternal grandmother. We're excited. I'm terrified, too, because I was an only child. I've never changed a diaper before, but my wife assures me I will take to it."

The reporter turned to Finley. "You are a photographer of some note, Finley. You're the one who designs all WEBA Productions' film posters and ad campaigns. What's important to show when you're creating a movie poster?"

Finley considered the question a moment and then said, "You want to convey as much of the tone and story as you can in order to entice a moviegoer to buy a ticket to the film. The poster needs to capture a moment in the movie which, once a fan has seen the film, every time he or she sees the poster for it, it will bring back a fond memory."

"You also photograph for magazines now, don't you? I recently saw a spread you did on Jack Calder."

Finley smiled. "Jack was the lead in Wolf's filmed version of *Hill Country Homicide*. It was a pleasure getting to know him and his family during that shoot. I was pleased that he asked for me to be the photographer for that interview."

The reporter glanced back at Holden. "Are you writing something new now? Maybe something Jack Calder might eventually star in?"

"I am working on something, Jane. Whether Jack will be interested in it or not, it'll be up to him and his agent to say."

The journalist thanked them for their time, and they continued along, stopping to pose for photographers.

Finley smiled up at him. "I'm used to being on that side

of the camera and not this one. There are so many photographers here."

"Wait until tomorrow. It's going to be a zoo compared to this."

Holden referred to the Academy Awards. They would be attending tomorrow night, alongside Wolf and Ana. *Mr. Hamilton's World* had opened early last November to great buzz. He had released his novel two months earlier, through a company he'd formed with Ana and Rey's help. The book had immediately landed on the bestseller list, with reviewers likening it to *Tuesdays with Morrie* and *A Man Called Ove*. When Wolf's film opened Thanksgiving weekend, it did terrific box office numbers, especially for a small, independent film production. Holden hadn't been surprised that the film had been nominated by the Independent Spirit Awards. What had taken him aback was when he'd received a nomination for Best Adapted Screenplay from the Academy.

He wouldn't worry about tomorrow night now. He'd become good about living in the moment, thanks to Finley's influence. Yes, they did plan for their future, but she had taught him to cherish the here and now.

They moved inside the tent, greeting people they had met at the previous year's ceremony. Holden received congratulations on his Oscar nom. He didn't think he would win tomorrow night, but he felt deeply honored to have received the recognition.

His cell buzzed in his pocket. He slipped it out and saw it was a text from Dax.

The gang is all at Hill Street Hangout.
We've gotten Rob to switch the channel
to your awards show. Knock 'em dead,
Holden.

He became emotional reading the text, blinking rapidly a few times to keep tears from falling. Finley's family treated him as one of their own, while her friends had welcomed him with open arms. He had become a part of their ever-expanding group, thanks to marriages and babies. Holden knew just how lucky he was.

They moved to their assigned table, greeting Grady Lancaster, a long-time character actor in movies, who had taken on the role of Mr. Hamilton, and Zane Adams, a newcomer who'd portrayed the character based on Holden in the film. Grady was up tonight for Best Lead Performance, while Zane had been nominated for Best Breakthrough Performance.

Holden recalled how nervous he'd been last year, waiting for his category to be called and shocked to his core when he actually won. He didn't think he would win this year because of the stiff competition, but he was more than pleased when he heard his name called forty minutes later. He leaned over and kissed Finley briefly before hurrying to the mike to give his acceptance speech.

"I had a wonderful man come into my life many years ago. His name was Mr. Hamilton, and *Mr. Hamilton's World* is a love letter to him. I wanted people to know about his generosity and spirit. Mr. Hamilton took a lonely, troubled kid and taught me to believe in myself. I wasn't the only person he mentored. Mr. Hamilton was generous with his time with many other people. This award is for all the Mr. Hamiltons out there. Keep doing what you're doing— because you are appreciated.

"I also want to thank my good friends Wolf and Ana Ramirez for bringing this small, intimate story to the screen. The two of you mean so much to me, and I treasure our working and personal relationships."

His eyes sought Finley and found her, seeing her beaming at him.

"Mr. Hamilton may have helped me reach my full potential, but it's the love of my life, my wife Finley, who has made me the man I am today. Finley loves me. She inspires me. She is my everything."

Holden held his trophy high. "I share this moment and this award with you, babe. I love you."

He left the stage, being steered to a staging area where he answered a few questions from entertainment reporters before returning to their table. Sitting, he took Finley's hand and gave her a lingering kiss.

"I am so proud of you, Holden," she told him, tears misting her eyes. "*Mr. Hamilton's World* has been my favorite thing you've written. I'm so happy you are being recognized for it."

The night grew even better, with Grady and Zane both winning. Wolf also won for his direction, while their film took Best Feature. That award was presented to Ana, as the movie's producer.

Wolf smiled at Holden. "*Mr. Hamilton's World* is the little engine that could," the director declared. "I hope the attention the film has received this evening will draw more viewers into theaters to watch it because the more who see it, the better the chances are that more Mr. Hamiltons will spring up in the world."

"Are you going to the after party?" Ana asked.

"No," he replied, answering for the both of them. "We're going to have our own private celebration."

Holden took Finley's hand, lacing his fingers through hers, and they strolled back to their hotel.

"Mr. Hamilton would be so proud of you, Holden," his wife said.

"He would be proud of the work I've done, but he would be even more excited to know I've found someone to share my life with. To know the husband I've become—and the father I'll soon be. I love you, Finley. Now and always. Thank you for helping me make our dreams come true."

Holden stopped on the sidewalk and kissed his wife, ready to meet each tomorrow with Finley by his side.

PREVIEW: LOVE IN EVERY BITE

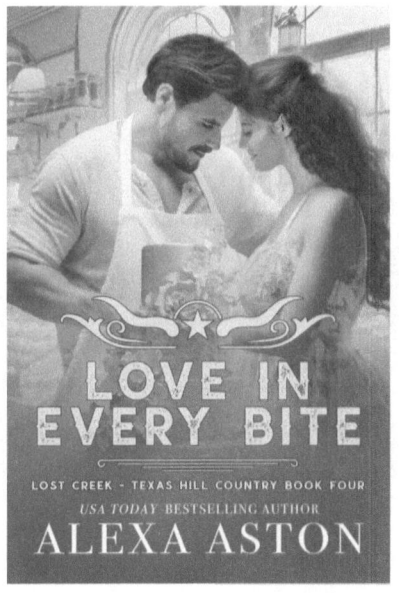

Read on for a preview of Love in Every Bite, book 4 in the Lost Creek, Texas Hill Country series.

PROLOGUE

MARCH—AUSTIN

*E*merson Frost glanced at the clock, knowing her friend Finley Farrow would arrive at any moment. She began wiping down the counter, eager to leave the bakery.

And hopefully land a teaching position in Lost Creek, Texas.

Her companion, a high schooler who was the niece of the owner, leaned against the wall, scrolling through her phone. The girl hated having to work here and did as little as she could.

The bell above the door chimed, and she glanced up, seeing Finley breeze in. Her roommate from their freshman year in college was a natural beauty, an inch taller than Emerson's own five feet and three inches, with blonde hair and startling aquamarine eyes. Although they had only roomed together that first year, Emerson knew she and Finley would be lifelong friends.

"You ready?" Finley asked, smiling.

"Let me get my things," she said, heading to the back, where she told Joe, the bakery's owner, that she was clocking out.

His wife, who was icing a cake, said, "Good luck with your interview, Emerson."

Emerson removed her apron, hanging it on the peg with her name above it. She picked up the sturdy brown paper sack with handles, which contained her interview outfit, PJs for tonight, and a few toiletries. Returning to the front of the bakery, she saw Finley buying cookies.

"I'll also need some kolaches," her friend said, picking out some in apple, pear, and cherry.

Finley paid for her purchases and then turned to Emerson. "I also got two bottles of water for us. Let's hit the road."

The pair went to Finley's new car, an early graduation gift from her parents, and got in. They drove through Austin, talking about the upcoming interview they both had tomorrow at Lost Creek Elementary, where Finley had gone to school.

Once they were on the highway, Emerson said, "I can't thank you enough for driving back to Austin to get me, Finley, and letting me stay at your house tonight. Your friendship means the world to me." Her voice wavered as her eyes misted over.

Her friend reached out and took Emerson's hand, squeezing it.

"I'm happy to do so, Em. Besides, we can be nervous about tomorrow's interview together."

She thought Finley had the job in the bag. Her friend's family owned a Montessori preschool in Lost Creek, and Finley had talked over the past few years about what a tight-knit community her hometown was. She would be certain to land one of the two open positions. Emerson only hoped she could be hired for the other one.

Already, she'd had two interviews this week, one with Austin ISD and another with a charter school in the area. She had presented herself as best she could, but both times, the person interviewing her seemed disinterested, as if they were merely going through the motions and had already decided upon another candidate for the teaching position.

"So, how have you been spending spring break?" she asked.

"I've read a couple of books. For fun. I haven't had time to do that since last summer. I also helped Ches and Sally with some inventory."

Finley's brother and wife owned Hill Country Water Sports, which was located on Lost Creek Lake. They rented equipment such as kayaks and jet skis.

"Other than that, I finished writing that final paper that's due for our Ed Leadership class. Have you finished yours yet?"

"I wrote it last weekend."

"Of course, you did," Finley said, laughing. "You always get every assignment done before anyone else."

Emerson had to. Working two part-time jobs while taking a full load of classes at UT meant she had to use her time extremely wisely.

"You'd be proud of me," Finley told her. "I've completed the rest of my lesson plans for the last month of student teaching and already submitted them to my cooperating teacher for approval. I'll be glad when we're done with student teaching. I'm itching to have my own students and do things the way I want and not how The Dragon wants them done. You are so lucky you did your student teaching in the fall and had a great mentor."

Finley called her cooperating teacher The Dragon with good cause. Emerson had completed her student teaching at the same elementary school and had been relieved not to be under The Dragon's supervision. Finley was a bright light and eager to teach, full of creative ideas, but The Dragon had tried her best to snuff out that light.

"How are things between you and Jeb going?" she asked.

As Finley talked, Emerson wanted to tell her friend she didn't think Jeb was good enough for her. The couple had been dating for the past three years, and Emerson had never warmed to Jeb. She thought the frat boy was a self-centered asshole who took his girlfriend for granted and would eventually break Finley's heart. When he did—and she was certain this was a given—Emerson would never say *I told you so*. She'd simply help Finley pick up the pieces and start again.

They arrived in Lost Creek, a place Emerson had visited once before during their freshman year. The town was as picturesque as its name, and the people she had met during that weekend were warm and friendly. It was one of the reasons she had applied for one of the openings at Lost Creek Elementary. She wanted to be a part of a community. Have a school family.

And maybe a family of her own someday.

Finley pulled up in front of the large ranch house her parents owned, and Emerson claimed her purse and sack from the back.

"I'll need to iron my dress," she told her friend.

They went inside the house, where Mrs. Farrow hugged her, saying, "I'm so glad you could come and stay with us, Emerson. It's so good to see you again. I only wish you could stay longer."

"I've got work, Mrs. F. If I didn't, you wouldn't be able to get rid of me. I'm just grateful Finley came back to Austin to pick me up for this interview since I don't have a car. Don't worry. I'll pay her for the gas."

Dianne Farrow pulled Emerson to her again, hugging her tightly. "Don't worry about that, honey. Let's get you set up in the guestroom. I'm making lasagna for dinner. Hope that sounds good."

"A home-cooked meal sounds wonderful," she replied, not recalling the last time she'd eaten one.

Even though she lived in the dorm, Emerson was not on one of the UT meal plans. She found she could eat more cheaply on her own. Joe was kind enough to let her have whatever she wanted from the bakery. The sports bar where she worked on weekends let her buy meals at half price. Between that and the small fridge and microwave she had in her dorm room, she got by.

She took her things from her sack, lamenting the fact that she'd never owned a suitcase. Once she landed a teaching job, a suitcase was on her wish list of items to buy. She would also need to buy a car. For the last four years, she'd gotten around Austin on a second-hand bicycle, but she would need more reliable transportation. She couldn't arrive at school looking like a drenched rat on rainy days, which had happened numerous times over the years as she'd ridden her bike to classes and various jobs.

Mr. Farrow joined them for dinner, asking both Finley and her all kinds of questions, trying to help prepare them for tomorrow's interview.

"You both gave very thoughtful answers," Mr. F told them. "Mary Miller would be a fool not to hire each of you on the spot."

"I know you're friends with Mary, Dad," Finley said. "Do you have any idea how many other candidates there are?"

"We haven't discussed it," he said. "Mary knows you're applying for the job. We've kept everything aboveboard."

Still, Emerson could see in Mr. F's eyes that he believed his daughter would be hired by the elementary school principal.

They finished dinner, and Emerson offered to do the dishes.

"No, you're a guest," Mrs. F said. "You need to relax tonight."

She and Finley decided to watch a romcom on Netflix, and Emerson ironed her dress as they did so. She had already polished her only pair of dress pumps.

The movie ended, and Finley said, "That was cute. I wish real life could be more happily ever after like that."

"Is something wrong, Fin?" she asked.

"I have a bad feeling about Jeb going to Wharton," her friend admitted, worry in her eyes. "I thought we would be engaged by now, Em. I assumed we'd get married this summer, and we'd both be moving to Pennsylvania. I'd teach while Jeb earned his master's degree. The fact that he's leaving Texas and I don't have a ring on my finger makes me feel that he isn't as committed to our relationship as I am."

"Has he told you he wants to break up?"

"No, but my gut is telling me it's going to happen." Finley wiped away a falling tear.

"Then you should break up with him," she advised.

Finley's eyes widened. "Why would I do that? I love him."

She could tell no matter what she said, Finley was going to have to figure things out on her own.

"It was just a suggestion. Maybe absence will make the heart grow fonder. There has to be something to those old sayings, or they still wouldn't be around."

They went to their separate rooms, and Emerson fell asleep immediately. She usually ran on empty, getting only three or four hours of sleep a night, so anytime she fell into bed, she slept like the dead.

She awoke early the next morning and showered, using the wonderfully scented shampoo and body gel in the guest bathroom. She dressed and then applied a bit of makeup, something she usually went without because it cost money she didn't have. This interview was a special occasion, though, so she swept on two coats of mascara.

She would put on lipstick after she ate breakfast and brushed her teeth.

In the kitchen she found a note for each of them from Mrs. F, wishing them good luck today. The Farrows would already be at the school they operated.

Emerson helped herself to a bowl of cereal and made a cup of coffee. Finley joined her, also drinking coffee, but said she was too nervous to eat.

They drove to the school, the place deserted except for two cars in the front parking lot. Most school districts in the Hill Country took the same spring break UT did, and so staff and students were gone this week.

They entered the building, and Finley directed them to the office, where one lone worker was tapping away at her computer. She glanced up and came around from behind the counter, hugging Finley.

"Oh, it's so good to see you again, Finley. I was thrilled to see your name on Mary's calendar."

The woman turned to Emerson. "Hello. I'm Sheila, the school secretary. Are you Emerson Frost?"

"I am. It's nice to meet you, Sheila."

"Emerson and I were roommates our freshman year," Finley told the secretary. "Before I left the dorms and moved to the sorority house."

"Well, I'm happy you both are here. If you'll have a seat, I'll let Mary know you've arrived."

Minutes later, Sheila escorted Finley in for her interview. Emerson sat, her mouth growing dry, butterflies raging in her stomach. She took out her phone and checked her email and then jumped around various sites, trying to keep her mind calm.

Forty-five minutes later, she heard voices and knew Finley had emerged from her interview. Moments later, her friend appeared in the office, accompanied by an older woman in her early fifties. The two shook hands.

"HR will be in touch about your contract, Finley," the principal said.

"Thank you, Mrs. Miller. I'm so happy I'll be a Lost Creek Lion again."

Mrs. Miller's attention now turned to Emerson. "And you must be Emerson Frost."

She shot to her feet, approaching the principal. Offering her hand, she said, "It's so nice to meet you, Mrs. Miller."

The administrator shook her hand and said, "Come back to the conference room. Let's get to know one another."

Her heart pounding, she followed the older woman down a hallway and into a room.

"Have a seat, Emerson," the principal said, indicating a chair at the conference table and taking one at the head. "Usually, I interview with teachers from the team our applicant would be a part of. With this being spring break, however, I didn't want to ask any of them to give up their much-needed time off."

"I understand, Mrs. Miller. Thank you for coming in during your break to interview me."

The gray-haired woman gazed at Emerson thoughtfully. She was used to being scrutinized and looked back steadily.

"Your grades are excellent, both in your education courses and your specializations of math and science. But you have no extracurriculars on your resumé, Emerson. That concerns me. No campus organizations. No community service. We here at Lost Creek Elementary are looking for well-rounded individuals to educate our students. Yes, mastery in content areas is important, but we are molding global citizens here. I'm only seeing you today at Finley's request. She insisted when I contacted her for an interview that you be granted one, as well."

Her heart sank, knowing she had only gotten her foot in the door because of her friend.

"I appreciate Finley championing me," Emerson said. "If you wish, we can end the interview now since you don't believe I'm what you're looking for in a Lost Creek Lion."

Mrs. Miller pursed her lips and studied Emerson. "Hmm. I didn't take you for a quitter."

"I'm not," she said quickly. "However, I don't want to waste your time, ma'am."

Again, the principal looked at Emerson, as if she saw through her. "Finley has always been a loyal little thing. I recall one field day when she was probably in first or second grade. She was winning her race and stopped right in the middle of it. Looked over her shoulder for her friend, who had fallen. Finley let the other runners pass by her as she trotted back and took her friend's hand. Pulled the girl to her feet. They crossed the finish line together, holding hands, the other girl no longer crying but beaming."

The principal smiled. "They acted as if they'd actually won that race."

"They did," Emerson said. "Friendship—and loyalty— won that day."

Mrs. Miller nodded approvingly. "Tell me about yourself, Emerson. Help me to see what Finley does."

She took a deep breath and decided full disclosure was the best policy.

"My dad went to prison for killing a man when I was nine years old. I never saw him again. He was stabbed by his cellmate when I was fourteen. My mom suffered from depression once he was incarcerated. She turned to drugs as an escape and died from an overdose when I was eighteen."

Emerson paused, gauging Mrs. Miller's reaction. The principal appeared unruffled, but she could see sympathy in her hazel eyes.

"Miss Kent was my third-grade teacher. She mentored me. Taught me how to navigate the world. Miss Kent believed in me. Long after my mother relinquished her parental rights and I was placed in foster care, Miss Kent was there for me. She took me to the school's clothes closet so that I had a few different shirts and a pair of jeans. A third-hand coat that kept me warm. She encouraged me to read, telling me I could see the world through books. And she urged me to pursue math and science, telling me I could be anything I wanted to be."

"Your Miss Kent was a wonderful role model for you," Miss Miller remarked.

"She married and her husband took a job in Fort Worth, so they left Austin. Still, she stayed in touch with me and continued advising me. Miss Kent was a Texas Longhorn, so I wanted to go to UT and follow in her footsteps. She guided me through the Texas Advance Commitment."

"Which is?" Mrs. Miller asked, clearly curious.

"I was valedictorian of my high school, which guaranteed my tuition would be paid for during my freshman year of college. It's only tuition, though. Not books or fees. Not room and board. The Texas Advance Commitment is a program which aids low-income students. In my case, I had no family income. In addition to paying for my tuition each semester while I pursued my teaching degree, I was eligible for additional grants and scholarships, which I took advantage of.."

"What about work-study programs or loans?"

"I didn't want to leave college awash in debt," she said frankly. "Loans were never an option to me. I also knew I could make far more money working off-campus though I did accept an on-campus housing scholarship." She paused. "That's why I have none of the extras you're looking for, Miss Miller. I've worked two jobs and carried a full load my four years at UT."

"That's impressive, Emerson. What jobs have you held?"

"The last two years, I've worked three mornings a week at a local bakery. I'm there by three those mornings, baking everything from donuts to cakes to pastries. Out the door by nine so I can bike to campus for my classes. Weekends, I tend bar on Sixth Street. I started as a server, but I subbed one night when a bartender was out and found the tips were way better. It's also close enough for me to bike to."

She sighed. "I don't even own a car, ma'am. When I land a teaching job, I want to buy a used vehicle, so I don't turn up to school looking like a drowned rat on rainy days. But I am a hard worker. Yes, academically I know my stuff, but I also have a deep love for children and know, especially at the elementary level, how much influence a teacher can have on her students. I want to teach life, Mrs. Miller, not just how to divide fractions and what the life cycle of a plant is. I want to be a role model. Help students to become life-long learners while they learn how important integrity and gratitude are."

Emerson paused. "I may not be your ideal candidate on paper, but I will work harder, longer, and more efficiently than anyone else on your staff. I want to be the Miss Kent to all of my students. I could have majored in anything—and Miss Kent often told me I should go into medicine or accounting. I wanted to make a difference every day, though, in a direct way, guiding young minds."

The principal placed folded hands upon the table, her gaze direct. "You are very forthright, Emerson. Your passion is obviously. I can see why Finley befriended you."

"I love Finley to pieces, ma'am, but don't consider me for this teaching position because of Finley. If I win it, I want it to be on my own merits."

Finally, the older woman smiled. Extending her hand, she said, "I would be honored to have you as a faculty member of Lost Creek Elementary School, Emerson. Finley has already accepted a position for fifth grade ELA and Social Studies. My other opening is third grade math and science."

A warm glow filled her. "That's what Miss Kent taught." She beamed at the principal. "Yes. I would be happy to teach little Lions in third grade."

Mrs. Miller rose, and Emerson sprang to her feet. Surprisingly, the older woman embraced her.

"Welcome to Lost Creek, Emerson. We are lucky to have you. I'll forward your information to HR. They'll send an electronic contract for you to sign. Once you're officially employed, I'll be in touch."

She left the conference room in a daze.

Finley shot to her feet when Emerson appeared.

"Well?"

Her gaze met her friend's. "I got it. I got it!"

Finley crushed her in a bear hug. "We'll be at the same school. And we can be roommates again. This is the best news ever. I love you, Em."

Emerson smiled at her friend. "I love you, too, Fin."

Get your copy of Love in Every Bite!

ALSO BY ALEXA ASTON

Hollywood Flirt

Hollywood Player

Hollywood Double

Hollywood Enigma

LAWMEN OF THE WEST

Runaway Hearts

Blind Faith

Love and the Lawman

Ballad Beauty

SAGEBRUSH BRIDES

A Game of Chance

Written in the Cards

Outlaw Muse

KNIGHTS OF REDEMPTION

A Bit of Heaven on Earth

A Knight for Kallen

SUDDENLY A DUKE

Portrait of the Duke

Music for the Duke

Polishing the Duke

Designs on the Duke

Fashioning the Duke

Love Blooms with the Duke

To Heal an Earl

To Tame a Rogue

To Trust a Duke

To Save a Love

To Win a Widow

THE ST. CLAIRS

Devoted to the Duke

Midnight with the Marquess

Embracing the Earl

Defending the Duke

Suddenly a St. Clair

STANDALONE ROMANTIC THRILLERS

Leave Yesterday Behind

Illusions of Death

ABOUT THE AUTHOR

USA Today and Amazon Top 100 bestselling author Alexa Aston lives with her husband in a Dallas suburb, where she eats her fair share of dark chocolate and plots out stories while she walks every morning. She enjoys travel, sports, and binge-watching—and never misses an episode of *Survivor*.

Alexa brings her characters to life in steamy historicals, contemporary romances, and romantic suspense novels that resonate with passion, intensity, and heart.

KEEP UP WITH ALEXA
Visit her website
Newsletter Sign-Up

MORE WAYS TO CONNECT WITH ALEXA